INSPECTOR FRENCH:
GOLDEN ASHES

Freeman Wills Crofts (1879–1957), the son of an army doctor who died before he was born, was raised in Northern Ireland and became a civil engineer on the railways. His first book, *The Cask*, written in 1919 during a long illness, was published in the summer of 1920, immediately establishing him as a new master of detective fiction. Regularly outselling Agatha Christie, it was with his fifth book that Crofts introduced his iconic Scotland Yard detective, Inspector Joseph French, who would feature in no less than thirty books over the next three decades. He was a founder member of the Detection Club and was elected a Fellow of the Royal Society of Arts in 1939. Continually praised for his ingenious plotting and meticulous attention to detail—including the intricacies of railway timetables—Crofts was once dubbed 'The King of Detective Story Writers' and described by Raymond Chandler as 'the soundest builder of them all'.

T0016665

Also in this series

By the same author

*with other Detection Club authors

FREEMAN WILLS CROFTS

Inspector French: Golden Ashes

COLLINS
CRIME
CLUB

COLLINS CRIME CLUB
An imprint of HarperCollins*Publishers*
1 London Bridge Street
London SE1 9GF
www.harpercollins.co.uk

HarperCollins*Publishers*
1st Floor, Watermarque Building, Ringsend Road
Dublin 4, Ireland

This paperback edition 2022
1

First published in Great Britain by Hodder & Stoughton Ltd 1940

A catalogue record for this book is
available from the British Library

ISBN 978-0-00-855412-5

Set in Sabon Lt Std by Palimpsest Book Production Ltd, Falkirk, Stirlingshire

Printed and bound in the UK using 100% Renewable Energy
at CPI Group (UK) Ltd

MIX
Paper | Supporting
responsible forestry
FSC™ C007454

This book is produced from independently certified FSC™ paper
to ensure responsible forest management.

Find out more about HarperCollins and the environment at
www.harpercollins.co.uk/green

Contents

PART I

As Betty Stanton Saw It

1

The Promise of the Job

When Betty Stanton, getting out of bed with a tremulous eagerness, pulled back the curtains of the small poorly furnished room and saw above the grimy brick court that the sky was blue and the sun shining, her spirits rose unwarrantably. It was an omen, she told herself. On such a morning things could not but go well.

She was desperately anxious, was Betty, that on this morning things should go well. Today a lot was at stake. On what happened within the next three or four hours her whole future might depend.

In the space of her not very long life—she would be thirty-two in a month—Fate had dealt her two devastating blows. Regrettably it is not uncommon for a sheltered woman to be robbed suddenly of her support and thrown out into the world to fend for herself, sinking or swimming as time and chance may befall her. But it is unusual for this calamity twice to overtake the same woman. Yet this was what had happened to Betty.

Her mother had died when she was a child and she, her

twin brother Roland and her sister Joan had been brought up by their father in their old-fashioned family place near Andover. Hubert Brand was a survivor of that fast vanishing race of country gentlemen who occupied themselves with sport and useless hobbies, living on capital amassed by more energetic ancestors. He died in 1930, when Betty and Roland were twenty-three and Joan twenty. Then the blow fell. No business man, but with a pathetic belief in his flair for finance, he had let his capital run through his fingers in unprofitable speculation. The three young people were almost, though not quite, penniless. The house and all their belongings had to go and to find jobs became for them the most urgent thing in life.

Roland and Joan had succeeded. Through the good offices of the family solicitor Roland had got a start in a bank, while Joan had been appointed assistant children's nurse on an Atlantic liner. But in Betty's case Fortune's wheel had given an unexpected turn, providing her with security in another way. John Stanton, a merchant living near Maidstone, had asked her to marry him and she had consented.

For eight years they had lived happily together. Though not exactly rich, Stanton was well-to-do and their home had every reasonable luxury. Both were fond of society and they entertained lavishly. Then Stanton had died and another blow, exactly similar to the first, had fallen on Betty. It was found that her husband, like her father, had been living above his income and instead of a comfortable nest-egg for his wife, he had left only debts. Again everything had to be sold and again Betty had to fend for herself. It was then that her former great trouble became her chief source of thankfulness—that there were no children from the marriage.

The next few weeks were to Betty a bitter experience.

She put up at a boarding-house in Brook Street, W.C.2, euphemistically referred to by its manageress as 'the Hotel'. Its sole recommendation was its tariff. If it was cheap, and it certainly was, even more certainly was it nasty. Betty haunted employment bureaux and even registry offices, but without success. Gradually she began to lose hope, for in most cases the reception of her reply to the first question asked, 'And what can you do?' brought the interview to an abrupt termination.

What could she do? she asked herself in growing despair. She could be a hostess of some kind no doubt, if she could summon up the necessary bright and cheery manner so soon after her great loss. But the people who wanted official hostesses wanted also testimonials. They had not known her own admirable ménage. All that she could hear of were vacancies for general servants, and though she was afraid that she was coming to it, she had not yet reached that level.

Then just as anxiety was sharpening into sheer terror she received a radiogram from her sister Joan from the *Nicarian*, homeward bound from New York and four hundred miles west of the Scillies: 'Meet ship arrival Southampton think job for you.' With tremulous hope she packed her bag and took an evening train to the great port. The night she spent at a small hotel near the docks. It was here that, after tossing for hours, she had pulled aside the curtain and been cheered to find the sky blue and the sun shining. She would want, she felt, all the extraneous aids she could get when in some three hours' time she boarded the *Nicarian* to learn her fate.

She made her preparations for the interview, as she did every thing, carefully and systematically. Concentrated thought had gone to the selection of her dress with the appurtenances thereof, and her make-up, scarcely perceptible as such, was an artistic triumph. After a glance into the hotel coffee room she decided to forgo the breakfast included in the terms she had paid and have a dainty meal at a fashionable restaurant she had patronized in happier days. The resultant stiffening of her self-respect would, she thought, be worth the money, and when after a cigarette, smoked delicately through a long holder, she set off in a taxi for the docks, she felt her preparations for the fray were as adequate as she could make them.

Indeed, as she stood on the wharf while the great ship drew slowly in, Betty Stanton was a sight upon which men's eyes tended to linger. Though substantially built, she had a good figure, naturally made the most of by her clothes. Her colouring was fair, a creamy complexion—so far as this could be seen—hair almost golden and eyes of a light blue. She looked fresh and wholesome and kindly, as indeed she was, and there was that invaluable suggestion of competence and sanity in her appearance which tended to inspire confidence. If within she was still quaking, without she showed a poise of complete self-assurance.

Gradually the space between ship and wharf narrowed, ropes were thrown, caught, made fast and drawn tight, till movement ceased and gangways were pushed aboard. Betty had not seen her sister's face among those which lined the various decks, but she had not expected to do so, believing that Joan's business would keep her at her post.

She pushed on board as soon as possible and cajoled a harassed-looking steward into leading her to the nurseries. There, as she had expected, Joan was awaiting her.

'My dear! How splendid to see you!' Joan cried, running

over and kissing Betty warmly. 'Sit down, won't you? Ten minutes and I'll be free.'

Betty sank into an easy chair while her sister settled some business with her subordinates. A year earlier she had been appointed head of her department and now a faint envy gnawed at Betty's heart as she watched her dealing with her staff. She looked so pretty and so competent. Clearly she was on the friendliest of terms with her helpers, yet she held her position with every word and movement. Betty knew she was better looking than herself: she was slighter, her hair really was spun gold, and her expression was jollier. But what Betty didn't appreciate was that she hadn't her own air of complete dependableness.

Joan presently dismissed her assistants and came across the room.

'You're looking well, Betty,' she said, with an appraising glance; 'much better than I could have hoped. So glad.'

'I'm all right and I needn't ask about you. You seem on top of the world.'

'I'm all right too. Busy: we had a bad trip: heavy weather all the way. But that may have been a blessing in disguise. It's where your little business came in at all events.'

'Oh, tell me, Joan.' Betty couldn't keep the eagerness out of her tones. 'Is it really a job?'

Joan made a deprecating gesture. 'Afraid that's too optimistic. But it's the chance of a job, and I think if you play your cards well, you'll get it.'

'Tell me.'

'It's a housekeeper's job, but a superior housekeeper and over a superior house. One of the passengers has inherited an estate and wants someone to run the house.'

'A man, of course?'

'A man, yes.'

'And unmarried?' Joan glanced at her, a mischievous light dancing in her eyes. Then evidently remembering what Betty had just suffered, she answered seriously.

'Naturally. He knows nothing about it, and if you get the job you'll have a free hand.'

'Who is he and where's the house?'

'He's now Sir Geoffrey Buller, and the house is in Surrey, somewhere near Ockham. He's just inherited, you understand.'

Hope began slowly to grow in Betty's mind. 'Tell me the story, Joan. It means a terrible lot to me.'

Joan looked at her sympathetically. 'You poor dear,' she murmured. 'Are things so bad with you? Have you been hard up?'

For a moment Betty did not reply. 'I've got thirty-four pounds in the bank,' she said slowly. 'That will last me about seventeen weeks or perhaps a little longer. Then, I'll get nothing—I'm down and out.'

'My dear!' Joan's voice was full of sympathetic concern. 'I had no idea! Of course I knew that you wanted a job, but I had no conception that it was urgent like this.'

Betty forced a smile. 'Well, it is. And now having said so I needn't refer to it again. Tell me about this Sir Geoffrey Buller.'

'I'm going to. But you do understand, Betty, that you'll never come short while I can help it. You know I've practically no expenses here and I'm saving nearly the whole of my salary. I've quite a lot saved as it is, and if you don't get this job we'll share it.'

Betty pressed her hand. 'Dear Joan, it's just like you, and I would ask you if I were in difficulties. But you know, I must get work. I can't live on you.'

'You'll get work all right,' Joan said with decision, 'even if this falls through. It's only just to fill the gap till it comes, and there you can count on me. And now for the story. It began with a slight accident which happened on the second day out. It was blowing half a gale and the ship was rather lively. Nothing to worry about of course, but unpleasant. Most of the passengers were in their berths, but some who weren't ill were creeping about, clinging to handrails and so on.

'I didn't see what happened, but I heard about it afterwards. During a heavy roll this man, Sir Geoffrey Buller, lost his hold and slid right across one of the saloons. It wouldn't have mattered—he didn't hurt himself—but unfortunately he landed against a sofa and hurt a child who was sitting on it. It was a small American boy aged five, and one of the bones in his forearm was broken. They got him to bed in his mother's cabin, but he had taken a fancy to this place and nothing would do him but that he must be brought here. No one wanted to turn the nursery into a hospital, but he was beginning to fret and they were afraid he would make himself ill, so a cot was put up in that corner and he was brought in.

'Well, all that's immaterial except that it brought Sir Geoffrey here. He was terribly upset about the accident and spent a lot of time trying to amuse the kiddy. That was genuine about him and it was all to the good. At least it was at first.' Joan hesitated, then went on as if unwillingly, 'I hate to say it, Betty, but afterwards I couldn't but see that the child was no longer the attraction. While he was always correct and there was nothing I could take hold of, I found it wise to provide myself with a job which would have to be attended to in case of need.'

'That's not very encouraging,' Betty put in.

'Well, I'm giving you the whole thing, the cons as well as the pros. It began by his telling me all about himself. Found me sympathetic, he said. As a matter of fact I was sorry for the man, for he did seem lonely. Didn't hit it off with the others somehow; I don't know why.'

'Seems high time the ship got in,' Betty remarked severely.

'I thought so too,' Joan grinned. 'Well, his story was rather a romance. His grandfather had broken with the family through marrying after his heart instead of his head. He had been brought up in Plymouth, as plain Geoffrey Buller of course, and apparently in a pretty small way. He went into a house agent's office, but I imagine from what he said, only as a clerk. Then a friend of his went out to Chicago, and after a while he wrote to Buller saying there were far better chances in America and to go out. Buller did so and got a job with a real-estate firm in Chicago.

'Then when he'd been out some four or five years he learnt that a cousin, Sir Richard Buller, had died near Ockham, and that as the family estate was entailed and he was the next of kin, he had succeeded to both estate and title.'

'Rather a surprise for him, that. Had he known of the possibility?'

'Oh, yes, but he had believed he was too far from the direct line ever to inherit. However, there it was. He naturally threw up his job and is now on his way home to take over.'

Betty, now that she could see what was coming, grew even more eager. 'Yes?' she prompted, as she struggled to keep cool. 'None of the family was left at Ockham, but there was a host of servants, apparently under the butler.

Sir Geoffrey was obviously dreading the whole thing. He explained that he wanted to fill the house and entertain his neighbours, but admitted he had no idea how to set about it. He wanted a lady to run things and give him some help and advice. In fact he—he asked me if I would go.'

'Did he want to marry you?'

Joan shook her pretty head. 'Nothing like it,' she answered, a little grimly. 'He would have been quite on for anything that might come his way, but one could see that already he was aiming higher when it came to marriage. No, I think what he said was quite true: that he really did only want a kind of superior housekeeper and social adviser.'

'And did you want to take it on?'

Joan smiled. 'For some reasons, yes. But not really. I'm too well fixed here. But I thought of you at once. I thought if you hadn't anything better, it might be useful. I imagine he'd be liberal about terms and all that.'

'It seems, Joan, like a glimpse into heaven.'

'Poor old Betty! Well, it's on the cards that you'll be appointed.'

'How does the thing stand? Did you mention me?'

'Of course; he knows by this time all about you. I thought it might put him off if I seemed to be pushing you, so I told him straight out that you were looking for a job and why. I said I would wireless you to meet the boat, and he said he would be glad of an interview before he went ashore.'

'Oh, then I'm to see him now?'

Joan glanced at the big clock on the opposite wall. 'In twenty minutes. I said you'd be here at eleven.'

'I just can't thank you enough, Joan.'

'More important still,' Joan smiled, 'I've ordered coffee for a quarter to. Buck you up for the fray.'

11

'Perfect.'

Joan moved uneasily and ceased smiling. 'Well,' she said, her apparent preface to every remark, 'I want to tell you everything, and there's another snag. Something I don't understand: it doesn't seem too straight.'

'I'm not a thought reader, my dear. You'll have to do better than that.'

'I'm not accustomed to dealing with low-grade intelligences,' Joan explained easily, continuing, 'I'll tell you what I saw, and you may draw your own conclusions. There's a man on board called Davenport: Mr Davenport. I've never spoken to him, but I'm told he's an artist, a painter in oils. Apparently he's an Englishman who has been over for some time in the States. Well, I was coming along the deck one night when, with the bad weather and so on, very few people were about, and I saw these two, Sir Geoffrey and Mr Davenport, in the lee of one of the deck houses deep in talk—intimate talk, you understand. They didn't see me. There was nothing in that of course, but here's where it comes in. A couple of days later I saw them introduced, and they pretended to be strangers.'

Betty's comment was interrupted by the arrival of the coffee.

'That sounds extraordinary,' she remarked, when the steward had gone. 'Sure you didn't make a mistake?'

'Positive. They were in the light of one of the deck lamps and I saw them as clearly as I see you.'

Betty was slightly puzzled, but she did not take the matter too seriously. Probably in spite of Joan's belief, she had made a mistake. But even if she were right, it did not seem to be very important. No doubt they would have some quite adequate explanation.

Further discussion was postponed by the arrival of Sir Geoffrey. He was of medium height and rather stocky build, with high cheekbones and a dark, saturnine face. His expression was sharp and there was in his eye that which gave Betty a feeling of slight disquietude. He was dressed, she thought, too well and he crossed the room with a pronounced rising motion in his gait.

'I can see at a glance it's your sister,' he said to Joan, in a curiously high-pitched voice, with just a suspicion of an American accent. 'How do you do, Mrs Stanton?'

'Sir Geoffrey Buller,' breathed Joan, and Betty held out her hand, though without getting up.

'My sister has just been telling me about you, Sir Geoffrey,' she answered. 'May I be the first on this side of the Atlantic to offer my congratulations?'

'Now that's very kind of you,' he returned, drawing over another chair. 'Don't go, Miss Brand,' he went on, as Joan got up. 'Nothing that I have to say to Mrs Stanton is private.'

'Sorry, but I've got one or two things to see to,' Joan smiled, tripping daintily to the door. 'You two have your talk and I'll be back presently.'

'Tactful, isn't she?' he squeaked—really his voice was rather like a squeak—then went on more seriously, 'Well, Mrs Stanton, she told you, I suppose, what I wanted to say to you?'

'I don't know that,' Betty smiled. 'She told me you were looking for a housekeeper, and as I want a job of the kind, I hoped we might come to terms.'

'A housekeeper?' he repeated. 'No; that's not quite the proposition. I want more than a housekeeper. I want a lady who will run the house, yes. But I also want someone whom

13

I can talk to occasionally and who will advise me on social matters. You can understand that I don't know much about the usages of that kind of society.'

This was promising enough. At least he was not giving himself airs.

'I could run your house, I feel sure. But with regard to advising you on social matters, I think you should have a man. What about a good valet?'

'A valet could keep me straight about the clothes I should wear and that sort of thing, but that's not what I should want the lady to help me with. I mean, questions like who should be asked on the same weekend and how they should sit at dinner: things like that.'

Betty smiled again. 'But, my dear man,' she almost said, though she changed it in time to, 'But, Sir Geoffrey, that wouldn't be a matter for me. You know your own friends and I couldn't presume to interfere about who you should or should not ask.'

He looked at her seriously, almost with a scowl. 'If you came, it would be your job all the same. I might have friends who were—what's the phrase?—mutually incompatible. You would have to sort them into lots which wouldn't jar, so to speak.'

Betty decided to leave her fences till she came to them. 'Oh well,' she agreed, 'I expect I could do that. And so far as seating people at table is concerned, I think I could manage it too. There again you would want compatible people to sit together, and where there was precedence to have it correctly observed.'

'That's it.' He seemed relieved and paused as if at a loss. 'I don't know that there's much I want to ask you,' he went on presently, 'because Miss Brand has answered most of my questions, but before you can decide, you might want to ask some of me. If so, please go ahead.'

'Well, I should want to know about my position in the house, also about salary and leave of absence and things like that, you know.'

He nodded. 'I can answer those straight away. Your position in the house would be that what you said about everything would go, subject of course to my reasonable requirements. Questions of leave of absence and suchlike wouldn't arise. You would be your own mistress and come and go as you liked, provided only that the house ran. You would have your own suite and in reason you could ask down any of your friends to stay with you if you were lonely.'

'I might abuse all this kindness.'

He smiled for the first time. 'Well, if you did, you would go,' he returned. 'But if you're anything like your sister I'm not worrying. Then salary. I'm afraid I don't know much about that. What about twenty-five a month and all found?'

'Pounds, or dollars?'

'Pounds of course.'

It was better, both in money and conditions, than Betty could have hoped. She wanted then and there to clinch the bargain, fearful only that out of further talk some hitch might arise. Yet her common sense told her not to seem too eager.

'That would be quite satisfactory as to amount,' she returned presently. 'What about the house money? Would I be expected to run the house on a given sum?'

'Oh, lord, no!' He seemed shocked at the idea. 'I'd give you a lump sum to start with. Then I should want you to keep a book or cards or something, and put down all you spend in each month, and at the end I should give you a cheque for the amount. Any other questions?'

She thought. 'I don't think so. That seems to cover everything.'

'Then what about it?' He seemed really eager. 'Will you— take it on?'

'I'd love it,' she said, though not too warmly. 'I'll take it and say thank you. I only hope I'll do what you want.'

'I guess you'll do it.' She was surprised by the satisfaction in his tones. 'Now let's see; we want to settle details—when you should come and so on.'

Their heads drew closer together and when Joan presently returned Betty had agreed to go to Ockham in three days' time, Sir Geoffrey sending the car to town to meet her.

It was with her heart overflowing with thankfulness, though slightly tinged with foreboding, that Betty returned that evening to London. Her first action was to withdraw her things from her hotel and move to one more in keeping with her new status. Once again she was too excited to sleep, but at least she tossed on a comfortable bed, in a clean and well-furnished bedroom.

2

The Start of the Job

Betty's thankfulness for the happier turn in her fortunes grew, if anything, greater during the three days left to her in town. Her relief was not merely on her own behalf. She had another worry that was no secret from her intimate friends, but unknown to the outside world. It concerned her twin brother. Roland had proved a disappointment. His acquaintances called him a ne'er-do-well, though she softened the word down into a 'misfit'. Artistic, with charming manners and kindly in all that did not incommode himself, he was yet selfish at heart, as well as being cursed with an almost ungovernable temper. Loving excitement and unable to bear the humdrum life of a bank clerk, the inevitable happened and he lost his job. He went to Paris, which he had known well in more prosperous days, and made ends meet by acting in a troupe which did occasional turns in the lower class music halls of the metropolis. In this precarious life he had often applied to Betty for help. Idolizing him as she always had—perhaps because they were twins—she could refuse him nothing, and while she remained

17

well-to-do she had pulled him through many a crisis. Her recent inability to help him had hurt her, but now she would be able to do this again.

Her satisfaction indeed was so great that she felt she must share her news or burst. She therefore went next day to call on her dearest friends, a couple named Barke. They had been living at Maidstone when, as John Stanton's bride, she had gone there eight years earlier. They had met at tennis and had quickly grown intimate, and when some five years later the Barkes moved to town, the friendship was not dropped. Though Betty had not told them how serious was her predicament, they knew she was left badly off and would be delighted to hear of her good fortune.

The family consisted of husband and wife and a married daughter living in Jamaica. Charles Barke was an artist of I distinction and Director of the Crewe Gallery. A Royal Academician, 'hung' each year as a matter of course and, a recognized authority on matters of art, he even made art pay. In appearance he was small and sturdy, with fair hair, a round face, observant blue eyes peering out through large horn-rimmed spectacles, and a belligerent expression oddly at variance with his gentle manner and kindly disposition.

Agatha Barke was what Betty called a dear. Also small, her looks were not her best point. She was stout and usually slightly untidy. But in character she was goodness and unselfishness personified. Her joy was to make other people happy, and she felt that no day was complete unless in it some lame dog had been helped over its stile.

When Betty arrived she found her dressed for out-of-doors.

'You provoking creature!' Agatha cried. 'Why didn't you ring me up? I have to go out in ten minutes. *Must* go: it's that wretched Collison exhibition and I have to open it. But look here, you come too! Then we can talk on the way.'

'Awfully good of you, Agatha, but I can't do that,' Betty returned. 'I just called for a moment to tell you of my good luck,' and she went on to give her news.

Mrs Barke beamed.

'My dear, I *am* glad,' she cried, and the warmth of her tone was like a cordial to Betty. 'And Charles will be delighted. You know, I get jealous sometimes, he thinks so much of you.'

'You're both too good to me for words,' and Betty meant it. 'How is Charles? I haven't seen him for some time.'

'First-rate. He's in Nimes. You heard about the find there?'

'No? What was that?'

'Six old canvases—in a small second-hand dealer's. They think one's a Raphael and that all are valuable. He's been asked to give an opinion.'

'His own special line.'

'Yes, he's in demand in such cases. In fact, he gets too many commissions of that kind now. He's been complaining that he can't get on with his own work and that he must begin to refuse them.'

Betty laughed. 'My goodness! Fancy *refusing* jobs like that! That's the reward of climbing to the top of the tree.'

Agatha made a face at her, then smiled affectionately. 'But you haven't heard *our* news,' she went on. 'We're off to America!'

'What?'

'America! A month's lecturing tour and holiday, six weeks altogether. I'm so excited I don't know whether I'm on my head or my heels.'

Betty jumped up and kissed her friend. 'Agatha! I'm so

19

delighted! You wanted that for a long time and I'm certain you'll love it. When do you start?'

'On Wednesday week. Just as soon as Charles can get away. He's been talking about it for ages, but it was just fixed up this morning. Yes, we'll love it. But there,' she glanced at her watch, 'I'm terribly sorry, but I must be off. Sure you won't change your mind and come with me?'

Two days later at the appointed hour of three in the afternoon, Sir Geoffrey Buller, resplendent in a new Rolls Royce, drew up at her somewhat modest hotel.

'How good of you,' she greeted him, 'to come for me yourself. I didn't expect this.'

'Unhappily,' he told her in his high-pitched squeaky voice, 'it's not so good as it seems. In the first place I've fired the chauffeur and the new one doesn't take over till tomorrow, and in the second I've just taken delivery of this car; in fact, I've been with a mechanic all morning learning about its inside.'

'Lucky for me at all events. The proper way to arrive anywhere is in a Rolls.'

'I hope you'll like it when you do get there,' he went on more seriously. 'It's a great big barrack of a place. Huge! It's like dining in a Zepp hangar in the evenings.'

'It's old, I suppose?'

'Before the Flood by the look of it. I don't know how old it is: fifteenth century, the butler says, but I don't suppose he knows.'

'Charming!'

'I'm not so sure,' he said doubtfully. 'It's a bit gloomy for my taste. And it wants a terrible lot done to it. I don't know how those people lived, my respected cousin and his crowd. You'd scarcely believe it, but there's not a private bathroom in the entire outfit. Not one in the house! What do you think of that?'

She smiled. 'I shouldn't have been surprised if you had said there was only one makeshift bathroom to do the whole establishment.'

'You're not so far wrong,' he agreed. 'There are five, but they're just what you say, makeshift. Look as if they were put in fifty years ago and not touched since.'

'Probably exactly what has happened. Are you going to put that sort of thing right?'

'Well, I fancy that if one's going to live in the place it'll have to be put into some sort of order. My heavens, those people had some funny notions. They've spent hundreds, *thousands* by the look of it, on the garden. There's a rock garden there would do for Buckingham Palace and Kew rolled into one: the stones must have cost hundreds, let alone the plants and the water supply and all the mainte- nance. Thousands poured out like that—and no decent baths in the house. Can you beat it?'

'Just the old ideas handed down from generation to gener- ation.'

'I don't know why they bothered with glass in the windows or electric light: though that's all a washout too. It'll have to be done again from A to Z.'

'You don't seem altogether smitten with your new abode,' she laughed, and though he turned it off with a joke, she believed her remark had gone home.

As they drove further she grew more certain of it. He was obviously disappointed. What he had expected, she didn't know, but it was evident he had not found it.

Yet when they reached Ockham and turned into the gates of Forde Manor, she could see no reason for disappointment.

On the contrary, first views at all events were charming. The drive curved past a little old huddled lodge—though probably without a bathroom of any kind—the overhanging timbering of which seemed scarcely able to bear the weight of wisteria and honeysuckle which clung to it. A belt of gnarled oaks screened the grounds from the road and then the drive reached open parkland. To the left were tennis courts and the extravagant gardens, the house showing as a grey mass some quarter of a mile further on. On the right the grass lawns sloped gently down to a quite decent sized lake.

'Oh,' cried Betty when she saw this last, 'is the lake yours?'

'Yes, it's all inside the property.'

'How delightful. That surely will make up for many bathrooms.'

'It's a catch, I agree,' he returned seriously. 'But there again there are boats and cushions and so on in the boathouse to carry a regiment of soldiers, but there's not an outboard motor in the whole concern.'

'They wouldn't have liked the noise.'

'But there are guns enough to arm the regiment. They didn't mind that noise.'

'Hush!' she returned with a scandalized expression. 'Have you forgotten that you're an Englishman? You're speaking lightly of sport. You may damn your government and cheat your baker and seduce your neighbour's wife, and no one'll think any the worse of you. But *sport*! My goodness, what are you thinking about?'

He laughed a little uneasily. 'I guess that's right,' he returned. 'I had forgotten about all this Test match stuff and so on till I got back and saw your papers.'

'*Your* papers.'

'Well—our papers then. It's different, over on the other side, but I suppose I'll get used to it again. What do you think of the house?'

They were now coming close to the front and Betty could see its entire extent. 'Why,' she cried, 'it's splendid! Magnificent! How can you feel disappointed about it?'

'I didn't say I was disappointed.'

'No, but your manner has. Why, it's grand.'

Though not perhaps one of the stately homes of England, Forde Manor was a really fine old pile. It was E-shaped, the main house having large projecting wings at each end, and a smaller one, the porch and probably a front hall, in the centre. It was built of old grey stone in the early perpendicular style. Its masses were admirably proportioned, the whole looking restful and dignified and ineffably secure.

The door was opened by the butler and they passed into a long hall with doors at the sides, a double staircase curving up to two surrounding balconies on first and second floor levels and a high timbered roof with central light. The walls were panelled in black oak and there was a huge open fireplace with a metal grate carried at either end on elaborate dogs. The furniture was sparse but in period, a black oak refectory table on a large rug in the centre, a few chairs, a tallboy, and some big game heads on the walls.

'You'd like to see your room, wouldn't you?' Sir Geoffrey went on. 'Then if you'll come down we'll have tea in this place next door,' he nodded towards the left; 'the blue drawing room, I believe.'

Betty was met at the first floor balcony by a superior-looking young woman who smilingly introduced herself.

'I'm Hawes, the head housemaid, madam. You wish to see your room?'

A good type, thought Betty as she smiled back. Honest, reliable and kindly. She felt instinctively that she and Hawes would get on, and this view became strengthened as they chatted.

The 'room' was at the end of the corridor. Betty was surprised and delighted to find that it was really a four-roomed suite consisting of two bedrooms, a sitting-room and one of the five bathrooms, though this latter could only be reached from the corridor. The furnishing was luxurious, but old-fashioned and rather sombre. The only thing lacking was a view of the lake, the windows being at the rear of the house and looking out over shrubberies and trees.

Tea was waiting in the blue drawing-room, so called from the shade of its Chinese carpet. Sir Geoffrey talked, not uninterestingly, about his life in America, and when they had finished he suggested a look over the place.

Fine as she thought the outside of the house, she was even more delighted with its interior. From the lofty central hall a corridor ran north and south along the centre of the house, beneath those on the upper floors. Off it opened an astonishing number of rooms. Beside the blue drawing-room there was another drawing-room, larger and more ornate in decoration, also a reception-room, a dining-room, a breakfast-room, a morning-room, a gun-room, a library, a study and some half a dozen others. Behind the hall were the kitchen and service pantries, which Mrs Jessop, the cook, would show her later.

'The two swell rooms are at the ends of the house,' Sir Geoffrey explained, as they reached a pair of doors across the corridor. 'They form those wings that project from the front. This one to the south is the ballroom, and the other used to be the banqueting hall and is now the picture gallery. Some room, isn't it?' He threw open the door.

Betty thought it was magnificent. About forty feet by eighty, it was lofty with a fine hammer-beam roof. All four walls except where the house joined on were pierced with windows, with stained glass showing idyllic or hunting scenes. Round the walls the old woodblock floor remained, but over the central area this had been replaced by a modern dancing-floor. The furniture was ordinary, but when Betty looked at the pictures she had eyes for nothing else.

'You've got some magnificent stuff there,' she cried. 'Surely those are invaluable?'

He nodded. 'So I'm told. I don't know a thing about pictures myself. But the butler tells me the best are at the other end of the house in the picture gallery. Come and have a look.'

'I promise myself a feast in here,' she returned as she followed him out.

'Then you're an expert?'

'Not I. But I'm fond of pictures and I have an artist friend, a Mr Barke, who has taught me a little. He's an enthusiast and you couldn't be in his company without getting enthusiastic too.'

'I wish I knew more about things,' Sir Geoffrey said plaintively. 'There's a lot of stuff in this place that's thrown away on me. I can't appreciate it.'

Betty almost began to like him. 'You'll soon learn,' she answered with conviction. 'You'll find these pictures grow on you. Then you'll wonder why you like them, and before you know where you are you'll be a connoisseur.'

He laughed, almost for the first time. 'I can see it happening,' he declared. 'This is the gallery.'

He threw open the door of the room forming the northern wing, and Betty caught her breath. The room was similar in size and construction to the ballroom, but here every available foot of wall space was occupied by canvases.

'I should want,' she exclaimed, as they walked slowly round, 'at least a week in here. What a priceless collection you've got!'

'I hope,' he said gravely, 'you'll have a good many weeks to look at them.'

'That's very nice of you,' she declared. 'But I won't see them now. I'll come back later and gloat over them.'

'Right,' he returned, apparently relieved. 'Care to have a walk round outside?'

'I'd love it.'

The terrace in front of the house was laid out as a formal Dutch garden, and though Betty did not particularly admire Dutch gardens, she had to admit how admirably the design suited its setting. The view across the lawns down to the lake was more in her line, restful and charming, fringed with great trees to right and left, and in the centre showing a vista of distant country beyond the lake.

The garden to which they now walked was what Betty called a dream. But it was not very different from other gardens, and presently continuing their tour, they passed the tennis courts and, crossing the drive, walked down over the grass to the lake. With the lake Betty was enchanted. It was roughly pear-shaped, with its lower broad end open to the house and lawns, and its narrower top surrounded by what looked like the beginning of a forest. They walked round it and inspected the boathouse, which was hidden by the trees from the main building. Betty, who was fond of boating, promised herself some delightful hours on the water. Finally they returned by the back of the house, where stood the garages.

'Lordly, aren't they?' Sir Geoffrey commented. 'There's room for twenty cars and fine space above them. Old hay lofts, I suppose. One thing I'll get here,' he went on, with more enthusiasm than he had yet shown, 'in one of those lofts: a workshop. I've wanted one all my life, and now I'll have it.'

'What kind of work do you do?' asked Betty.

'All kinds,' he grinned. 'Woodwork, metal work, electrical gadgets. I'm happier at that sort of thing than at anything else.'

That night as Betty turned in, she felt that the lines had fallen to her in marvellously pleasant places. She would never, she told herself, have such a chance again. If she couldn't make good and be happy here, it would be her own fault and she would deserve anything which might come to her. Soon she had completely settled down. She was tactful, and without interfering very much with anyone concerned, she contrived to introduce a number of improvements into the running of the house. These she would like to have discussed with Sir Geoffrey, but ten days passed before she found an opportunity. It proved gratifying in that he expressed his approval of all she had done, but unsatisfactory because she could get no hint from him as to his future intentions. During the discussion on the *Nicarian* he had been full of plans for entertaining: house parties as well as luncheons and dinners. Now his interest in these seemed largely to have died.

'Just go right ahead as you are,' he said eventually. 'I

don't know yet what I'm going to do. Time to make alterations when they become necessary.'

Betty thought this closed the discussion, but after a pause he went on. 'That respected cousin of mine must have been the hell of a queer guy. I've been going into the finance of this estate, and I will say,' his voice grew emphatic, 'that I never could have figured anything being let get in such a mess. There just aren't any accounts, not what you'd call accounts; no records of what was spent on various items, nothing! It just isn't believable.'

Betty looked up interestedly. 'I suppose the late baronet had so much that it didn't matter,' she suggested.

'That may explain, but doesn't excuse it, as Gladstone said in 1888. Well, I reckon everyone ought to know just how far he's solvent. But that didn't seem to have worried him.'

'There must have been plenty of money. One can see that from the way everything has been kept up—except, of course, the bathrooms.'

'Oh yes, that's right enough,' he answered unsmilingly, 'there's plenty of money and it hasn't been stinted. But imagine not knowing just how you stand! Can you beat it?'

'You'll put that right at all events.'

He smiled at that. 'I don't know if that's one below the belt,' he returned, 'but I certainly will. And it doesn't stop there. What do you think of having all that valuable stuff and pictures and so on, and none of it properly insured or only for a fraction of its value? I know nothing of costs myself, but I've been making inquiries.'

'I expect your predecessor took the view that as the pictures were irreplaceable, no money would make good their loss.'

'I wondered that at first, but I don't think so. I believe it was just slackness. Anyway, that's a darned silly notion. If you lose a valuable possession, why shouldn't you get its money's worth, even if that won't replace it?'

'I see your point,' she told him as she carefully fitted a cigarette into her long holder. 'It's just, I think, a different way of looking at things. There are two sides to every question, you know.'

'There are to this one, at all events,' he agreed, 'my late cousin's and mine.'

'That sounds very uncompromising.'

He lit a cigarette in his turn. 'Well, I reckon I must do something about it, and that's why I opened the subject: to tell you what I've decided. I'm having the entire outfit revalued: house, furniture, pictures and everything else. Some experts are coming tomorrow. They may be here some days. I thought you'd wonder what they were doing, so that's it.'

Next day two well-dressed, prosperous-looking men arrived and were shown over the house by Sir Geoffrey. He introduced them to Betty as Mr Merton and Mr Wilberforce, and asked her to help them in every way possible.

'We won't give much trouble, Mrs Stanton,' Merton assured her. 'Really all we want is acccss to the various rooms. We're just going to have a general look round now; then in the morning we'll start on the inventory.'

'It will take you some time, won't it?' she answered.

'There's a good deal to be done.'

'Ten days to a fortnight, I should imagine. But I needn't say,' he smiled, 'we'll not be longer than we can help. The pictures will take some time. What do you say, Wilberforce? Mr Wilberforce specializes on that kind of thing.'

'Yes,' said Wilberforce. 'I've not seen the pictures here, but I'm told they're very good.'

'They're magnificent, just delightful.'

Wilberforce looked at her speculatively. 'You're an enthusiast?' he suggested. 'Do you paint yourself?'

'No, but I'm fond of pictures and I've picked up a little through my friend Mr Barke.'

'Mr Charles Barke?' asked Wilberforce with more interest.

'Yes,' said Betty. 'Do you know him?'

Wilberforce nodded. 'Rather. Mr Barke is the ultimate authority in my walk of life; the last and highest court of appeal. I've been present when he's been examining canvases, deciding if they were genuine and so on, and I can tell you it's been a pleasure to watch him.'

Rather generous, thought Betty, from one art critic of another. She smiled at Wilberforce.

'May I come sometimes and watch you work?' she asked, 'or would I be too dreadfully in the way?'

He made the required reply as if he meant it, and the three men drifted on.

Next morning the two principals, each followed by retainers, arrived early and began operations. They were very thorough, going over with care everything on the estate. The work took exactly ten days, as Mr Merton had estimated.

Betty had some talk with each and found them pleasant and well informed. She was interested to learn that they were acting for the Thames & Tyne Insurance Company, with whom Sir Geoffrey was taking out a revised policy. This new one would be founded on the carefully estimated value of the actual articles insured, instead of on the round and wholly inadequate figure previously adopted.

Betty was sorry when the work was done. Though she wouldn't admit it even to herself, she was finding life at Forde Manor a trifle lonely. Her occasional chats with the two men had been a pleasure.

3

The Progress of the Job

Betty by this time felt as if she had spent half her life at Forde Manor. Save for that slight loneliness, she found the job ideal, and every day which passed made her feel more and more thankful that she had obtained it.

Only on one point was she dissatisfied, and that a matter which was not even her business. Sir Geoffrey was obviously unhappy. He had lost his optimistic eagerness and appeared to be worrying over some secret misfortune. Had it not been for Joan's warning, as well as what she had herself seen in his eyes, Betty would have tried to comfort him. But she was afraid to seem too sympathetic. Then at tea one afternoon he made an enlightening remark.

'How do you get to know people in this blessed place?' he asked. 'I've been here now ten weeks and I've scarcely spoken to a soul bar the newsagent and tobacconist and some of the other tradespeople in the village.'

'Well,' she answered, hoping she had not hesitated, 'it's not so frightfully easy. British reserve and all that, you know.

They're delightful of course when you know them, but sometimes it's hard to break the ice.'

'Now just what does all that mean?' he returned. 'Are you suggesting I won't be able to make friends with them?'

As she looked at his undistinguished features and listened to his squeaky high-pitched voice with its suggestion of working-class America, she realized that that was exactly what she was suggesting. But she couldn't hurt his feelings.

'Of course not,' she lied bravely, 'but you'll find it hard because you don't go in for the things that they do. If you were a crack shot or golfer or tennis player, you'd meet them on their own ground. As it is, you've no very obvious points of contact.'

He made a joking reply, but his air of disillusionment remained. Indeed, sometimes he looked so worried that she felt it must be due to something more pressing than his failure to enter the local society.

It was partly to help him in this respect and partly to gratify herself, that a couple of days later Betty made a suggestion. The Barkes had just returned from America and she had been intending to go to town to see them. Now it occurred to her that instead, they might be asked down to lunch at Forde Manor. Charles Barke, she knew, would enjoy seeing the pictures, while Agatha would be interested in the house, even if only as the scene of her new job.

'I should be very pleased if they'd come,' Sir Geoffrey answered when at tea that afternoon she broached the idea, 'but they're your friends and you'd have to do the asking.'

'Write,' she directed, 'a short note to Mr Barke saying that I said he might be interested in the pictures and asking him and Mrs Barke to lunch on whatever day you select.

I'll enclose it in a letter from myself, so it will really be a joint invitation.'

The visit took place on the following Friday. The Barkes turned up shortly before one and their obviously genuine admiration of the place pleased Sir Geoffrey and reduced his inferiority complex. Lunch passed off successfully enough. The Barkes were full of their trip, which appeared to have been an immense success. The lecture tour had taken them down to Florida, and for a week they had basked in the winter's summer of that favoured land. Charles had been gratified by the attention given to his lectures and Agatha by the kindliness and hospitality which greeted them on all hands.

'We had a great time,' Charles declared. 'You also liked the country, Sir Geoffrey?'

Sir Geoffrey had liked the country. He listened with just the right comments, then as their tales drew to an end, began to talk himself. He didn't pretend to knowledge which he had not got, but spoke with some shrewdness on his experiences in Chicago in real estate. This interested Barke, who had been to Chicago on a previous visit, and the two men were soon chatting like old friends. Betty and Agatha Barke always had plenty to say to one another.

They had coffee on the terrace, then after a stroll down to the lake, they turned to the ostensible object of the visit. Here again the affair clicked. Barke was impressed by the two great rooms and enthusiastic about the art collection.

'I knew you had some fine stuff here,' he told Sir Geoffrey, 'but I didn't realize it was as good as it is. I quite envy you.'

'I wish I knew more about art,' Sir Geoffrey bemoaned. 'The collection's a bit lost on me. I like the pictures, you understand, but not enough to enthuse.'

34

'If you like them,' Barke returned, 'your appreciation will grow the more you look at them.'

'One side of them I can appreciate all right, the financial,' Sir Geoffrey grinned. 'I had them valued and reinsured lately and I was staggered by the prices put on them.'

'Genuine old masters run into a lot of money,' Charles agreed. 'That Holbein, for instance, should be worth quite a tidy sum, and the Van Dyck,' he pointed as he spoke to a three-quarter length portrait of a nobleman in velvet and lace, 'is one of his best.'

They had tea after the inspection and then the Barkes drove off. It was not till a week later that Betty saw either of them again, when she lunched with Agatha in town.

'Wonderful pictures, those,' Agatha remarked as they discussed their visit. 'Charles raved about them. And poor Sir Geoffrey was right; he doesn't at all appreciate them.'

'What do you think of him, Agatha?' Betty asked with some curiosity.'

'Much more prepossessing than I expected from your description,' Agatha returned slowly. 'But he won't be taken up by the local bigwigs, if that's what he wants.'

'You think not?' Betty's sympathetic heart made her sorry to hear so decided an opinion.

'I'm sure of it and Charles says the same. "It's no use his trying," Charles said. "He seems a decent sort of fellow, but he's not the type." As Charles points out, he lives in another world and speaks a different language.'

'I'm afraid you're both right,' Betty admitted. 'But he will be disappointed and disappointment is unpleasant to watch. I think he's really hospitable and was looking forward to entertaining the countryside, and now it looks as if he's not going to do it.'

Agatha shrugged. 'There are plenty of people—nice people—whom he could entertain. I don't know that I feel so sympathetic.'

From the first moment they had met, Betty had noticed a strain in her friend's manner and now she asked if anything was wrong. For a moment Agatha did not answer, then just as Betty began to think she had been indiscreet, she explained.

'Nothing to do with me in a way,' she said, 'but Charles has been so worried. It's a profound secret, but you're safe.'

'My dear, if it's a secret I don't want to know it. It was only—'

'No, I'll tell you; I'd like to and Charles wouldn't mind. It's about Mr Lorrimer. You know; you've met him here. That tall young man with the blue eyes and the BBC announcer voice.'

'I remember. Charles's second in command?'

'Yes, he's assistant director at the Crewe. Or rather *was*, for that's the trouble. Charles has just had to sack him.'

'Oh, I'm sorry.' Betty hated to hear of unhappiness anywhere. But she could not see why Charles and Agatha' should be so much upset. 'What was the trouble?'

'Money, I'm afraid. It was when we were in America. It occurred to Charles when he came back to make a rough Check of the books, as he does occasionally. Well, he couldn't balance the figures, and to make a long story short, Lorrimer had been cooking them.'

This was more serious than Betty had somehow expected. 'Oh, that's bad, Agatha,' she answered. 'Had much disappeared?'

'Nearly two hundred and fifty pounds.'

'Horrible! And that young man! I couldn't have believed it.'

'Charles thought he was led into it without exactly meaning to steal. He's fond of women, you know. What we both think is that he got into some harpy's clutches and couldn't resist her demands. Such a pity! Charles was upset because he and Lorrimer's father were such friends. He brought him into the Crewe and to some extent felt responsible for him. You understand?'

'Of course. Is the father alive?'

'No, fortunately in a way. He'd be terribly cut up over this.'

'Horrible for Charles. But is he not prosecuting? I should have thought he'd have no option.'

'No, he's not. Lorrimer appeared so repentant and begged so hard for time to repay the money that Charles didn't know what to do. He thought if Lorrimer were sent to prison he would be ruined for life, and he remembered his promise to his father to do what he could for him. On the other hand there was his duty to the Crewe: he could not allow it to be swindled.'

'Very difficult, but I should have thought the Crewe would have come first.'

'It did. Very strictly between ourselves, Charles paid the debt himself. Then he gave Lorrimer six months to find the money, holding the threat of prosecution over him. Lorrimer doesn't know the debt is paid.'

'How handsome of Charles and how just like him! And what is Lorrimer doing? Has he private means, or how will he pay?'

'I don't know, but I think he has a little money. He's going to Paris and says he'll get work there among the ateliers: a tutor probably, with perhaps copying in his spare time.'

'Well, I think it was extraordinarily good of Charles. I don't believe there's another man in the world would have done it.'

'Nonsense! Charles liked him and found him very helpful. But altogether it has been an unpleasant fortnight for Charles since we got home. But there, that's enough of grousing. Let's talk of something pleasanter. What's the news of Roland?'

The inquiry, Betty thought, was just like Agatha, or for the matter of that, like Charles. Always kind! She was glad the Barkes knew all about Roland—except perhaps how much money she had given him. Their sympathy had been a support to her. And when Charles's frequent Continental business took him to Paris, he usually contrived to meet Roland.

'I had a letter about ten days ago,' she answered gratefully. 'Things appear to be looking up. He has a scheme for joining in a small company to tour the suburban music halls. Thinks it would do well.'

'Does he want you to put money into it?' asked Agatha, who had less use for Roland than her husband.

Betty smiled rather unhappily. 'He needn't. I have none to give him.'

'Just as well, my dear. You spoil him. He'd be far better standing on his own feet.'

'I don't think I do, Agatha. I know he was wrong to lose his job, but he'd had a very rough time in Paris and he's trying so hard to pull up.'

'If he does, it'll be thanks to you. You're much too soft hearted.'

'You old hypocrite!' Betty laughed. 'As if you wouldn't share your last crust with a beggar!'

For some days after Betty's visit to Town things went on uneventfully at Forde Manor. No other visitors came to meals or to see the pictures, but Sir Geoffrey now began leaving home more frequently, spending long days in London and weekends in Paris. Betty remained rather worried about him, for in spite of her efforts to cheer him up, he was undoubtedly growing more and more depressed.

Betty herself, while remaining profoundly thankful for her job, was finding her loneliness increasing. It was this loneliness and the time which lay heavy on her hands which redirected her thoughts to an old and cherished project. She wanted to write a novel. The theme was to be the successful struggle of a girl against poverty, and she had devised what she believed was a striking and original plot. Now the urge to put it all on paper took possession of her, and she presently went off to the nearest stationer's, bought some ruled quarto sheets and a new fountain pen, and set to work.

It proved an even greater interest and pleasure than she had expected, and on fine mornings when her housekeeping was done, she would take a boat out on the lake, and sitting on a pile of cushions, allow it to drift while she covered sheet after sheet of her new paper with her angular and rather untidy writing. She began with a Synopsis, which took several days to lick into shape, then when the great morning came on which she wrote 'Chapter I' at the head of a sheet, she felt that the keel of the magnum opus was at last visible on the stocks.

It was just a week later that she made a discovery which for the moment gave her a rather nasty shock. On her daily inspection of the picture gallery she noticed something unusual, though for a moment she could not think what it was. Then suddenly she realized: the Van Dyck was missing!

Its loss was not apparent at first sight, as the adjoining pictures had been moved so as to cover the vacant space. Whoever had taken it had therefore done so deliberately and unhurriedly.

For a moment she stood motionless, overwhelmed with dismay. How could anyone have got into the room? The door was always locked at night and it certainly had not been forced. Leaving the gallery, she locked the door, put the key in her pocket, and set off to look for Sir Geoffrey.

She found him writing in the library. He looked up as she entered, and his evident surprise increased as she carefully shut the door behind her and advanced into the room.

'Good morning,' he greeted her, getting up and pulling round an easy chair. 'You look as if a disaster of the first magnitude had occurred.'

'I'm afraid one has,' she answered. 'I went into the picture gallery this morning on my usual rounds and—' She paused, then added in a low urgent tone: 'Did you know that the Van Dyck is missing?'

For a moment he looked embarrassed. 'I'm sorry,' he said. 'I meant to tell you, but it slipped my memory. May I congratulate you on your supervision? It only went away yesterday afternoon and you discover it first thing this morning. Pretty good!'

She felt relieved, though still puzzled. 'Oh, if you know, it's all right. I thought at first it had been stolen.'

'No,' he smiled, 'not so bad as that. The fact is I'm having it cleaned. I've been advised that some of the pictures are in a very filthy state and that a bit of cleaning wouldn't do them any harm.'

Betty stared. She knew that the question of the cleaning and restoring of oil paintings was very controversial and that different artists held different views upon it. But to interfere with the Van Dyck seemed absolute sacrilege! And though she knew she was no judge, she didn't think it had needed cleaning.

'Oh, Sir Geoffrey,' she exclaimed, 'are you sure you're right? I mean, it's not my business of course, but it's so easy to damage a picture, and to damage a Van Dyck would be so irrevocable and so—so, forgive me, so unpardonable.'

'It's good of you to warn me,' he returned, 'but, you know, I'm not trusting to my own opinion. I've had what I'm told is the best advice. However, I'm impressed by what you say, and I'll certainly not get a second one done unless this turns out O.K. Perhaps your friend Mr Barke would advise me then?'

Betty laughed. 'I can tell you what his advice would be,' she declared. 'Except in the case of actual injury, he would be dead against doing anything. It's one of his obsessions. He's against unnecessary cleaning or renovation.'

'Then we must just wait and see how this turns out.'

She wished he would cancel the work till Charles could advise him, but she felt she could scarcely suggest it. She wondered who had recommended it. Only Mr Wilberforce, she imagined, as so far as she knew, no other artist of repute had visited the collection. She had asked Charles about Wilberforce, and he had said that he was a sound man and an expert in his own line. So perhaps the idea was not so bad as she had feared.

At the end of that week they had their second visitor. Betty had just finished her inspection and was about to sally forth with her manuscript when the butler called her to say that there was a Mr Davenport on the phone. He was asking for Sir Geoffrey, who had gone down to the village.

Betty took the receiver. 'I'm afraid Sir Geoffrey's out at the moment,' she explained. 'I'm the housekeeper and if you like I can give him a message when he comes in?'

'Thanks. My name is Davenport and I met Sir Geoffrey when crossing the Atlantic in the summer. He asked me to call if I were passing, and it was just to say that I shall be in your neighbourhood in the afternoon and would look in if Sir Geoffrey was not busy.'

'I'm sure,' Betty returned, 'he would be delighted.' As she spoke she heard Sir Geoffrey's voice speaking to the butler. 'Hold on for a moment,' she added. 'Sir Geoffrey's just coming in.' Then putting her hand over the mouthpiece, she went on: 'It's Mr Davenport who crossed with you on the *Nicarian*. He wants to call this afternoon if you can see him.'

'Davenport?' Sir Geoffrey queried. 'Oh yes, I remember. I'll speak to him.'

She heard him as she was leaving the hall. 'Hullo, Davenport! Very glad to hear of you again. And you say you'll be able to look in today?' There was a pause and he went on, 'Splendid! But couldn't you come to lunch?'

On this she waited to hear if special arrangements were to be made for the meal, and when Davenport accepted the invitation she turned back to the kitchen to give the necessary instructions.

She met him at tea. He was a curious-looking man. Small and inclined to stoutness, he had small round features, round eyes, a round mouth and a little round spud of nose. All these were grouped closely together in the centre of his round face. He had just been looking at the pictures.

'A splendid collection,' he exclaimed when introduced. 'I paint myself and I'm lost with envy of Buller.'

'Yes, isn't it grand?' Betty returned, 'and so well hung. The light is good in these rooms.'

Davenport agreed, rubbing his hands together. 'You know,' he went on, 'with the utmost respect to our host, I don't think it's right that such pictures should be privately owned. They should be the property of the world.'

Sir Geoffrey smiled. 'The world has no gallery to hang 'em in!'

'I mean, they should be the property of the nation. You know. The painter's nation preferably.'

'That's just what my friend Mr Barke says,' Betty put in. 'He thinks that great works of art should be available to everyone.'

'Mr Barke?' Davenport asked. 'Mr Charles Barke?'

'Yes,' returned Betty. 'Do you know him?'

Davenport shook his head. 'I don't, I've just come back to this country after some years in America. But of course I know his name. Everyone does.'

'But surely,' Sir Geoffrey interposed, going back a step in the conversation, 'there's not much to all that. These pictures are privately owned and in a private house, but anyone who wishes to see them can do so by asking leave.'

Davenport again rubbed his hands. 'Ah, but that's just it,' he declared. 'They shouldn't have to ask leave. They should have the right to walk in when they liked. You know. As they can into the National Gallery.'

'Just what Mr Barke says,' Betty added.

They discussed the point for some time, then Sir Geoffrey began to ask his visitor about his American experiences. 'I was in Chicago in real estate for several years. What part of the country were you in?'

'The south. I lived at Baton Rouge for three years, then

drifted about through Louisiana and Florida, painting and so on. I'm fond of sea and river scenes. I've done a number of the Mississippi and the cays off Florida.'

'Never been north?'

'Never been north or west. I've wanted to go to California, but somehow I've never been able to manage it. You know. You plan these things, but they don't always come off.'

Betty was interested and wished to ask Davenport where his pictures could be seen, but she hesitated. Somehow she did not take to him personally. There was a shifty look in his eyes which was unprepossessing. She felt in her bones that he was untrustworthy, then chid herself for letting a mere fancy influence her against him.

Outwardly he was much more a man of the world than Sir Geoffrey, but in spite of that, her feeling against him was so strong that she made no advances of any kind, and as soon as she decently could, she said goodbye and went back to her room. Shortly afterwards she heard his car starting up and then the sound faded as it went down the drive.

That was the first and last visit of Davenport to Forde Manor, and so far as she knew, Sir Geoffrey never paid a return call. In fact, as later she looked back over this part of her life, she realized that Davenport was the last visitor ever to be given lunch in the old house of Forde Manor.

4

The Loss of the Job

One morning two or three weeks after the disappearance of the Van Dyck, Betty was called by Sir Geoffrey to the picture gallery. 'Well,' he said, pointing, 'what do you think of it?'

The nobleman in velvet and lace was once more hanging in his old place, but a rather different nobleman. He was much brighter in colour, with stronger and more vivid tones. In parts which had formerly been dark and confused by shadow, details were now visible. To some extent Betty thought this was an improvement, yet the picture as a whole seemed to have lost character. It was less mellow, and the brighter colours struck her as restless and crude.

She did not know what to answer. Sir Geoffrey was so obviously pleased with it and there was so little about the place which appeared to give him pleasure, that she did not want to damp his enthusiasm. 'I'm not sure,' she said slowly. 'I like seeing more of the detail, but it looks a little too much brightened up. You like it yourself?'

'I do,' he admitted. 'But of course I'm not a judge.'

'I wish Mr Barke could see it,' Betty went on, 'but he and Mrs Barke are just leaving for a tour in the East and I'm afraid he wouldn't have time to come down.'

'I should be pleased to have his opinion when he comes back,' Sir Geoffrey said politely. 'I'm getting one or two more done and then he could see them all.'

Betty felt she ought to protest, but after all it was not her business, and while she deliberated he changed the subject and the opportunity was gone.

During the next few weeks a number of other pictures were done, and the more she saw of them, the more strongly Betty felt that the work was a mistake. The pictures definitely were not improved. She was perturbed also by Sir Geoffrey's choice. Broadly speaking, those which had been done were among the best of the collection. They included an admirable Goya, an undoubted Franz Hals, a Murillo, a Fragonard and a small Teniers. Terrible if they were really being damaged, yet once again it was Sir Geoffrey's responsibility, not hers.

Time passed with increasing speed until November came in and Betty realized that she had been for six months at Forde Manor. She was liking the job more and more. Its advantages of a comfortable home, light duties and a settled income—the greater part of which she was saving—remained unaltered, while its earlier drawbacks of loneliness and boredom she had now entirely overcome. She could not be bored while she had for a spare time occupation the Great Work—which had now reached Chapter IX—and as for company, she had scraped acquaintance with a number of the local people and could always count on a cup of tea or a game of golf if she wanted either.

One unexpected friend she had made was Mrs Relf, the

woman who lived in the Forde Manor gate lodge. Relf was a quiet individual with a pleasant smile who was employed at the Manor as a sort of handy man. He did everything that was no one else's job. He looked after the boats and the lake sluices, stoked the central heating furnaces in the winter, knew where the switches and valves were situated, besides doing all sorts of small repairs both inside the house and out.

Betty had first got to know his wife when, caught one day in a shower close to the lodge, she had asked for shelter. She had taken an instantaneous liking to the kind, motherly woman with her soft Western accent—she was from Somerset—and her look of placid and dependable competence. She liked also the neatness of her dress and the spotless cleanliness and comfort of the kitchen. And when she had talked to her for a little—it was a long shower—she began to respect her for the breadth of her views and the charitable way she spoke of others.

All this time the deterioration in Sir Geoffrey was slowly continuing, and much as Betty regretted it, she did not see how she could help him. Gradually from moody he had become positively morose. He spent long periods alone in his workshop, which at least he ought to have enjoyed, as he turned out some beautiful work both in wood and metal. But otherwise he seemed increasingly unhappy. He now made no attempt to hide his disappointment at not entering the local society and seldom referred to his neighbours without some sarcasm or bitter gibe. Also he had grown more secretive, more furtive, more unwilling to speak of himself or his concerns. But he must, Betty felt sure, have friends somewhere. He was away much more, and so far as she could gather, the principal loadstone was in Paris.

At times Betty grew seriously upset as she thought over the situation. That things could go on indefinitely as they were, seemed impossible. A breakdown of some kind was inevitable.

In December it came. One afternoon at tea Sir Geoffrey told her quite casually and unemotionally that he was fed up with Forde Manor and had decided to leave. He would sell the entire place, lock, stock and barrel, and return to America with the proceeds. The one thing he would regret, he went on handsomely enough, would be to say goodbye to her, as she was the only person who had been really friendly to him since he had re-entered Britain.

'Of course,' he added, 'there's no hurry. I don't know what you'll want to do; go to friends or look out for a job or what, but whatever it is you'll have plenty of time to make arrangements. So don't let the idea upset you.'

It naturally did upset Betty, profoundly. Her search for a job was still too recent for her to have forgotten its terror. Now this would start all over again. It was true that she was in a much better condition to meet the strain' than she had been six months earlier. All the same, to lose a job which suited her so ideally was a cruel blow.

She would have liked to have seen the Barkes to obtain their possible advice and certain sympathy. But they were in India and now talked of going to the Malay States. Betty felt driven back on herself, for though she had plenty of friends, she was not on such intimate terms with any of the others.

Then a further consideration struck her. Her book! She had got on well with it during these last months. Eighteen chapters out of an estimated twenty were finished. And they were good chapters, so she was convinced. Indeed, she was amazed at how good they were. Nothing gave her greater pleasure than to read over some of the earlier passages. She loved the sound of the words, she thrilled again at the skilfully built up crises, she was moved afresh by the pathos of the sadder scenes. Excellent work, certain of success!

And now the whole thing would be stopped. Its completion would be deferred, perhaps indefinitely. She certainly couldn't write during the strain of looking for a job, and perhaps not even after she got one.

And there was another point. If the book were a success it would bring in money. What a pity if she could not have the time to finish it! It would not take long. Three or four weeks and the thing should be done.

It was then that her three great ideas occurred to her. First she thought, why not finish the book before looking for a job? She could well afford it. She had now £150 to her credit in the bank. The book once finished, she could close down temporarily on her writing.

Presently followed the second. Why should she not stay in this charming district which she knew and so greatly liked? A couple of rooms in some small house should not be hard to find.

The third completed the cycle. Mrs Relf's! The gate lodge was a good-sized house, and as the Relfs' son was away from home, only the elderly couple occupied it. Would Mrs Relf take her?

Next day she put up her idea to Sir Geoffrey. He gave it his unqualified approval, then paused and said seriously: 'There's no bathroom in that lodge.'

She laughed, then after agreeing that it was no laughing matter, went on: 'I would have to do with what a lot of my ancestors had to do with: a portable bath. Sad and wholly to be deplored, but I'm afraid necessary under the circumstances. Of course, Mrs Relf mightn't have me.'

He was still thinking. For a time he didn't answer, while he glanced speculatively at her out of the corner of his eyes. She thought he looked unpleasantly shrewd, but when she heard what he had to say her delight overwhelmed every other feeling.

'I'll tell you what I'll do,' he went on at last. 'I can see an unexpected advantage to myself in this. I'll build a bathroom at the lodge and I'll pay whatever Mrs Relf charges you, if in return you'll keep an eye on the place till it's sold, It wouldn't mean very much, just a look over the house every now and then to see that the central heating was properly kept up and that damp wasn't getting in, and perhaps a word to the gardener if he got slack. Also I should want you to show round prospective purchasers.'

'Why,' she cried, 'that would be perfect. But it's not a fair arrangement. You wouldn't be getting anything like a return for your money.'

'I think I should,' he declared and again there was something in his manner which she found vaguely repellent. 'I'm not proposing to pay you a salary, you know; only Mrs Relf's charges. However, that's my side of it, and if I'm satisfied you needn't worry. The question is, what about you?'

'Satisfied?' she repeated. 'I should just think so! More than satisfied. Why, it's perfectly ideal for me. That is—' she hesitated.

'What's the snag?'

'Well, it's just that I couldn't promise to go on indefinitely. It might be some. time before the place was sold, you see.'

'Naturally. You stay as long as it's convenient to you, and

if you leave,' he smiled slightly, 'my payment to Mrs Relf stops.'

'Then I accept,' she declared warmly, 'and thankfully.'

'Right,' he returned, 'that's settled: Now I'll tell you what I propose. I'm fed up with the place and I want to get out of it. I'll ask you to supervise the dismantling or packing up or whatever you do to the rooms. By the time that's finished the household staff will have worked their notice and they can clear out and I'll close the house. I'll keep the central heating going, as I'm advised it would be worthwhile for maintenance reasons. Also the garden should be kept up, as the first sight of a place has a deal to do with a person's reactions to it.'

'Sound psychology,' she smiled.

'Business at all events,' he returned.

Half an hour later Betty found that Mrs Relf was even more delighted with the prospect than she herself, and a firm arrangement was made.

Events then moved quickly. No structural alteration to the gate lodge was found to be necessary and by some miracle the bath was ready within the week. In due course Betty moved to her new quarters, finding them extremely comfortable. Forde Manor was put on the agents' books and its sale widely advertised. First Sir Geoffrey and then the servants left; she and Relf presently became the joint caretakers, and in a very few days she had settled down to a new phase of her life.

To the book the move proved very advantageous. Not only had she more time on her hands, but she was now able to plan her day with system. Finding that she could do better work in the mornings, she set apart the time between breakfast and lunch for the actual writing. After lunch she relaxed. It was then that she made her inspection of the house and grounds, called to see her friends and took such exercise as she desired. In the interval between tea and dinner she revised her morning's work and considered next day's quota. This second spell she did not mind breaking if she wanted to go to town or take a holiday, but the morning she did her best to keep inviolate. Her book remained her great thrill, and while she was working at it she envied no one in the world, not even Sir Geoffrey, who was in Italy.

He had taken up his quarters in Rome for the time being. Betty wondered if he were trying to get into English society there. If so, she hoped he would have more success than in Surrey. She had had a letter from him announcing his arrival and saying that he was considering moving on for a week or two to Capri. He kept her informed of his whereabouts, as one of her duties was to forward his correspondence.

During this period Betty was rather worried about her brother Roland. She had had a further long letter from him about his idea of forming a troupe to tour the Parisian suburban music halls.

'I would manage it myself,' he wrote, 'and I've two splendid people in my mind for the leads, man and woman. Also for the three other parts we would need: six would be enough to start with. I've been round and I've found eleven houses that would give us one turn a week—if they liked the show, of course. That would be practically two turns a night, or four where there were double houses. With luck we might get on the air also. There's money in it, old girl, if only we could get going. But that, as you can imagine, is the snag. My share would be £120, and I haven't a bean. I know you've been having bad times yourself, but if you could do anything for this, you'd be no loser. Any help you could give us would remain your property, upon which we would pay interest as a first call on profits . . .'

She sighed as she thought it over. The letter was so like Roland: enthusiastic, but with an enthusiasm carefully controlled, plausible, persuasive, with a superficial air of hard-headed business ability. These traits no longer took Betty in. She felt sure that when the time came the leading lady would have left for America or the managements of the eleven music halls would have mysteriously filled their programmes. Never mind. Dear Roland! How gladly she would give him the money, if only she had it to give.

But she had, though of course £120 would make a big hole in her savings. She wished she knew more about the scheme. She did not exactly disbelieve Roland; it was just that his artistic imagination sometimes strained the facts. Often under similar circumstances she had thought of going over to Paris, but there were reasons against it. First there was the expense. Next, she shrank from seeing the conditions under which she believed Roland lived. And lastly, it would be no use for her to look into any of his schemes. In his presence she lost her critical faculty and he could put anything over on her that he chose.

On the other hand she believed from the tone of his recent letters that he was doing better. If so, and if this new scheme would give him a real chance to get his head above water, well, he ought to have that chance.

She would have liked to consult the Barkes about it, but though they were on their way home, some time would still elapse before they arrived. She therefore replied to Roland that she was not at present able to advance £120, but that she would be glad if he would keep her advised about the idea, as she might later be in a position to do so. Roland didn't always reply to this kind of letter, but he did so on this occasion, so warmly and without further begging, that she could scarcely resist sending him the entire sum.

For Betty the time now began to pass very quickly indeed. Towards the end of January, Sir Geoffrey came home. He stayed in London and ran down occasionally to visit his beloved workshop and have a chat with Betty. So far not a single offer had been received for the place, though a number of people had inspected it. Then about the middle of February, Sir Geoffrey went back to Rome, which he appeared really to have liked.

Once again Betty settled down to work. She had now finished her first draft and was hard at work revising. This she found even more engrossing than the original composition, and the days fled happily by.

In the first week in March the Barkes returned, and from the note Betty received from Agatha it was evident that their Eastern tour had been even more successful than that to America. Agatha asked her to go up and see them and she decided to do so next day.

They were naturally full of the trip and during lunch the talk was of India and the Malay Archipelago and the people they met on the various boats. Then they discussed the closing of Forde Manor and Sir Geoffrey's reactions to Rome, finally turning to Betty's more personal affairs.

'I was wondering if Charles would do me a great favour,' she adventured when she thought the time was ripe. 'It's rather a lot to ask, I'm afraid.'

'Don't be silly,' Agatha adjured her. 'Of course he'll only be delighted.'

'Dear people,' Betty returned gratefully. 'I know how good

you both are. It's about that scheme of Roland's. I told you something about it,' and Betty explained the further details she had learnt.

'A hundred and twenty.' Charles looked grave. 'That's a lot of money.'

'I don't think it is really,' Betty said more eagerly. 'You see there are not only all the clothes and so on, but he has to live while they're getting under way.'

Charles looked dubious. 'I'm afraid,' he was beginning, when Agatha interposed in her brisk forceful way. 'You needn't say anything. Don't you see that she had decided to back Roland? Haven't you, my dear, or am I wrong?'

'I should like to,' Betty admitted, 'if only I was sure of the facts. I don't mean,' she added hastily, 'that I doubt Roland. Only as you know, he gets carried away.'

'We understand,' Agatha nodded.

'I wondered, Charles, whether next time you were in Paris, you'd let Roland call on you and hear what he has to say?'

'Of course,' Charles declared warmly. 'You'd like me to report to you?'

Betty shook her head. 'I want much more than that, I'm afraid. I want to give you the money before you start and to ask you either to hand it on to Roland or to say nothing about it as you think best.'

Charles gave a short laugh. 'But, my dear Betty, that is asking rather a lot,' he said ruefully. 'You want to make me responsible for handing over most of your capital to a scheme of which I can't possibly judge the chances of success.'

'No, it's not that.' Betty spoke earnestly. 'I've already taken the decision. I'm going to pay unless there is some special reason why I shouldn't. All I ask is that you hear Roland and hand him the money unless there's something that strikes you as actually fishy.'

Charles was unwilling, but Agatha plumped for Betty's plan and insisted that he must carry it out. 'I'll do my best,' he agreed at length, 'but I can't guarantee that my decision will be wise. You'll have to take the chance of that.'

'I'll take it and thankfully,' Betty assured him. 'And I just can't say how grateful I am.'

'Right,' he smiled, though still rather ruefully, 'I'll let you know when I'm going over.' Presently the conversation swung back to Forde Manor.

'It doesn't seem as if Sir Geoffrey was going to sell it,' Betty declared. 'It's been on the market now for nearly three months and there hasn't been a single offer.'

'Too big for most people,' Agatha suggested.

'I should think so,' Charles agreed, 'and not in a good place for a residential hotel, which is about all it's good for. I'm not surprised he's having difficulty.'

Betty chuckled. 'He said it would make a swell roadhouse,' she told them, then suddenly remembering that her story would interest Charles, she went on: 'But I didn't tell you about the pictures. He's had a lot of them cleaned.'

Charles Barke stared. 'Cleaned?' he repeated. 'Very few of them wanted cleaning. He hasn't done any of the good ones, I hope?'

'I'm afraid he has. You remember the Van Dyck and the Goya? He's had them done, as well as several others.'

'Good lord! What was he thinking about?'

'He was told they wanted it.'

'No doubt. But not by anyone really qualified.'

'That's what I thought you'd say,' Betty answered. 'Also

56

he's done that small Teniers. I don't know if you remember it? And a Murillo and a Fragonard, as well as several others. He's done over a dozen altogether.'

This roused Charles, as Betty knew it would. 'It's a crime,' he declared hotly, 'that ignorant fools like Buller should have control of such work—work that they can neither understand nor appreciate. Have they been much damaged?'

'I'm afraid they've not been improved,' Betty admitted. 'You can see more detail, but they somehow look cruder. I don't know exactly what it is: the suggestion of complete perfection is gone.'

Again Charles raved. 'That's worse than ever! They've been restored. The man should be locked up in Broadmoor.'

'They mayn't be so bad as I think,' Betty went on. 'I'm not a judge, as you know.'

'They're worse, I should imagine, Charles returned gloomily, 'and I don't expect it would take a judge to see it.'

'Why not go down and have a look at them yourself?' Agatha suggested.

'Yes, come down, both of you,' Betty returned warmly. 'I was going to ask you to come and have tea in my gate lodge in any case. Now you'll have a motive and I'll get you.'

'I'd like that,' Charles admitted. 'As you may know, I've taken a strong line about unnecessary work of this kind, and I'd like to see if these support my case. But I can't spy on this maniac.'

'Nonsense,' said Betty firmly. 'Coming to tea with me would seem perfectly natural, even if it wasn't'—Agatha made a face at her—'and when you're there you'd obviously like to have a look at the pictures. No spying about it.'

'Of course not. Don't be silly, Charles,' came the wifely closing of the argument. 'Let's see now, this is Wednesday. When can we go?'

Charles took an engagement book from his pocket. 'I'm lunching with the Spencers at Woking on Monday,' he said presently. 'I am advising him about a Claude that he wants to sell. You're coming too, by the way, Agatha. Now suppose we come home via Ockham that afternoon and call on Betty?'

'Quite an idea,' Agatha approved. 'That suit you, Betty?'

Betty declared that it was idyllic perfection for her and the talk drifted back to the Eastern tour.

5

The Precursor of Tragedy

On the following Saturday there was a letter from Charles. Agatha was down with 'flu and rather ill. There was no chance of her being well enough to leave her bed on Monday, but he, if he might, would come alone.

It was the seventh fresh case of 'flu Betty had heard of that day. For two or three weeks an epidemic had been raging, and now it seemed to have reached its climax. It was not a serious type, but it left its victims weak and acutely sorry for themselves.

So far Betty had escaped, but next day, on the Sunday, she developed a suggestive lassitude with accompanying headache. She fought it off, but it persisted, and that night she went early to bed, having taken quinine and hot drinks.

The post on Monday morning brought a letter from Sir Geoffrey. He wrote from a hotel in Capri, where, he said, he was spending a fortnight with some Americans whom he had met in Rome. After inquiries about herself and the Manor, he went on: 'I have mislaid a certain paper, a testimonial from my employers in Chicago, which I require in connection with a company out here. I am thinking of buying an interest in it, on condition that I am made a director. I want to prove my business ability. It has occurred to me that this paper may be in one of the drawers in the old bureau in the library. I thought I cleared out everything valuable from those drawers, but might not have done so. The key of the bureau is on the smaller of the two bunches you hold. I should be grateful if you would have a look, and if you can find the testimonial, please send it here under registered cover.'

Betty felt somewhat better, and after breakfasting in bed she got up and went over to the Manor to look for the paper. She was still a little shaky and it was an effort to concentrate on what she was doing.

She quickly found the key of the bureau and began to work. In accordance with an apparently immutable law of the universe, the document was in the last drawer she opened. She replaced the papers she had disturbed and locked the bureau. Then enclosing the document with a short note to Sir Geoffrey, she went over to the post office, registered the letter, and returned to the lodge.

She was tired by her walk, though the distance was not great. The day was unpleasant, heavy and muggy, with a blustering wind from the west which drove before it a fine and very wetting rain. Indeed, when she reached her room she frightened herself by suddenly feeling faint. Mrs Relf shook her head reproachfully.

'You didn't ought to have gone out at all, mem,' she admonished her, as she poured her out some brandy; 'not with 'flu coming on or whatever it is. And if you take my advice you'll go straight back to bed and I'll bring you up a bit of lunch later.'

'But Mr Barke is coming to tea,' Betty protested.

'Well, it's not for me to say, mem, but you tell me his number and I'll ring and put him off. Or if you wish, I'll see he gets his tea here, all just as if you were down yourself.'

'I'm sure you would, Mrs Relf. But I mustn't give way like that. I'll go and lie down and get up again before he comes.'

It was not long, however, before she realized that she was too ill to entertain Charles. She therefore called Mrs Relf and asked her to ring him up and put the visit off. The lodge was on an extension from the Manor, but on the closing of the latter, the extension had been left switched through, so that the lodge was directly connected with the exchange.

The visit off her mind, Betty turned in and found that bed was the place for which she had been unconsciously longing all the morning. She listened dully to Mrs Relf's voice telephoning the message, then gave herself up to the luxury of thinking about nothing whatever. Presently she fell asleep.

She woke feeling a good deal better, though with no desire to get up. The house was very still, but presently she heard Mrs Relf moving in the next room and called her in.

'Oh, mem, you're looking more like yourself,' she was greeted. 'Maybe it's not the 'flu after all.'

'I don't believe it is,' Betty answered bravely, though she had little doubt that it was a mild attack. 'I'm feeling better. Did you get through to Mr Barke?'

'No, mem, he called here about an hour ago. He had left home when I rang up, and the message was not repeated on. He was sorry to know you were laid up, but he wouldn't allow me to wake you.'

'Oh,' Betty cried, 'I'm so sorry I was asleep. He's coming back to tea, I hope?'

'I asked him, saying I knew you would wish me to. But he wouldn't come. He said he hoped to pay another visit with Mrs Barke when you were all right again.'

'Yes, I hope he'll do that. Too bad; I wanted him to see the pictures.'

'He saw them, mem. He asked me and I sent Relf with him.'

'Oh, good! That was quite right.'

So he had seen Sir Geoffrey's improvements. Betty wondered what he had thought of them. That he had disapproved, she could have sworn.

She spent the rest of the day luxuriously in bed. For once she was content to lie still without thinking even of her book.

That night she had a rather unpleasant dream: not the usual nightmare in which she was trying to run through a glutinous sea or with impossibly heavy weights attached to her feet, but still disagreeable enough. She was in some large, dark and dangerous space, trying desperately to find an EXIT notice which she knew was there, but which she could not see because she was blinded by some unknown operator flashing a gigantic torch at intervals into her eyes. She would all but catch the letters with their message of safety, when flash! another beam would strike her, leaving everything else a pitchy black.

Presently she struggled into half wakefulness. The flashing was still going on. It was, she now saw, not bright like a torch; rather was it a faint continuous light which increased and diminished irregularly and to a small extent.

She opened her eyes. The room was dark, but the square

of the window was faintly illuminated. As she gazed the light waxed slightly, then waned again.

For a moment she lay pondering the strange phenomenon. Then suddenly she was wide awake. Leaping from bed, she tore aside the curtain and gazed out.

The sky to the northward—in the direction of the Manor—was dully red, and the branches of the trees between her and the house showed in sharp black tracery against it. Then slowly the light increased and for a moment a brilliant spot showed through the branches, flickered and faded back as before.

'Fire!' she screamed as she began wildly to throw on some clothes. 'Fire! Fire! The Manor's on fire!'

As she raced down to the telephone she heard exclamations and movement in the Relfs' room. She had scarcely discovered that the telephone was dead when Relf appeared, stumbling downstairs.

'The Manor!' she repeated. 'It's on fire and I can't get through. Your bicycle! Give the alarm!'

He nodded and dashed out, while Mrs Relf, hurriedly buttoning on some clothes, appeared on the stairs. 'Oh, mem,' she cried, 'it's the Manor! Oh, this is awful!'

'Come and see if we can do anything,' Betty shouted, wrapping a coat round her and thrusting her feet into gumboots.

'Don't go out, mem! Don't go out!' Mrs Relf implored as she hurried after her. 'You'll get pneumonia.'

But Betty was already out of earshot, running fast but rather unsteadily towards the house. The drive swung outwards towards the right, approaching the Manor in a wide curve, but there was a direct path through the garden, and this Betty took. At every step the light grew brighter and she could now see a huge column of smoke trailing away towards the right. The wind was still blowing gustily from the west, though less strongly than on the previous day. The rain, now that it might have been helpful, had stopped.

The garden path brought Betty out at the end of the house, where the great bulk of the ballroom wing stood up black and square against the brightness. Fortunately it, at least, was not yet on fire, and ideas of saving the pictures leaped into Betty's mind. Then she rounded its projecting corner to where she could see the front of the house, and at once stood stock still in horror.

The entire centre of the building was ablaze. For half its length smoke was pouring from windows and roof, while the block containing the porch and hall was a raging furnace. The roof light over the hall had gone and from the opening were issuing the huge balls of flame, like rapidly rising and vanishing balloons, which had lit up her bedroom. A fierce and steady roar came from the building, with sharp crackling like rifle fire. As Betty watched, a light sprang up in a bedroom near the hall, the glass in the window fell with a crash, heard faintly above the general noise, and a tongue of fire shot out.

Betty felt paralysed. What could be done against such odds? The fire was simply eating the house. It was spreading from the centre in both directions, more quickly with the wind towards the picture gallery, but still quickly enough towards the ballroom. Far back as she was standing, the heat was already intense. As she watched, the next window in the line fell out. No wonder the telephone was dead. The extension switch was in the central hall: in that glowing mass of flame.

Now she was joined by Carson, the gardener, who lived

along the road not far from the lodge. Some neighbours followed him, also wakened by the glare.

'Oh, Carson,' she cried, 'the local brigade will never be enough! Hurry and ring up London!'

'The local brigade's coming. We've sent for them.'

'It won't be enough! Ring up London! Quickly, Carson! Don't delay a moment! Tell them two lots of engines will he wanted, one for each end. And tell them,' she halted him with an imperious gesture as he moved off, 'tell them there's a lake a couple of hundred yards from the house.'

The gardener waved his arm and disappeared, while Betty turned to the little knot of neighbours, five men and two women, who had arrived.'

'Oh,' she panted, 'the pictures! They're worth thousands! Hundreds of thousands perhaps! We must do something before the brigade comes!'

A large well-built man, whom she suddenly recognized as the postman, stepped forward.

'We'll do what we can, mem,' he declared. 'Where are they kept?'

'In the two wings,' Betty pointed. 'The side doors will be locked. Can you get ladders and break the windows and pass them out that way?'

The postman, an old naval rating accustomed to prompt action, took charge. 'Here you, Bill,' he shouted, as one of the under-gardeners hurried up, 'we want to break in through that there window to get out the pictures. A ladder and an axe! Look slippy, now.'

'Aye. Lend a hand, chaps!' The under-gardener ran off, beckoning towards the yard.

'The windows look middling high, mem,' the postman went on to Betty. 'Can we reach them from the floor inside?'

Betty doubted it, and another man was dispatched to bring a second ladder.

'How'll we know the valuable ones?' continued the postman, glancing appraisingly at the slowly approaching furnace. 'We'll never get them all out.'

'I'll get in and show you here. But the best are in the other wing. If you could start some men here, we could perhaps get another ladder and try there.'

Just then appeared on his bicycle, solid and comforting-looking, a policeman. Betty turned to him.

'We've sent both for the local brigade and to London,' she explained, quickly, 'and we're going to break in here to get some of the pictures out. But the best pictures, worth thousands, are in the other wing. Can you help us there while Mr—' she pointed to the postman, 'does what he can here?'

As she spoke, a little knot of men appeared round the corner of the ballroom, running with two short ladders. One of these was quickly put up at the side of a window and the postman, seizing the axe which another man had brought, climbed up and began smashing out the window. The second ladder was pushed through and fixed in position and the postman disappeared inside.

'Can you do the same at the other wing?' Betty implored the policeman. 'There's a long ladder in the yard and you could cut it in two. I want to show them the best pictures here and then I'll follow you.'

For a moment she thought the policeman was going to be official. He had taken out his notebook and was turning over the pages. Then to her relief he put it away.

'Reckon that must wait,' he answered, with a crooked smile.'

'We'll do what we can.' He turned to a knot of fresh men who had just arrived. 'Come along, lads, and lend a hand to save the pictures. Worth a dozen fortunes, they are.'

Meanwhile Betty had climbed to the window, and having with difficulty transferred herself to the second ladder, got down into the ballroom. It was brilliantly lit up by fire through the windows in the wall which gave on to the front. But it was still cool, and though the flames seemed to be perilously near, there might be time to save the best of the collection.

Now Betty suddenly realized that she had undertaken a difficult task. It wasn't easy at a moment's notice to decide the relative excellence of the pictures. Three, a Holbein, a Poussin and a Morales, were outstanding, but after them the choice was not so obvious.

'Those three first,' she therefore decided, 'and after them as many of the others as you can manage. I must go to the other wing.'

The postman helped her out and she stood for a moment to recover her breath, before hurrying round by the yard to see how the policeman and his helpers were getting on. She could see some of them across the space of Dutch garden and lawn in front of the house, indefinite figures dancing in the heated air, lit now by the blaze, hidden now by coils and wisps of smoke. The fire had by this time become an awesome sight, though magnificent also. It had spread with almost incredible speed. The entire spine of the building, the upright stroke of the E, was now alight and belching forth huge clouds of smoke along its whole length. At least a dozen more windows had fallen out and showed as rectangles of blinding light, from which great tongues of flame were shooting out and disappearing up into the air, while showers of brilliant sparks floated away into the distance. The grounds and trees down to the lake were now illuminated by the fierce glare, as if floodlit by red-beamed searchlights of continually varying power. The roar of the flames was indescribable, the crackling menacing and horrible. Fanned by the still considerable wind, the fire was travelling more rapidly towards the far wing, and Betty got a shock when she realized how terribly near it had reached the picture gallery.

She was just about to turn away when there came a terrible rending, tearing noise which rang out high above the general din, and as she stood motionless, gazing, she saw with horror the roof of the central hall slowly disappear. It crashed down inside the building and a spurt of flame, solid and bigger than an ordinary house, rolled up to the sky, while sparks and burning fragments poured like fireworks from the windows.

Then suddenly the light went out of Betty's world. She struggled for a moment to keep her grip on things, but without success. Dimly she was conscious of the ground swinging about, then coming up to meet her, and then a great blackness shutdown on her and she sank slowly into oblivion.

6

The Aftermath of Excitement

Aeons later Betty gradually became conscious.

A general feeling of discomfort slowly clarified itself into aching limbs and head and a feeling of lassitude amounting almost to pain. She endured this for some time, then as her consciousness returned more fully, she opened her eyes.

She was lying in her bed at the gate lodge. It was day, for light was behind the drawn blind, though whether morning or afternoon she could not tell. No one seemed to be about: at least the house was very still. After some more aeons she began dreamily to consider what might have happened.

An accident presumably? No broken bones, she hoped. Experimenting, she tried gingerly to move her legs and arms, and was gratified to find she could do so. Then it must have been some illness, though she couldn't remember getting ill. No doubt she—

Suddenly recollection flashed across her. Ah, now she had it! The fire! Forde Manor; burnt down! She shivered with horror as she recalled the dreadful scene, the fierce leaping flames, the lurid glare, the terrifying crackling. Oh, ghastly, hideous! When she thought of it she felt physically sick.

But try as she would, she could not recall how it had all ended. She remembered the pictures. They were trying to save them. But had they succeeded? She didn't know.

Then a wave of thankfulness swept over her. What an overwhelming mercy it was that the house had been empty! The fire had spread so rapidly that the servants' bedrooms might have been cut off before the alarm was given. How unthinkably awful that would have been. Indeed she might have been in danger herself. She might not have wakened till the staircase had become impassable! Again she grew sick and faint at the idea.

Presently she heard a stealthy footstep in the next room. So she was not alone. More faintly than she knew, she called out. The steps became louder and in a moment Mrs Relf appeared. She smiled at Betty.

'Oh, mem, that looks better,' she declared, advancing into the room. 'I'm glad to see you're yourself again.'

'The fire?' Betty gasped. 'What happened?'

'Burnt out,' Mrs Relf returned solemnly. 'A terrible sight. The whole place gutted. Not a room or a roof left bar the garage.'

'The pictures?'

'All destroyed except about two dozen from the ballroom. A terrible loss!'

Betty groaned, staring helplessly at her landlady. Then her thoughts took another turn. 'What day is this?' she asked in a puzzled tone.

'Tuesday. You haven't been ill long, if that's what you mean.'

'Tuesday. Then the fire was—last night?'

'Early this morning. But they didn't get it out till midday.'

It was now after three o'clock, as Betty with raised head could see from the clock on the chimneypiece. She moved more energetically.

'I don't remember the end of it. Tell me, was I ill? How did I get here?'

'You fainted, and no wonder. You didn't ought to have got up at all, mem, and that's a fact.'

'I remember nothing after seeing the hall roof go down. What happened then?'

'That was when you fainted. They saw you fall and some of them picked you up, and then I told them to bring you here and we got you to bed and Relf went for the doctor.'

'Gracious,' Betty grimaced, 'was I all that trouble? Well, go on about the fire. Did the engines come from Town?'

It appeared that just as Betty had fallen in her faint, the local brigade had turned up. They had a stretcher as part of their equipment, and while she was being lifted on it, the brigade had got their hoses going. But it was like playing on a haystack with a penny squirt. The fire was much too fierce for their efforts to make any difference, and it was only when the engines arrived from London that adequate measures could be taken.

But it was then too late. By that time the whole roof of the 'spine' had gone and both wings were blazing furiously.

The policeman and his helpers had had, Mrs Relf explained, bad luck. They could only find a long ladder and precious minutes were lost looking for a tool to cut it in two. When it was at last in position and the gallery window was broken, a rush of thick smoke poured out. No one could have lived in it, and the attempt to save the pictures had to be abandoned. Only twenty-five had been saved, all from the ballroom.

To Betty this seemed an absolute calamity. The destruction of the house was bad enough, but at least it could be rebuilt. But the pictures were irreplaceable. The loss was not only that of Sir Geoffrey's or his insurance company; the whole world was the poorer. What a confirmation it all was of Charles Barke's oft expressed opinion that such works of art should not be left in private hands, but should be kept in national homes properly secured against fire!

The thought of her employer raised a new question. 'By the way, has anyone wired to Sir Geoffrey?' she asked.

Mrs Relf showed some slight embarrassment. 'Yes, mem,' she said, moving uneasily. 'Relf and Mr Carson thought that should be done and I—er—took the liberty of looking among your letters on the table there to see if I could find the address. I thought you wouldn't mind.'

'Of course not. That was quite right. Did you find it?'

'Yes, mem. I found it and Mr Carson wrote the message and Relf took it to the post office. Italy, it was.'

'Yes, Capri. That's all right. There's been no reply?'

'No, mem; not yet.'

Some two hours later a message was received. It read: 'Distressed at news. Arriving tomorrow. Buller.'

He must be coming by air, Betty thought, as she rather painfully racked her brains as to whether any other step should be taken before he arrived. Eventually she concluded that there was nothing which could not wait. It certainly was a relief that he was coming so soon.

That evening the doctor called again.

'You've been fortunate,' he told Betty, when he had made his examination. 'You might well have got pneumonia running about like that when you had a temperature. But you're none the worse. You've got 'flu, but it's a mild attack and you'll probably be about again in a day or two.'

Betty didn't really feel so badly and that night she slept reasonably well, awaking almost normal in the morning.

Now at last she began to think of how the fire would affect herself. For one thing her job was gone. Sir Geoffrey couldn't retain her to look after a non-existent house. Here again she had been fortunate. The book was all but finished. Only three chapters had still to be revised and more than half of the final typing was done. This work Betty had given to a girl in Ockham and she was making a neat job of it. It warmed Betty's heart to see the pile of typescript grow, and the adding to it of each completed chapter as it came in gave her a thrill of real delight.

But these pleasures were now coming to an end. In a week the typing would be finished and the book would start off on its adventures. Then would begin the nerve-racking period of waiting to learn its fate, of which she had heard so much. She had already selected the publisher to whom she would first send it, and from frequent rehearsing knew by heart the covering letter she would write.

Indeed, as soon as the book had gone, life would deteriorate from every point of view. That dreadful hunt for a job would begin again, for she daren't bank her future on the chance of her writing being a success. If a miracle happened and it became a best seller: well, that would be all joy and she could give up housekeeping for other people and start a second book. But could so great a miracle really happen?

Her thoughts strayed back to Sir Geoffrey. What a calamity this was for him! He had hoped to sell, and now not only was the house destroyed, but the place was rendered practically valueless. Fortunately the insurance had been put right; at least she presumed the new policy had been completed. But even if he got a substantial sum, it wouldn't be the same thing. The place would be left on his hands as a continual drag.

After lunch Mrs Relf appeared, labouring under excitement. Sir Geoffrey, it seemed, had arrived and was below, asking whether she would see him.

'Of course,' said Betty. 'Show him up.'

Mrs Relf, apparently slightly scandalized, vanished, and presently Sir Geoffrey knocked and entered. He was not looking his best. To Betty he seemed more furtive and ill at ease than ever.

Surely, she thought, he was not embarrassed by seeing her in bed? And when he spoke, his high-pitched squeaky voice with its American twang seemed to grate on her more than ever. But his words were pleasant enough.

'Well,' he greeted her with a crooked smile, 'this is an unexpected meeting.'

She held out her hand. 'You got back quickly. How did you manage it?' She pointed to a chair. 'Won't you sit down?'

'Thanks.' He moved the chair, as if casually, but she noted that he turned it with its back to the light. 'I flew. By a stroke of luck the message came in time to let me catch the boat to Naples, and the boat just caught the plane, so I hadn't to waste any time.'

'You came right through?'

'I couldn't. I slept in Paris last night and came on by the first plane this morning. And how are you? I was sorry to hear you weren't too fit.'

'It's nothing; just a touch of 'flu. By the way, are you afraid of it? If so, you'd better not stay.'

He smiled. 'I'm not afraid. Besides, it's all over the country. In Italy too; all over Europe, I believe.'

She nodded. 'I'm so distressed about this business,' she assured him. 'I just can't say how sorry I am.'

'Yes, it's a bit of a knock. But before we go any further there's something I can't say either: I can't say how grateful to you I am for all you did. I've been hearing about it.'

'It was nothing, and in any case you surely wouldn't expect me to lie here in bed and not see what was going on.'

'But you did much more than see what was going on. Your decision to call the London brigades and your attempt to save the pictures! It was just splendid.'

'It didn't do much good, I'm afraid.'

'That wasn't your fault. It was just bad luck that the thing wasn't seen earlier. An hour earlier and the wings might have been saved.'

'The pictures!' she exclaimed. 'That's what's so dreadful—all those gorgeous pictures being lost.'

'That's so,' he agreed. 'And yet it might have been a deal worse. Have you thought what might have happened if the house hadn't been empty?'

She shivered. 'I know. That's one thing we can't be too thankful for. Tell me, what does the place look like? Can you go into the ruins yet?'

'No, they're still smouldering and there are a couple of firemen in charge. But I don't think it's necessary. There's nothing left to burn.'

'Dreadful! Is it really as bad as that?'

He made a gesture as if of horror. 'It's the worst case I've ever seen. Completely gutted. Nothing left but the walls and some heaps of smouldering debris.'

'The roof?'

'All gone. And the stonework round the doors and windows cracked and chipped. It's really a rather horrible sight.'

'The pictures that were saved?'

'They're all right: stored in my workshop. Twenty-five— out of a hundred and eighty-nine.'

'It's just too horrible.' She paused, then went on. 'There's only one redeeming feature in the whole thing: that you had amended that insurance. The policy was complete, I suppose?'

'Oh yes, six months ago and more. Yes, that part of it's all right. And arising out of that, there's another thing I'm thankful for: that I wasn't here when it happened.'

Betty stared. 'What do you mean?' she asked more sharply.

He shrugged. 'Well, it might have looked badly, mightn't it? Just note the sequence: I inherit; I don't like the place; I reinsure; it's burnt down. Uncharitable people might think they were clever in putting two and two together.'

She felt rather horrified that such an idea could have occurred to him. 'Oh, I think that's dreadful,' she exclaimed. 'You mean that people might have thought that you set it on fire for the insurance? I'm sure no one would have imagined such a thing.'

'People are ready enough to imagine things like that.'

'Oh no! Besides your sequence is wrong. You inherited; you reinsured,' you found you didn't like the life here; and—the house was burnt. A slight change, but one which makes all the difference.'

He seemed relieved. 'Good of you putting it like that. Not

that the question arises, for I could have scarcely set it on fire from Capri.'

She smiled. 'Then why talk nonsense? All the same, is there any theory of what did happen?'

He shook his head. 'I'm afraid not, so far. It seems that it started in the central block somewhere near the service rooms. At least, the man who wakened Carson says so. He saw it from his house and ran down. If so, it suggests the central heating. There may have been some timber too near the flue.'

'Surely if so, the house would have gone up before this?'

'So one would say, but I understand fires have occurred from this cause years after the houses were built. Then it might have been an electrical short. Do you happen to know if the current was on or off?'

'Switched off at the main switches. I saw to it myself when we closed the house and I was looking round only last week, Thursday or Friday, I think, and I particularly noticed the switches were off.'

'Then that settles that. We needn't worry about the cause because the insurance company will make an inquiry into it.'

'Oh. Will that be soon?'

'I imagine so. They wouldn't want to wait till all the facts were forgotten.'

'Of course. Then I'd better make a note of everything I did in the house during the last few days.'

'Yes, if you will. In fact, I'm asking everyone concerned to do so. Well, let's talk of something else. I'm afraid this will make a difference to your plans. By the way, it's rather late to ask, but how is your book?'

'Finished!' she declared, and she could scarcely keep a

ring of pride out of her voice. 'Or just finished. Another week and it will be out of my hands.'

He seemed interested and asked for details, which under the circumstances Betty thought considerate. Then he reverted to her plans.

'I'm afraid, you know, there's no more to be done here. I don't yet know what I'll do, but,' he smiled grimly, 'it won't be necessary to look after the house any longer.'

'Of course I understand that,' she assured him. 'In any case, I was going to begin looking for a job directly I got the book off.'

'Well, you mustn't be in a hurry. Legally you're due proper notice and I don't mind the present arrangement running on for a few weeks more if it's a convenience to you.'

It was kind of him. Indeed he had always been kind to her and she wished she did not feel that barrier of—was it merely indifference? No, she had to admit to herself that it was actual dislike. Though she had never seen his ugly side, she could not but feel that he had one.

But he was chatting on. 'Seen your friend Mr Barke lately?' he asked. 'I always look back with pleasure to his visit here.'

'Not very recently,' she answered. 'But he's been here; as a matter of fact on Monday, the day before the fire. He was coming to tea and I put him off because I wasn't well, but he didn't get the message.'

'Oh, he was here, was he? Then you didn't see him?'

'No. I was so cross with Mrs Relf. He came here to the door, but I happened to be asleep and she didn't wake me.'

'Good for her. Pity all the same that he had his journey for nothing.'

Betty smiled. 'Well, he didn't quite. Feeling sure that you

78

wouldn't mind, he asked Relf to let him have another look at the pictures. He does love them so much, you know.'

Sir Geoffrey took out his cigarette case and in opening it fumbled suddenly and dropped it. The cigarettes fell out in a little cascade.

'Oh, sorry,' he apologized, 'that was stupid of me. I took out the case automatically, for of course I didn't intend to smoke here.' He stooped and began picking up the cigarettes. 'So Mr Barke had another look at the pictures? I'm delighted. He was very welcome.'

'Thank you, I knew you'd feel like that and I was going to suggest a visit to them before tea. He knew that too, otherwise he would never have asked Relf.'

'You were both absolutely right. Unhappily it doesn't matter now, but if this disaster hadn't occurred, I should have much liked to hear his opinion of the cleaning of some of them. We discussed it, you remember?'

'I'm sure he would have liked a chat about it. As you know, he has taken up rather a decided line on the subject. When I mentioned that you had had some cleanings done he was interested. I know he wanted to see how far the results supported his theories.'

'And you don't know his opinion?'

'No, and I don't expect to till I see him. He is a pleasant visitor, but a terrible correspondent. I'm expecting him down again shortly. He told Mrs Relf he'd come with his wife as soon as I was all right. She's also got 'flu at present.'

'Not badly, I hope?'

'I'm afraid she has rather. Not serious, I expect, but worse than the average.'

'I'm sorry. Well now, let's see. Is there anything else we ought to discuss?'

'I don't think so,' Betty answered slowly. 'I found that testimonial, by the way. I sent it off on Monday.'

'Oh, thank you. That was good of you. It was a company that some Americans I met in Rome were thinking of starting, to run oil from the States to Italy. I thought it would interest me to be on the board, if I decided to live in Rome. Now I don't know what I shall do.'

He chatted for a little longer, then after urging Betty to stay where she was till she felt perfectly well, he rose.

'I shall be in London,' he said as he opened the door, 'at the Brooklyn, near Marble Arch. If you want me, you'll find me there.'

He was taking it well, Betty decided, as after he had gone she thought over the interview. Of course the loss of the house was not nearly so heavy a blow as it would have been had he always lived there and got to love the place. And the destruction of the pictures wouldn't affect him as it would a connoisseur. His distress was probably nothing like so keen as his predecessor's would have been under similar circumstances.

Betty's attack of 'flu proved milder even than the doctor had forecast and on the next afternoon she insisted on getting up, and in spite of the protests of Mrs Relf, going out to see what was left of Forde Manor.

It was indeed a horrifying sight. The walls alone stood, bare and gaunt and blackened, with cracked and split stone dressings and gaps where the cornice had been dragged away when the roof collapsed. Within were heaps of wreckage, mostly brick and stone from internal walls which had fallen, but with occasional objects of twisted metal and quantities of broken glass. In one place Betty saw the remains of the study safe and in another three sticklike objects which she eventually identified as the barrels of shot guns. Even after so much time had passed, faint traces of smoke still hung about the larger heaps.

Late that afternoon she received a reply-paid telegram: 'Unexpectedly crossing Paris tomorrow. Have wired Roland. If you desire will advance him money if satisfied with scheme. You refund me later. Charles.'

Without hesitating Betty replied: 'Please do as you suggest. Immensely grateful. Betty.'

A warm sense of pleasure flowed into Betty's mind as she contemplated the bestowal of her gift. How surprised and delighted Roland would be! What a vista of hope it would open up to him! And how good of Charles to undertake the task! He certainly was kind.

She longed to write to Roland, a letter overflowing with good will and affection, expressing the hope that the gift was opportune and that the venture would be a huge success. But of course she could not, lest Charles should decide to withhold the money.

On the following morning a brief confirmatory letter came from Charles. It was dated Thursday night and he said he had received her telegram and would carry out the money business as best he could. Then he went on: 'I wonder if you could possibly come up tomorrow and stay with Agatha till I get back? Of course if you are well enough. I am not very happy about her. She is still far from well and it would be a great ease to my mind if I knew that you were in the house. Don't trouble to telephone, but if you can manage it just turn up. Having had 'flu yourself, you won't be afraid of infection.'

For once, Betty thought, duty and inclination pointed in the same direction. She enjoyed staying at the Green House and she was glad to be able to oblige Charles. Having rung up Sir Geoffrey she went up to Town after lunch.

When she reached Chelsea she was more glad than ever that she had come. Agatha was worse. She was lying half asleep and took very little notice of Betty. Kate, the Barkes' elderly retainer, was obviously frightened and seized on Betty with relief.

'Has the doctor been here today?' Betty asked.

'Yes, m'm, early this morning.'

'I think he should see her again. Let me have his name and I'll ring him up, and if she's not better, I'll ask him to send a nurse.'

The doctor's report was reassuring. Though Agatha's attack was sharp and there was some fear of pulmonary complications, she was otherwise fit and he didn't think these would materialize. In the meantime she would be the better of professional aid and he would send a nurse. An hour later a pleasant looking middle-aged woman arrived and took charge.

Betty was thankful to be there and able to help with the nursing, but as she sat staring into the fire after dinner that evening, her thoughts were not with Agatha. In Paris, Charles and Roland would by now, she felt sure, have had their meeting. How she wished she knew what had taken place! She hoped against hope that one or other would ring her up, though she knew it was unlikely. If not, there might be a wire in the morning, or at least a letter in the evening. At all events she longed before anything else that the events which had taken place in Paris that day might be the beginning of a period of real happiness and prosperity for Roland.

How maliciously Fate must have smiled at her innocence!

7

The Dawn of Suspense

The Barkes' residence in Wilton Road, Chelsea, was aptly named the Green House. It was really a green oasis in the surrounding brick and mortar desert. It stood in its own grounds, a microscopic estate admittedly when compared with the broad acres of Forde Manor, but large by Chelsea standards. From all windows could be seen greenery, or at least this was possible in summer, and from the sitting-room the foliage was so plentiful as to screen all adjoining buildings.

For the next two days Betty lived a happy and carefree life in this haven. Agatha was better, although still dazed and unwilling to talk. Her lungs had remained unaffected, and the doctor believed that in two or three days she would be herself again. Betty, thrown on her own resources, quickly reproduced the routine of the gate lodge. In the mornings she monopolized the sitting-room. In that charming apartment, long and low and high windowed, with its old well-matched furniture, its comfortable cushions and its bright fire, she pushed rapidly on with the revision of her final chapters. She could not help feeling a certain relief at Agatha's indisposition, though she had the grace to be ashamed of herself therefore. But fond as she was of her, she knew that once Agatha was about she could no longer work. For Agatha, the personification of cheery good fellow-ship, could never sit alone if she could find a companion, nor remain silent so long as there was anyone to talk to.

Saturday and part of Sunday passed in this blissful way, and then on Sunday afternoon an event took place which opened up a new and very disquieting chapter in both their lives.

It was about three o'clock and Betty was lying back in her chair before the fire, trying to screw up energy to go for her afternoon walk, when she heard a ring. There was a murmur of a man's voice, then heavy steps crossing the hall.

'Two gentlemen to see you, ma'am,' explained Kate, throwing open the door.

Of the men who entered, the first was stoutish and slightly below middle height, with a clean-shaven good-natured face and honest but extremely shrewd blue eyes. The other was tall and strongly built, with an air partly martial, partly deprecating. Plain-clothes policemen, Betty thought instantly.

'I'm sorry, madam,' began the short man in a pleasant voice, 'for this intrusion. I wanted to see Mrs Barke but I understand she's ill?'

'Yes, she has a bad attack of 'flu.'

'So the maid said. But perhaps you, madam, could help me. You're Mrs Stanton, the maid said?'

'Yes.'

'A relation, perhaps?'

'No,' she answered, presuming that an explanation of the

interrogation would presently be vouchsafed, 'just a visiting friend of the family. What can I do for you?'

'We've called to ask for a little information. We are police officers from Scotland Yard. My name is French—Chief Inspector French, and this is Sergeant Carter.'

Betty strove to hide her surprise. 'Well,' she answered equally pleasantly, 'I don't know what information you want that I can give you, but I'll do my best. Won't you sit down?'

'Thank you, madam.' They seated themselves and French paused while Carter took a notebook from his pocket and opened it on his knee.'

The visit had aroused astonishment in Betty's mind, but as she looked at the men's expression this turned swiftly to foreboding. The fire! There was some trouble at Forde Manor because of the fire, and the police had been called in. An idea which had already slightly worried her flashed back into her mind. It surely couldn't be that Charles had switched on the electric light and somehow caused a short circuit? But no, that was impossible! Even if he had switched it on, it could not have done any harm.

But it was not about the fire that French spoke. 'A word from you may settle my business,' he said. 'I hope it will. Can you tell me if Mrs Barke has heard from Mr Barke since he went to France?'

Betty stared. 'I know she has not,' she answered promptly.

'When does she expect him back?'

'When she sees him. I mean, he didn't know himself.'

French glanced at his assistant. 'Do you know what was the business which took him over?' he went on.

Though Betty had no idea where these questions were tending, a feeling of misgiving arose in her mind. Charles's business? Why, to give her £120 to Roland! Then she saw she was wrong. That was only a friendly errand undertaken because he had had to go in any case. She need not mention Roland. Indeed, an unaccountable presentiment urged her not to do so.

'No,' she answered, 'I have no idea. But I can't tell you whether Mrs Barke knows.'

French nodded slowly. 'Now, Mrs Stanton, I have to tell you something which may be a shock to you.'

Betty's face grew more anxious as she looked at her questioner.

'The fact is that Mr Barke left his hotel rather suddenly and has not returned and I wondered if Mrs Barke knew where he was? Or perhaps you?'

'I?' said Betty sharply. 'No, I know nothing. What does this mean?'

'Mr Barke crossed by the service leaving Victoria at nine o'clock on Friday morning,' French went on gravely, 'and arrived in Paris at three forty-eight. He went direct to his hotel, the Vichy, which as you probably know is beside the Place de Lafayette and near the Gare du Nord. He registered and told the clerk to send his luggage up to his room, as he wished before going up himself to pay an urgent call. He then left the hotel and—he has not returned.'

Betty felt the blood drawing away from her heart. 'Not returned?' she repeated as if in a dream. 'Then where is he?'

'That's just it, Mrs Stanton.'

'You don't mean,' Betty didn't realize the sound of her own voice, 'that he has—disappeared?'

French, she saw, was unobtrusively watching her every movement. Oh, why couldn't she be normal?

'Well,' he said reassuringly, 'it's true that nothing has been heard of him since he left the hotel. But don't let that upset you, madam. It doesn't follow that anything is seriously wrong.'

Betty thought she had experienced fear when her money had been at its lowest ebb. Now she realized that she had never known what it was like. A cold terror seemed to be closing down on her, paralysing her in its icy clutches. Charles had disappeared, and Charles—she could scarcely put it into conscious thought—Charles had intended to meet Roland. In spite of herself hideous pictures grew in her mind. Charles meeting Roland—with the money. Charles refusing to pay it over—as well he might have done. Roland disappointed—and Roland's terrible temper! Oh, no! Horrible! How could such a thought have entered her mind? Roland would never—*never* do a thing like that!

But she was mad to let herself go in this way. Her frightful idea was false and she would only make this policeman suspicious. Desperately she fought for self-control.

'That's a great shock to me,' she said in tones which she tried to make steady. 'Mr and Mrs Barke are my dearest friends and I just can't face anything having happened to him. Tell me more details. How did you know about it?'

'The hotel manager informed the French police,' French answered. 'When Mr Barke did not return that night he thought nothing of it, but when the next day passed without news he began to wonder. However, he waited till lunchtime today, then thought he ought to make a report. The French police phoned over to us to make inquiries at his home, and here we are.'

Betty felt numb. Charles was extraordinarily methodical and thoughtful for others. He hated to change his plans and he would never have broken an engagement without ringing up and explaining. And he was no subject for loss of memory. Besides, he had a notebook in his pocket bearing his name and address, as well as his cards. No, something dreadful must have happened. 'It sounds terribly bad to me,' she murmured.

'Well, we mustn't anticipate trouble,' French returned with a look that was almost kindly. 'But now I should like to ask my questions.'

Betty nodded. 'Ask what you will and I'll do my best to answer you.'

'Well, it would be a help to know Mr Barke's business in Paris. You say you can't help me there, but with your knowledge of Mr Barke, can't you guess what kind of thing it might have been? I know of course that Mr Barke is a famous artist, as well as being Director of the Crewe Gallery, but I know nothing of the details of his life.'

Thankfully Betty felt that she was once again regaining herself control. 'He frequently went abroad to look at and perhaps buy pictures for the Crewe. Then he was often consulted on questions about pictures: whether they were genuine old masters or copies, and so on. He was supposed to be the final court of appeal on such matters, at least in this country.'

French nodded. 'Now that's helpful, Mrs Stanton. That's just the sort of thing I want.'

'There were the Nimes pictures, as an example. Half a dozen pictures were found in Nimes which looked like old masters. He was called in. He decided that they were all copies.'

'I see. Very specialized and valuable knowledge. Mr Barke then told you what he had gone to Nimes for.'

'He told Mrs Barke and I heard of it.'

'Quite. Was it usual for him to tell Mrs Barke?'

'Unusual, I should say, unless as in that case the matter was of general interest. He usually said "Business" but seldom explained the details, and of course in this case there was a special reason why he should not.'

'You mean that Mrs Barke was ill?'

'Exactly.'

'And what did he say to you, Mrs Stanton?'

'I didn't see him. I had a note from him asking me to come here to keep Mrs Barke company while he was away, but he made no mention of business.'

'I see. When was that?'

'On Friday morning. I came here after lunch that afternoon.'

French nodded. 'Quite.' He paused, slowly turning the leaves of his notebook, then began again, 'When did you see Mr Barke last?'

'About ten days ago. I came up here and lunched with them.'

'Then where are you living?'

'I've been at the lodge of Forde Manor, near Ockham.'

'Forde Manor? Do you mean where the fire was?'

'Yes.'

'Then surely,' French's voice took on a new respect, 'you must be the Mrs Stanton who was mentioned in the papers as having acted so splendidly in directing salvage operations?'

Betty smiled. 'I was in charge there,' she admitted, 'and naturally did what I could: I'm afraid with poor success.'

'I read about it. A fine piece of work, if I may say so.' French paused, then turned back to business. 'Then you saw Mr Barke about ten days ago and you received a letter

89

from him on Friday morning asking you here. Had you any other communication with him during this last ten days?'

Betty hesitated. This was critical. Then she plunged. 'Not directly, but I should perhaps tell you that when we met he arranged to come down to see me at Forde on Monday afternoon—that was last Monday.'

'Oh, and did he not do so?'

Betty explained.

'There were fine pictures at Forde Manor, I saw by the papers,' French went on. 'Was Mr Barke interested in them?'

'He saw them, if that's what you mean, in a quite personal capacity—just for the pleasure of looking at them. Twice he saw them. Once some eight months ago with me and again last Monday with the caretaker, Relf. But there was no business motive behind the visit.'

'As far as you know?'

'As far as I know, of course.'

'Then I'm afraid it won't help us much. By the way, I forgot to ask: does Mr Barke often go to Paris on business?'

'Fairly often. He goes all over the Continent.'

'Do you know where he usually stays in Paris?'

'I'm afraid I don't.' French nodded. 'Thank you very much. Now just two other points. First, I should like to know whether Mr Barke told Mrs Barke about his business in Paris, and secondly, I should like permission to go through Mr Barke's papers. I wonder if you could see Mrs Barke on these points?'

'Oh,' Betty returned, 'I don't think she should be told about this: not at present at all events. She's very weak.'

'Yet a hint of Mr Barke's business might enable us to find him, and if he should be in difficulties, police help might be invaluable. I'm afraid I must ask you to try.'

'If you think so, I will. But I'm doubtful of the result.'

'I suggest,' French went on, 'that you don't mention Mr Barke's disappearance. Simply say that some business question has arisen at the Crewe and they want to get in touch with him. Say they want to know where he went to and when he will be back, and if she doesn't know, that they would like to look his papers through in the hope of finding out.'

'All right,' said Betty with some relief. 'I'll do what I can.'

She greatly disliked the deception, though she thought it justified. However, she needn't have worried; Agatha took no interest in the questions. She simply shook her head when asked about Charles's movements and nodded when the search of the papers was mentioned, immediately going off again to sleep.

Having shown French Charles's desk in the library, Betty returned to the sitting-room and gave herself up to an attempt to weigh the new disaster. She was sure from her knowledge of Charles that he would never voluntarily have left his friends a prey to anxiety: if he had not given notice of his whereabouts, it was because he could not. And if he had met with an accident someone would have found him. It looked terribly bad.

In spite of all her striving, the idea of Roland kept thrusting itself back into her mind. Roland wouldn't do a dirty or a crooked thing—or would he not?—but she couldn't forget his terribly quick temper. A moment's rage; and something might happen which could never be undone. But, she told herself again and again, she mustn't think these hideous thoughts. The idea was not—could not be—true. Roland, her own twin brother, could not be a—*murderer*!

With misgivings she thought of her own part in the affair.

She had deliberately kept back what might be vital evidence from the officers of Scotland Yard. If that awful thing were true, what would be her position? Bad, she was sure. But she didn't care. The first thing was to protect Roland. No breath of suspicion must arise that could touch him. Then she felt sick with horror as she thought of the fear her action implied.

Next came a revulsion of feeling. How wicked, how absolutely criminal she had been to doubt Roland! Roland would never be guilty of such a thing! It was she who was evil to have thought it. There was some quite different explanation.

Another name flashed into her mind. Lorrimer! Lorrimer had left the Crewe in the belief that unless he paid £250 within six months, he would be prosecuted for theft. He believed also that this necessity depended on Charles and Charles alone. If Charles were eliminated the question would never arise.

Oh, horrible! What had happened to her? Why did these dreadful unsought thoughts fill her mind? Lorrimer, if a trifle secretive, had always appeared a normal, decent sort of man. It was inconceivable that he, any more than Roland, should be guilty of such a crime.

She wondered if there was not still a possibility. Could Charles have penetrated into one of those dark Paris slums and been murdered for the money which a man of his appearance would certainly have about him? Then she remembered that he had disappeared about four in the afternoon. in broad daylight. Of course he might have gone to see someone and come back late at night . . . But to go deliberately into unnecessary danger would be equally unlike Charles . . .

Her thoughts swung back to her own position. She would, she supposed, have to tell Agatha. That wouldn't be easy. Dear Agatha who had been so good to her and who was so fond of Charles! How terribly upset she would be!

An hour, two hours, passed and then French returned from the study. 'I've been through all the likely papers,' he explained, 'and I'm sorry to say I've found nothing to throw light on the affair. I may have to make a further search later. Have you been able to think of anything that might help?'

'One thing occurred to me,' Betty answered, 'but I fear it won't be helpful. On last Monday, before Mr Barke paid his visit to Forde Manor, he lunched with some people at Woking—Mr and Mrs Harold Spencer, I think. Then as I told you he was with the Forde Manor caretaker, Relf, while looking at the pictures. Mr Barke may conceivably have spoken to one of these about his journey.'

French glanced at his watch. 'May I use your telephone? I'll ring up Woking. It may save going down.'

A few minutes obtained Harold Spencer's statement. Charles had said nothing about a visit to Paris and Spencer had not known he was going.

'Is Relf on the telephone?' French then asked.

Betty explained about the connection having been destroyed in the fire.

French got up. 'Then I'll send a man down in the morning. Now I'll wish you good evening and assure you that directly I get any information, I'll pass it on to you. And if you'll take my advice, you won't worry unduly. As I said before, there's no evidence to suggest that anything serious has happened.'

That evening Agatha was much better and after consulting

the doctor Betty did one of the most difficult jobs of her life and told her what had happened. Agatha was dreadfully upset. She at once took the most pessimistic view and nothing would convince her that Charles was alive.

But she was no more able than Betty to answer French's questions. She knew neither why Charles had gone to Paris, nor when he had intended to return. To Betty's overwhelming relief, it was also evident that she knew nothing of the proposed meeting with Roland.

'Chief Inspector French is rather a surprise,' Betty remarked later on that evening. 'I thought police officers were overbearing and aggressive and treated everybody as if they were criminals under suspicion. But no one could have been more polite than he was. I thought him even kindly.'

'I'm glad this is being handled by someone who'll be sympathetic.'

'Yes, and he's no fool either. His eyes are extraordinarily shrewd.'

Agatha made a gesture of anxiety and despair, as if to Change the subject. 'I dread the night,' she muttered in a low voice. 'I know I shall not sleep.'

'Don't let me leave you for a while,' Betty suggested. 'Tell you what, I'll make some tea. Or would you rather have whisky?'

'Tea, I think. A cup would be rather nice. Getting it will be something to do at all events. Make it there and I'll watch you.'

The occupation, slight as it was, gave them relief and the hot stimulant soothed their nerves. Their fright somewhat receded and they talked more normally.

'What a week this has been!' Betty remarked. 'First that awful fire, and now this.'

'Worse for you than for me,' Agatha returned, 'for I hadn't the fire. It must have been absolutely ghastly.'

Betty shivered. 'I hate to think of it, and I can't get it out of my mind. I haven't slept properly since. I lie awake and hear the roaring and the crackling and see the roof of the hall going down. That was the worst thing, the roof going down.'

'You poor thing!'

'I don't know why it should upset me now; it didn't at the time. It's ten times worse now even than when I first woke and saw the light in the sky.'

'There was so much to do that you couldn't think about it.'

'Perhaps so. At all events I felt neither fear nor excitement: only anxiety that we shouldn't be able to deal with it. Then the moment I saw it I realized we could do nothing.'

'Except save the pictures.'

'I mean, nothing to save the house. The pictures, yes. I was terribly disappointed about that. I hoped we should have got more of them out.'

For another hour Betty talked, trying to keep Agatha from thinking. Then when both were feeling exhausted, she turned in, hoping against hope that they might get some sleep. Both were astonished to find next morning that they had slumbered dreamlessly through the night.

8

The Deferring of Hope

In spite of her good night, Betty felt next morning bowed
down with the weight of approaching calamity. There was
the uncertainty about Charles which she shared with Agatha.
Agatha was brave and did not complain, but Betty could
not but realize how acutely she was suffering. Her own
burden was almost heavier. Still there was no news about
Roland, and to her uncertainty was added a cold and
numbing fear. She would have given a year's salary to know
what had taken place in Paris on the previous Friday.

On that Monday there were two callers at the Green
House. Sir Geoffrey was the first. He was shown in after
lunch. Agatha's improvement had continued and she was
up when he came. She was really not in a state for visitors,
but she did not like to make a pointed withdrawal and
indeed enjoyed the talk.

'Glad to see you about again, Mrs Stanton,' he greeted
Betty, then turned to Agatha. 'You were laid up too, were
you not, Mrs Barke? I hope you're better?'

Betty thought him looking tired and worried, but it was

evident from the way he chatted that he had not heard about Charles. She would have told him, but she thought the discussion would be painful to Agatha. However, Agatha herself presently broached the subject.

'You find us in an unhappy state, Sir Geoffrey,' she said. 'My husband—Tell him, Betty.'

'Yes, we're terribly worried about Mr Barke,' Betty exclaimed, going on to recount what had happened.

Sir Geoffrey was obviously upset. He expressed his sympathy and regret in unmeasured terms.

'How did you come to know about it?' he asked presently.

Betty glanced at Agatha. She wasn't sure if her friend would like French's call mentioned. Then she thought it could not be kept hidden. 'The hotel people informed the French police,' she therefore told him, 'and they rang up Scotland Yard. A Chief Inspector came to tell Mrs Barke and to make inquiries.'

Sir Geoffrey shrugged. 'Terrible for you both! Well, the matter is in the best hands at all events. But I suppose from what you've already said he hasn't discovered anything?'

'He can't have, for he said he would let us know immediately he did so.'

'I can't say how sorry I am. I hope you will understand that if I had had the slightest idea of it, I never would have dreamt of coming bothering you with my own affairs.'

'We're glad to see you,' Agatha answered, 'not only personally, but because anything which takes our minds off our trouble is a help. You have matters to discuss with Mrs Stanton? Would you like to go into the other room where you won't be disturbed?'

Sir Geoffrey was horrified at the idea. He had very little to say about business and none of it was private. But he had the tact to go on to it at once and cease discussing Charles's fate.

'Just one or two points, if I may, Mrs Stanton,' he explained. 'The first is about the inquiry. The insurance company are making an investigation into the cause of the fire, and I'm afraid they'll want to ask you a few questions.'

'I should be glad to help,' Betty answered, 'but I'm afraid I can't tell them anything useful.'

'Well, you'll hear from them. Their man will probably call on you.'

'Right. I'll do what I can.'

'Sorry you should be dragged into it. However, there it is. Then I wanted to ask you about your plans. I'm afraid that until the inquiry's over you'll be unable to go away, and I am prepared to settle Mrs Relf's bill till then, if that would be a convenience to you.'

Betty considered this handsome and said so, but before she could go on Agatha interrupted her.

'I'm sure it's very kind of you,' she declared firmly, 'but she's going to stay here. Yes, you are,' she went on to Betty, who demurred faintly. 'I just couldn't do without you. If eventually you want to look for a job, you can do it as well from here as from Forde Manor.'

'It's awfully good of you,' Betty was beginning, but again Agatha cut her short.

'Good!' she repeated. 'What nonsense! That's settled, and no more talk about it.'

'Very well then. Thank you very much; I'll stay. Now we've talked enough about me. What are your own plans, Sir Geoffrey, if you've yet made any?'

'I have, though only tentatively. My present idea is that as soon as the inquiry and so on is over I'll take whatever the insurance people pay and go back to America. Though, as I told you, I'm English, I find now I can get on better in the States.'

'And Forde Manor?'

'I won't rebuild. I'll try and sell the grounds as they stand. If no one wishes to rebuild, I daresay the land might be bought for farming.'

'Oh, what a pity that would be! All that beautiful lawn and those gardens!'

He shrugged again. 'If anyone feels that way about it, he can prevent it happening.' He got up. 'I must be getting along now, but tell me, before I go, what about your book?'

'Good of you to ask,' Betty smiled. 'The revision is finished and I'm just waiting for the typing of the last chapters to send it away.'

'I needn't say I wish it the best of luck. Well, we'll probably meet again over the inquiry.'

'One thing I omitted to mention,' Betty said, as she thanked him, 'I should like a testimonial, if you think I deserve one.' She smiled again.

'Glad you mentioned it,' he returned. 'I'll send it along. Goodbye, Mrs Barke. I do hope you'll soon have good news. Goodbye, Mrs Stanton, and I can't begin to thank you for all you've done for me.'

'You know, he's a curious mixture,' Agatha remarked when the door had closed. 'He's polite and kindly and he doesn't say anything that one could object to, and yet—I don't know what it is, but there's something. He's not, well, attractive.'

Betty made a gesture of agreement. 'I know, Agatha. That's just what I've always felt. I can't put my finger on anything particular, but in spite of his kindness I've never liked him.

And that seems the general feeling towards him at Ockham. It was of course the reason why he didn't get into the county set, not that he had been in real estate in Chicago.'

'He seems to me to be furtive: yes, I think "furtive" is the word. However, we needn't worry. I don't suppose either of us will see much more of him. And the job was a help to you while it lasted.'

'Absolutely ideal. I'm terribly sorry it has closed down.'

Not half an hour later Betty had another caller. She had gone upstairs with Agatha, who wished to lie down, when a card was brought to her: 'Mr Thomas G. Shaw. The Thames & Tyne Insurance Company, Ltd.' Nerving herself for what she felt would prove an ordeal, she went down.

She was slightly. surprised when her caller levered himself out of the most comfortable armchair to greet her. She had expected a neat, well-dressed man of the business type with shrewd eyes and a superficial polish covering a rather hard efficiency. Mr Thomas G. Shaw had none of these qualifications, at least outwardly. He was above medium height, thin and stooped, and stood with his knees slightly bent. His face was narrow and hatchery and he had one of those heads which overhang at the back like the counter of a ship. A pallid complexion, a long draggled moustache and a rather untidy sports coat surmounting particularly lengthy plus fours, did not tend to make him more impressive.

'A washed-out looking nonentity,' Betty said to herself and immediately grew more at ease. 'You wished to see me,' she went on aloud, glancing from the man to his card.

'Mrs Betty Stanton?' he asked in a drawling yet not unpleasant voice, continuing as she nodded, 'I've been sent here by the Thames & Tyne to ask you one or two questions about the fire at Forde Manor. As you probably know, the house and contents were insured with my company.'

Betty took a chair by the fire, indicating another for him. 'I was expecting you,' she answered. 'Sir Geoffrey Buller told me a representative of the company would call. I'll help you in any way I can.'

He collapsed into the chair, as if a two-foot rule had been quickly folded. 'Thank you,' he said. 'I should explain that it's my job to make a full report; cause, damage done, personal injuries, salvage efforts; everything the manager can ask—and a lot that he forgets and the directors think of. But I'll be no longer than I can help.' He looked at her mildly over the edge of his glasses.

'All right. I understand,' she returned. With his drooping moustache and his overhanging head he looked so like a great bird that she felt she would scarcely be surprised if he were suddenly to flap a pair of draggled wings.

'Now what would be the least trouble?' he went on in a mournful sing-song tone. 'Perhaps you'd tell me what happened in your own words? That might save the deuce of a lot of questions.' He looked at her as if propounding some interesting but purely abstract hypothesis.

The suggestion appealed to Betty, though she thought it a curious standpoint for an investigator to take up. However, she doubted if it mattered much what she said, as she could scarcely imagine his making a valuable report. All the same, she told her story as fully as she could.

While she spoke he gazed dully into the fire, but she decided that he must have been listening, as he now asked her to excuse him while he made one or two notes. He seemed to write slowly and lazily, but she noticed that he was using shorthand, and his memoranda might therefore have been comprehensive enough.

'Thanks,' he said at length, 'but we can't avoid all questions—unhappily. Can you make any suggestions as to the cause of the fire? Don't worry about evidence: guesses will do for me.'

She shook her head. 'I can think of nothing,' she answered decidedly. 'It's a complete mystery to me.'

He nodded. 'You said,' he went on, 'that when you saw it first the centre block was alight and that the fire spread from there to the wings. Did it spread equally quickly in both directions?'

'No, it reached the north-east or picture gallery end soonest. I understand that's why none of those pictures were saved.'

'But mightn't the fire have started to the north of the centre?'

She hesitated. 'I don't think so. Besides, there was a reason why it should travel more quickly northwards: the wind was west or south-west.'

'That's rather important,' he returned. 'You think the fire started in the centre block. Well, you're quite right. The smoke was noticed from another house quite soon after the place got alight, and it was coming from the centre block only.'

'If you knew that, why did you ask me?' Betty not unreasonably demanded.

He smiled. 'Routine,' he explained easily, 'we're slaves to it. Besides,' his smile robbed the words of offence. 'look at the side light it throws on your reliability as a witness. Now let's go a step further. What was there in that central area that might have started the thing?'

'There were the central heating and the electric mains,' she replied readily, 'but I don't see that either could have caused the outbreak.'

He peered at her above his glasses. 'You don't, madam? Now would you just tell me why not?'

'Simply because both have been there for many years, and if they were defective, the house would surely have gone up before this.'

He cocked his eye at her. 'Not necessarily, you know; not necessarily. Numbers of large country houses have been mysteriously burnt within the last decade, in which neither the central heating nor the electric fittings had been altered for years previously.'

'Then I'm afraid I don't know what happened.'

'No one does so far. Now will you tell me about the central heating. I understand Relf was in charge?'

'Yes.'

'What's your opinion of Relf? A good man?'

'First rate: good at everything, carpentry, painting, glazing, mason work, as well as looking after machinery.'

'Reliable?'

'Completely.'

'That was my impression of him. He told me the boiler was in a cellar beneath that central wing and that it burned anthracite. He said that there was no woodwork or other inflammable object in the place at all. Can you confirm that?'

'Yes, I can.'

'When did Relf do his firing?'

'Twice a day, morning and evening.'

'And were those the only occasions on which he was in the house?'

'So far as I know, yes.'

'Very well, let's pass on. You say the electric mains were also in that central block?'

'Yes, the switches were on the wall beneath the back stairs, almost exactly over the boiler cellar.'

'What did these switches control?'

'Everything: the entire house.'

'And can you tell me if they were on or off?'

'Off.'

'All of them? You're quite sure, I suppose, Mrs Stanton?'

'All of them and I'm quite sure.'

Shaw moved deprecatingly. 'I'm not questioning your statement, but wouldn't light be required in the cellar? How did Relf see to do his stoking?'

'He used a hurricane lamp—just to enable the electricity to be cut completely off.'

'I follow. Then I suppose he used the lamp to get from the entrance door to the cellar?'

'Yes, he did, of course,' Betty answered uneasily.

'Another source of fire, wasn't it? Hurricane lamp carried through the house—over wooden floors perhaps?'

'Well, yes, but I don't think the oil could have been spilled from such a lamp.'

'I don't say it did, but something very unusual did happen. Where was the oil kept, do you know?'

'In a ten-gallon drum in the cellar.'

'And cans of oil were carried in over wooden floors to fill the drum at regular intervals, I suppose?'

'No. It was filled when the house was closed down, but was not all used. At least, I passed no requisition for more oil. Relf will know all about that, though I don't believe it could have had anything to do with the fire.'

He smiled. 'I don't myself, Mrs Stanton, but it's a possibility. Please remember, I'm only trying to collect facts.'

'Sorry,' she apologized.

'Not at all. Now that gets us back to electricity. When did you yourself last see that the switches were off?'

For the first time Betty hesitated. She knew they were off all right, but she was worried as to whether Charles might not have had them turned on. She was growing more anxious also about her replies, for her opinion of Shaw had altered considerably since the interview began. In spite of his appearance, he seemed anything but a fool.

'I saw them turned off when the house was closed,' she presently answered, 'and since then I have noticed twice or three times that they were off when I was in that part of the house; I can't say exactly when.'

'After what you have said, I need scarcely ask if you turned them on yourself since the house was closed?'

'No, of course not.'

'Quite. Well, could anyone have turned them on? What about Relf?'

'Relf could of course, but I'm sure he never would have.'

'Now, Mrs Stanton, think carefully of this. Was anyone' else in the house recently, besides yourself and Relf?'

Put in this direct way only one answer was possible. 'Apart from Sir Geoffrey, the only person I know of was my friend, Mr Barke,' and she went on to tell of Charles's visit.

He did not seem impressed. 'Well, we can get that from Mr Barke and Relf,' he said casually and was going on with another question when she interrupted.

'I'm afraid you can't,' she explained. 'It's not yet generally known, but Mr Barke has disappeared,' and again she went on to give the details.

Shaw showed merely a polite interest until he heard that Chief Inspector French had the matter in hand. Then he brightened up.

'I know him well,' he told her with the nearest approach to enthusiasm he had yet shown. 'A thundering good chap. A bit slow, but thorough and as decent and straight as they're made. I'll never forget my first introduction to him.' He put down his notebook with an air of relief, as if welcoming a few moments' relaxation. 'We were on a job together, at least he was on it, a case of theft, and I was watching the affair on behalf of my Company, which had insured the stolen property. We went to get some lunch on the first day and on the way we met a man, a disreputable looking creature next door to a down and out. He looked at French as if he knew him, though he didn't speak. But next moment French spotted him and we stopped. "Well, John" or "Tom" or whatever it was, said French, "what are you doing here?" The man started on a hard luck story, just the standard rigmarole, out of a job, sick wife, no coal in the house, all as per sample. And what did French do? He didn't tell him to stop begging or he'd have him run in. He took a ten-shilling note out of his pocket and handed it to him and told him to call at a certain address where a man was wanted, promising he would write and recommend him for the job.'

'I should have called that weak-minded, not charitable,' Betty remarked, seeing that a comment was expected.

'Exactly what I thought,' Shaw returned, 'but I was wrong, and so would you have been. That's not the whole story. Over lunch French told me that the man had got out of Dartmoor only a few weeks previously, where he had been for burglary. It was French's evidence which had convicted him. He said he knew the man's story was true; he couldn't get a job and his wife was ill. He didn't know about there being no coal in the house, but he thought it not unlikely. I'll not quickly forget what he said. "If that chap doesn't get a bit of help he'll go back to Dartmoor, and the fault won't be his. It'll be yours and mine and the next man's." And he added what I knew myself, that most old lags want nothing more than to go straight and that they'd make specially trustworthy employees, but people won't have them and there's nothing for them but to go back to crime.'

'Did the man get the job?'

'I don't know. I only tell the story to illustrate the kind of man French is.' He sighed and reluctantly picked up his book. 'But I suppose this is wasting both your time and my own. Let's see, where were we? Oh yes, you were saying that Mr Barke went in to see the pictures and of course might have turned on the light, though you think that unlikely. Well, I can find out from Relf if he did. And may I, just before we leave the point, express my sympathy with you and Mrs Barke in this anxious time. Now what about Sir Geoffrey? You said he also had been in the house since it was closed.'

'Oh yes, but I couldn't tell you just when. He naturally went in and out when he chose.'

'When was the last occasion?'

Betty considered. Then she took her engagement book from her bag and turned the leaves. 'About a month before the fire,' she answered. 'Then he went out to Italy. He was in Italy all that month, till he was wired for after the fire.'

'Huh,' Shaw grunted as if disappointed. 'Nothing there.'

For a moment Betty thought he had finished, but she was speedily undeceived. In his slow, apparently inconsequent way he went on to obtain from her a description of the house and furniture as it was at the time of the fire, questioning her particularly about panelling, wooden ceilings and curtains. He asked what specially inflammable articles the house contained, oil, petrol, candles and so on, and where these were stored, made sure there was no gas on the premises, and obtained from her thumbnail sketches of Relf, Carson and Sir Geoffrey.

'Now at last he's done,' she thought when these last were duly noted.

But he hadn't. He paused, consulted his book, then started off as if with a new lease of life. 'You're fond of pictures, Mrs Stanton?'

Betty agreed.

'Then no doubt you grew familiar with those at Forde Manor? A good collection, I understand?'

'On the whole, yes,' she responded judicially. 'There were a number of really good and valuable pictures, but there were also several of a very ordinary type.'

'A description of most collections, isn't it? Did Sir Geoffrey make any changes in connection with pictures?'

Betty hesitated. 'Don't you think you should ask him?' she presently essayed.

'I see you think he did. For your peace of mind I may tell you that I've done so. But I want your confirmation, Routine again.'

In spite of the man's inconsequent and rather friendly manner, Betty shivered. There seemed something sinister in this system of questioning; something as comprehensive as the universe and as relentless as Fate. Against it nothing could remain hidden. All the same there was no reason why she shouldn't answer the question.

'I'm not sure what you want to know,' she said. 'He had some pictures cleaned, if that's what you mean.'

'That's what I mean. Fifteen, he told me,' and he read out a list which Betty recognized as correct.

This at last was the end. With an apology for the time he had taken, Shaw once again levered himself out of his chair.

'You lost nothing in the fire yourself?' he asked as she also rose. 'None of your own personal property? Because if it was in the building it would be covered by the policy.'

'Nothing,' she answered. 'I left with the others and was staying temporarily in the Relfs' cottage.'

He nodded. 'Well, Mrs Stanton,' he declared. 'I have to thank you for helping me so pleasantly. Often people are obstructive and it makes an inquiry a loathsome job.'

She smiled. 'I can imagine it.'

The next day was a thrilling one for Betty. By the early post the last three chapters of her book came in from the typist, and she spent a fascinating morning in getting the completed work off to the publishers. What a joy there was in checking over the chapters to make sure that all were there, in squaring them up evenly, in binding them in a cover, even in handling and looking at this complete and perfect article which she, by her thought and work, had created out of nothing whatever! Then there was the wrapping of it up in paper, the writing on it of that magic name borne by the publishers to whom she had decided to entrust it, and the carrying of the precious burden to the post office, where registration took on the nature of a sacred rite. The only pang was in the handing of it over to the attendant, while the careless way in which he dropped it under the counter shocked her profoundly. She brightened up, however, when she remembered that the carbon copy was still at the Green House, waiting to be bound and put away.

But even this delightful task could not be made to occupy longer than the next morning, and when it was done Betty felt lost; as if a whole piece had gone out of her life. She decided to wait for a day or two and then set to work in real earnest to look for a job. With her Forde Manor experience, Sir Geoffrey's admirable testimonial and her more self-reliant manner, she felt she would produce a very different impression on the heads of employment bureaux than nine months earlier. That afternoon the Scotland Yard inspector called again.

But he had no news, merely asking more interminable questions. This time he saw Agatha also, but he seemed only to repeat to her the questions Betty had already answered.

When that evening Betty spoke about looking for a job, Agatha made an outcry. She would have none of it. 'Here you are,' she declared firmly, 'and here you stay: for the present at all events.' This to Betty was like a glimpse into paradise, and after a half-hearted protest she accepted the invitation.

Gradually the days began to drift by. Neither she nor Agatha heard from French, nor, so far as they knew, was any progress made in clearing up the mystery of Charles's fate. Tacitly the two women assumed that he was dead, and the assumption drew them closer together.

PART II

As Chief Inspector French Saw It

9

The Opening of the Case

Chief Inspector Joseph French had had a busy winter.

In the autumn he had been engaged on the case of the good ship *Hellénique*, when he had succeeded in bringing to an end the unseemly activities of the great liner. This affair had proved the prelude to that of the murder of John Stott near Portrush in Northern Ireland, in which, in collaboration with District Inspector Nugent of the Royal Ulster Constabulary, he had achieved the arrest of the murderer. But once this was effected, as it was in the middle of October, French found that his connection with the affair was practically over. Usually the investigation of a case, even when brought to the stage of making an arrest, is only part of the work to be done. Not infrequently it is a small part. When the suspect has been 'brought in', there begins the marshalling of the evidence against him. This preparation for court is quite as important as the pre-arrest inquiry. In all serious cases it is undertaken in collaboration with the Public Prosecutor's department and it always is a big job, involving a lot of work.

But the Stott murder having taken place in Northern Ireland, the trial was also there and all this preparation was therefore undertaken by the local authorities. French had little to do with it beyond handing over his notes to District Inspector Nugent and later going over to give evidence at the trial.

On returning to London he had had a period of routine work at the Yard, after which he was put in charge of a case of immense national importance, though few of the public even knew that it had taken place. This was the Martini case, an affair which caused the heads of the Air Force to sleep uneasily for several weeks. In it the discovery of a code letter, obtained by the searching of suspected premises, enabled French to capture the agent of a foreign government as he was leaving the country with the plans of a new and extremely hush-hush anti-aircraft gun in the lining of his suitcase.

After that a paternal department thought that a fortnight's holiday was due to the saviour of his country. It was just after his arrival home from a trip to Portugal that he was given the case of the disappearance of Charles Barke.

It began with a telephone call as he was finishing lunch on the first Sunday after his return. A message had come in from the *Sûreté* and the Assistant Commissioner, Sir Mortimer Ellison, who happened to have looked in on other business, would be glad to see French about it.

'Back as soon as I can, Em,' he said to his wife as he hurried off.

'Well, French,' Sir Mortimer greeted him twenty minutes later. 'Settled down to work yet after your globe-trotting? Or is that an untactful question?'

French knew his superior officer. 'Fortunately highly tactful, sir,' he declared unctuously.

'Found the place had gone to the dogs since you left, I suppose? I think you said you came back overland, through Paris?'

'Yes, sir. My wife was with me and we rather got it in the Bay going out and didn't want to have the dose repeated.'

'Quite right, put it on the wife! I do myself. Now about Paris. As it happens, it's rather a pity you didn't stay there.'

French's eye twinkled.

'I didn't come back to work solely from a sense of pleasure, sir.'

'No? You surprise me. Well, you might have been useful in Paris all the same. However, you needn't go back. Read that,' he tossed over the memorandum of a telephone conversation, 'and do what you can about it—in London. You've not taken over any other case, I think?'

'No, sir. I've just been squaring up some routine stuff that had got behind.'

'Place gone to the dogs: what did I say? Very well, read that message, and if there's anything you want to talk about, come in again.'

French, accepting the hint, tactfully withdrew to his own room. There he examined the memorandum, which read:

Telephone message received at 12.19 on Sunday, 17 March, from the Chief Officer, the *Sûreté*, Paris, to the Commissioner of Police, New Scotland Yard, London.

At 9.40 this morning the manager of the Hôtel Vichy, situated in the rue des Alpes, close to the Place de Lafayette, reported that an English man named Charles Barke, of London, had arrived there a few minutes before 16.00 on the previous Friday afternoon, saying that he had just come from London. He booked a room and registered, asking that his luggage be sent up. He noted the number of the room and said that he wished to pay a call before going up himself, and that he would be back presently. He went out, though no one saw in which direction he turned. Since then nothing has been heard of him.

At first the hotel management supposed he had been incidentally delayed, but when this morning came and they were still without news, they reported to the police. An officer was sent to the Vichy who found the missing man's passport, which had been issued in London, and which gave the full name, Charles Gresham Barke.'

All due measures for tracing the missing man have been put in force in Paris, so far without success, and it is thought that the explanation of the affair may lie in London. Hence passing on of information to Scotland Yard.

In addition to what is already being done, any specific inquiry suggested by London will be made.

Replied: that Yard would look into the affair and report back to Paris.

Not a particularly interesting problem, French thought, as he read the message for the second time. Probably the explanation was simple. This man, whoever he was, had met with an accident or lost his memory or stayed overnight with friends. Or perhaps he had wanted to give his wife' the go-by and start another establishment. At all events there was no reason to suppose he had met with foul play. Probably a waste of time bothering about it.

However, that was the A.C.'s pigeon and the A.C. must

be humoured. French picked up his telephone directory and looked up Barke. There were two Charles Barkes, one living at the Green House, Wilton Road, Chelsea, the other in Great James Street, W.C.1, though whether either was the man who had registered at the Vichy there was no means of knowing.

The name Barke seemed vaguely familiar to French though he could not remember in what connection. He put down the directory and opened a *Who's Who*. There it was, of course! The man he had heard of was an artist, and this might well be he. Carefully he read the paragraph:

'BARKE, Charles Gresham, M.A. OXON, A.R.A. 1932 R.D.I. A.R.B.S. 1934: Artist and Director of Crewe Gallery since 1935. *b*. London 1884, *s*. of late Wilfred Barke, London. *m*. Agatha Joyce Willcox, 2nd d . . . H'm. H'm. *Educ*. H'm Asst. Director. H'm. Drawings and paintings in public galleries. *Publications*: The Flemish School; The Restoration of Oil Paintings; Rubens; H'm. *Recreations*: golf, travelling. *Address*: The Green House, Wilton Road, Chelsea. *Clubs*: Arts, Travellers.'

The other Charles Barke not being mentioned in *Who's Who*, French decided to take this one first, and having instructed Sergeant Carter to accompany him, he set out for Chelsea.

A very few minutes in the pleasant sitting-room of the Green House, while he questioned Mrs Stanton—Mrs Barke being too ill to see him—convinced him that this Mr Barke was the man he sought. He felt also that the Barkes must be 'nice people'. The house was comfortable, restful and homelike, and though, of course, without meeting the occupiers he couldn't be sure, this fact as well as Mrs Stanton's personality in a way guaranteed them. French greatly admired what he saw of Mrs Stanton. She was, he thought, a lady of the best type, good looking, straight, and decent, and by no means a fool, and clearly much attached to her host and hostess. Affection from such a character precluded anything very far wrong with the recipients.

From Mrs Stanton and the maid French learnt the following facts:

1. That the Charles Barke of the Vichy Hotel was the Barke of the Green House and the Crewe Gallery.
2. That he had left home to catch the 9 a.m. from Victoria on the previous Friday, which was the service by which he had reached Paris.
3. That he was methodical and thoughtful of others and that it would have been foreign to his character not to have informed his hotel management of any change of plans.
4. That he carried his name and address on objects in at least two separate pockets.
5. That he had not mentioned the purpose of his visit to Paris. He seldom did explain the precise object of his journeys, and on this occasion there was an additional reason why he should not have done so, in that Mrs Barke was too ill to discuss it.
6. That his business was usually in connection with pictures: the sale of his own or purchases for the Gallery, or pronouncements as to authenticity.

7. That he had no secretary at home, but had a staff at the Gallery, some of whom would probably know his Parisian business.

8. That he did not make a practice of staying at any one hotel in Paris, though he seemed to go more frequently to the Ambassadors than elsewhere.

9. That he had seen the pictures at Forde Manor on the day before the fire, but not officially or by request of their owner.

10. That Mrs Stanton was the Mrs Stanton who had been in charge at Forde Manor and distinguished herself during the fire.

With permission French then examined the missing man's papers, from which he found one or two other items of interest:

11. On his desk engagement pad he had noted 'Woking 1.30 p.m.' and 'Forde Manor about 3.00' for that Monday, 11 March, and 'Victoria, 9.00 a.m.' for Friday 15th.

12. There was no hint of what the Paris business might be anywhere among the papers.

13. There were only a few unpaid bills and these for comparatively small amounts.

14. Barke's income tax returns for previous years showed that he was in receipt of some £3,000 a year, approximately made up as follows: Crewe directorship £1,050, sales of his own pictures £1,000; professional fees £500; investments £500; while Mrs Barke appeared to have about £500 a year in her own right.

15. Barke's bank book showed a comfortable current balance of £640.
16. His current cheque book was missing.
17. The blocks of his earlier cheque books showed no large recurring payments to self or other individual.
18. There was no reason to suppose he had taken a large sum of money or other valuables to Paris.

French was looking grave as he returned to the Yard. The case now seemed more serious than he had at first supposed. Sunday afternoon as it was, he went to his room and sat down to think the thing out and decide on his next steps.

In such an affair voluntary disappearance, accident, illness, loss of memory, kidnapping and murder must all be considered. Were there any indications as to which of these was the most likely?

First as to voluntary disappearance. The general atmosphere of the home and the personality at least of its visitor and maid, as well as their evident feeling for Barke, made domestic unhappiness unlikely as a motive for voluntary disappearance. Further, the absence of large financial payments to 'self' or other persons was a strong indication that the man was not maintaining a second establishment. His finances moreover were on an exceedingly sound basis so that there could be no urge to escape from monetary embarrassments. On the whole French felt that he might provisionally eliminate voluntary disappearance.

Accident or loss of memory seemed quite as unlikely. Barke had carried his name and address both in an engagement book and on the visiting cards in his wallet. Had an accident taken place, the fact would therefore almost certainly have become known.

But with voluntary disappearance, accident, and illness eliminated, only crime remained: kidnapping or murder. Of these, the first, to say the least of it, was uncommon; therefore the broad probabilities pointed to murder.

If so, the affair was urgent. But the solution surely lay in Paris, and his first duty must therefore be to telephone a *précis* of his discoveries to the *Sûreté*. He drew a sheet of paper towards him and began to write.

By the time his message was drafted it was getting on to seven o'clock, and feeling that he had done enough for a Sunday afternoon, he went home.

Nine-thirty on Monday morning, the hour of opening, saw him passing through the ornate portal—no one could have called it a door—of the Crewe Gallery. He asked for Barke's chief assistant and was shown to the office of a Mr Oliphant. Oliphant proved a stout consequential little man with a Shakespeare beard and thick rimless glasses.

'Good morning, sir,' French began, handing over his official card. 'It's really Mr Barke that I want to see. Can you tell me anything as to his whereabouts?'

'We're expecting him in any time now,' Oliphant answered, glancing at a clock on the mantelpiece. 'He generally comes about a quarter to ten.'

'He's at home then, is he?' went on French.

'He was to be here this morning. He went to Paris on Friday but he expected to return on Sunday.'

'I see, Mr Oliphant, that you haven't heard the news. Mr Barke has disappeared,' and French went on to summarize what had occurred.

Oliphant was obviously astonished, though no great signs of sorrow were in evidence. Indeed, a rather eager excitement presently showed in his manner. French rather unkindly wondered if he was already considering his chief's possible successor.

'It is of importance, therefore,' French went on, 'that the police should know the business that took him to Paris, so that inquiries may be made in the right quarters. And that's the reason for my call. I hope you can help me, Mr Oliphant.'

The little man sat back in his chair. 'I'm afraid that's just what I can't do, Mr French. Mr Barke didn't say what he was going over for.'

This was a blow to French. 'I take it he has a private secretary?' he suggested. 'Perhaps she would know.'

'We can soon find out.' Oliphant spoke into a desk telephone and in a moment a tall, good looking young woman entered the room and stood looking questioningly at its occupants.

'Is this a secret, Mr French?' Oliphant asked. 'I think we should tell Miss Redpath. She's as much in Mr Barke's confidence as anyone. This is Mr French from Scotland Yard, Miss Redpath.'

French bowed slightly. 'It is a secret, Miss Redpath,' he told her, 'but I'll tell you in strict confidence.'

She took the news very differently to Oliphant. 'Oh,' she cried in evident horror, 'you don't mean that anything's wrong; that anything has happened to him? He's not *dead*?'

'We've no reason to suppose so,' French assured her. 'Something of course has happened and we're trying to find out what it is. And that's where we want your help.'

'Oh,' she cried again, 'I do hope he's all right. He's so kind. We'd never get anyone like him again.'

French fancied that a momentary flash of resentment showed in Oliphant's eyes at this speech, but it disappeared so quickly that he could not be sure.

'Don't imagine things,' French said encouragingly, though he felt the words should be addressed to himself. 'What we want you to tell us, if you can, is what business took Mr Barke to Paris on Friday last.'

'But I don't know,' returned Miss Redpath with a little gesture of helplessness. 'He didn't tell me.'

'Oh?' said French. 'Do you mean that he gave you no hint of any kind?'

'Absolutely none at all.'

'No letters? No papers that might throw light on it?'

'None.'

'What did he say about it?'

'Just that he was running over to Paris on Friday and hoped to be back on Sunday and that he'd be in on Monday morning as usual.'

'Was that usual?'

'To run over to Paris?'

'No, to do so without mentioning the reason.'

Miss Redpath looked at Oliphant. 'Very unusual, I should say. Would you agree with that, Mr Oliphant?'

'I should,' the assistant answered decidedly, evidently pleased to be once more taking the floor. 'Almost invariably he discussed his business with me before starting. This time was quite an exception. He gave me no hint at all.'

'Yes, that's correct,' Miss Redpath added. 'Besides, there were usually letters to be written making appointments and so on.'

'Very well,' said French, seeing it was hopeless. 'If he didn't say, he didn't and we can't do anything about it. But there might be a letter in his desk for all that, or a note in his engagement book. What about having a look?'

'We can look,' agreed Miss Redpath, after an interrogatory

glance at Oliphant, 'but I'm positive we'll get nothing. He doesn't lock his desk and I know everything that's in it.'

French saw that the search was thorough, but in spite of it, nothing helpful was found.

'Can you tell me the hotel he usually stayed at?' he went on.

'When people were meeting him he usually went to the Ambassadors. When he was alone, so to speak, he had no fixed rule. He went to different places.'

'Ever know him to stop at the Vichy?'

'The Vichy?' She pondered. 'I don't remember that name, but of course he might have done it for all that.'

An attempt to trace the calls Barke had paid, and the callers and messages he had received during the previous week leading to nothing, French turned to a further point.

'I want you, please, to prepare a list of Mr Barke's Paris acquaintances, both individuals and firms, as far as you can make it up.'

'I can get that from the letter book, though I don't suppose it'll cover everyone he knew.' She paused, looking rather hesitatingly at Oliphant. 'I suppose I should put in Mr Lorrimer's name? He was in Paris, wasn't he?'

The suggestion seemed to embarrass Oliphant. He glanced at the girl sharply. French could have sworn there was some understanding between the two which he did not share. However Oliphant's pause was only momentary.

'I really don't know,' he said vaguely. 'I heard he went to Paris when he left here, but I don't know if it's true.'

'Who was Mr Lorrimer, sir?' French asked.

'My predecessor. He resigned some eight months ago.'

'Would you kindly tell me the circumstances?'

Again there was that sharp exchange of glances and again

a certain hesitation in Oliphant's reply. 'I'm afraid I can't,' he replied. 'He just resigned. He didn't tell me his reasons.'

'Nor me,' added Miss Redpath, French thought with relief.

He wondered if there was something here that both wished to keep to themselves, and his questions grew more searching. He did not learn a great deal from them, but the little they did reveal was suggestive. Lorrimer had been chief assistant for five years, and was a young man—thirty-three, the office record showed—for such a position. He was good at his job and pleasant-mannered and easy to get on with. That referred to his hearing in the office. Of his private life neither knew anything, as he was of a secretive temperament. He seemed to like the work, and Oliphant thought he had done it quite well. He had taken charge while Mr Barke was in America, and then, just after Mr Barke got back, he had resigned. He had not worked out a notice, but had gone at once. Oliphant didn't know his reasons, as he had said, but he presumed he had wanted to go earlier, but thought he ought to hold on till the chief's return. Oliphant believed Barke had been sorry to lose him. He had told them one morning that Lorrimer had left and was not returning, but had vouchsafed no explanation and had not further referred to the subject except when arranging his, Oliphant's promotion. It was Lorrimer himself who had told them he was going to Paris. That was on his last evening when he was saying goodbye. Miss Redpath had asked for his address and he had given Hôtel Sand, rue Rollin, near the Pantheon, but there had been no letters to forward there, nor had Lorrimer written since he left.

It was lunchtime when French left the building, having first obtained from Miss Redpath the list of Parisians with whom Barke had had recent dealings. This business of

Lorrimer had aroused his interest and he felt that it might be a productive line of inquiry. He rang up the *Sûreté* and repeated the list, asking that special attention should be given to the movements of Lorrimer on the afternoon of Barke's arrival.

The next item on his programme was a call at Barke's bank. As he asked no questions, the manager was friendly and agreed to advise the Yard if any of the missing man's cheques should be presented.

From the bank French went on to Barke's solicitors, Messrs Quilter, Hepworth & Quilter, of Lincoln's Inn. There he saw a Mr Rathbone, one of the principals.

'I'm afraid Mr Barke's business was handled by our senior partner, Mr Wellesley,' Rathbone explained when French had stated his business, 'and he's in hospital—just met with an accident. However, I know something of Mr Barke's affairs. What exactly did you want to know?'

'Anything that might throw light on his disappearance or help me to trace him,' French answered, going on to ask all the questions which seemed relevant.

Rathbone was clearly anxious to assist, but he had little to tell which interested French. He knew of nothing which might make Barke wish to disappear, nor of anyone who might wish him harm. On the contrary, all his information tended to show that Barke was happily situated and generally liked.'

What, French wondered, should be his next step? He wondered indeed if there was anything more that he could do. Did not the whole solution lie in Paris, and must not the investigation be carried on there? The information he had already obtained should enable the French police to get on the trail. And he had not been long getting it. Indeed, he didn't think he had done badly in the time.

There was just one matter upon which he had not checked up: Barke's visit to Forde Manor. Apparently it could not have affected the disappearance, as Mrs Stanton had said it was a purely private call. Barke had had a look at the Manor pictures certainly, but this was a perfectly natural act. It was his business to know where good pictures were to be found, in case they should come on the market.

But though French reasoned in this way, he could not get the visit out of his head. It was the one suggested line of inquiry which he had not followed up, and though he did not believe anything would come of it, he felt he would be to blame if he did not put the matter beyond doubt. To ease his conscience, therefore, he decided to run down to Ockham next morning and have a chat with the caretaker, Relf.

10

The Inauguration of an Alliance

The next morning was fine and the country was showing a delightful suggestion of spring, as French turned his car off the Guildford road at Ockham Common and inquired his way to Forde Manor. At the lodge he parked, and calling on Mrs Relf asked if he could have a word with her husband.

'He's down at the lake, sir,' she answered, 'where the stream runs out. He's been having trouble with the weir.'

This was just what French wanted. He set off, considering himself accounted for and free to look at anything which interested him.

He was at once struck by the beauty of the place and in particular by the magnificence of the trees. He was fond of trees and those under which he now walked were patriarchs of their respective families. They arched high across the drive like the vaulted roof of a skeleton cathedral. Then coming to the open ground he gazed down in admiration over the sloping lawns to the lake beyond. The water looked cold and forbidding, but it was relieved by a broad band of gilding across its widest part, a gift from the sun which shone beyond it, low down in the sky. At the end was the tiny figure of a man, digging on the bank. French walked down.

'Good morning,' he called. 'Are you Relf?'

'Yes, sir,' the man returned as spade in hand he slowly approached.

'Having trouble here?' French went on to show interest and create a propitious atmosphere.

'Yes, sir,' Relf repeated. 'The water's been undermining this here end of the weir and I'm making it up. You have to keep on top of a job of this kind. If I let it go too far it wouldn't be long till the lake was emptied.'

'Is the lake artificial then?'

'Made in King John's time, they tell me. I've heard the old master say so more than once, that was Sir Howard before the present man, Sir Geoffrey, came over from America.' The words were correct, and yet the man's contrasting feelings towards his two employers were as clear as if he had delivered a lecture on the subject. French congratulated himself that Relf should be not only talkative but transparent. He chatted on about the repairs, then turned to business.

'I called to get some help from you, Relf. I'm Chief Inspector French from Scotland Yard, and it's nothing about yourself or Sir Geoffrey or this place or the fire. It's about Mr Barke.'

Relf's expressive countenance registered increasing surprise as he listened to this gambit. 'That's the gentleman what was down to see Mrs Stanton the day before the fire? I don't know nothing about him, sir.'

'No,' French agreed, 'but I think you can help me all the same. I'd better tell you in confidence,' he went on with an air of great candour, 'that Mr Barke has disappeared. No one knows what has happened to him. I'm trying to find out everything he did recently in the hope of tracing him.'

Relf shook his head. 'I'd be sorry to hear there was anything wrong with him,' he declared. 'A nice gentleman, pleasant spoken and all that, though,' he added as if from an afterthought, 'he'd be bound to be all right if he was a friend of Mrs Stanton's.'

French smiled. 'I agree with you, though I've seen less of her than you. However, that's not the point. I want you to tell me exactly what took place on that Monday afternoon. Did Mrs Stanton ask you to show Mr Barke the pictures?'

'No, sir, he spoke to my wife and she sent him down to me. I was giving the boats a go-over, for though there was no one in the house, everything had to be kept right in case there would be a sale. Mr Barke said he was an artist and that Mrs Stanton had been going to let him see the pictures, but as she couldn't do so and he was down here specially for the purpose, he hoped I would.'

'And you did?'

'Yes, sir. I thought it would be doing the right thing to oblige him.'

'I'm not suggesting it wasn't. I only want to know what happened.'

'Well, we went in and I soon saw he had been there before. "Where's the Gorah?" he asked. "You had a fine Gorah here and it seems to be gone." Well, sir, I couldn't tell him, I didn't know nothing about those pictures, you understand. And then he said something about a dyke. I couldn't make out what it was.'

'A Van Dyck,' French suggested.

130

Relf nodded. 'That's right,' he admitted. 'A picture, I suppose?'

'A picture painted by a man of that name.'

'That so? Well, he seemed to miss two pictures, the Gorah and the Dyke one.'

'Yes?' French encouraged.

'Then he looked round and found what he wanted. He went over to a picture. "The Gorah," he said. "Hell!" he said, but sort of to himself. I don't know what it was all about, but it seemed to upset him and he went on muttering.'

'What did he mutter?' asked the puzzled French.

'One word I heard was Van something. Not Van Dyck as you mentioned, but something else. Then he said, "That's private ownership for you!" I heard that clearly. Then he sort of turned to me and said, "Fools rush in." I thought for a moment he was off his chump, if you will excuse me saying so.'

'That word wasn't "Vandal", I suppose?'

'"Vandal" it was, sir: that's right.'

'And what then?'

'The same thing happened before a lot of other pictures. He saw something he didn't like, but he didn't explain to me what it was. He found the Van Dyck and it was the same with that. I couldn't make out what was wrong.'

French was by now completely mystified. What could Barke have seen in another man's collection, with which he himself had nothing to do, to cause him annoyance or distress? He wondered if Betty Stanton knew, and made a note to ask her.

He bade good day to Relf, but before leaving the grounds he decided to walk up to see what was left of the house. The ruins looked tragic enough from the lake, but it was not till he got closer that he realized how complete was the

131

destruction. Never had he seen such catastrophic devastation. As he gazed at the gaunt blackened walls with their starkly staring windows and cracked stonework he shivered. The place seemed a symbol of death and it cast its dreadful shadow over all its surroundings.

He walked along the ruined front, then turned round the gallery wing to have a look at the rear. As he did so he stopped suddenly and stared. There approaching him was someone he knew. With an exclamation of pleasure he stepped forward, his hand outstretched.

'Shaw, by all that's wonderful!' he exclaimed. 'Are your people interested in this?' He jerked his thumb towards the ruin.

'I might ask the same of you,' the newcomer answered, 'and with more reason. How did your lot get in on it?'

They shook hands, smiling genially at one another.

'In on it?' French repeated. 'We're not in on it—if there's anything to be in on. I'm down here on another case: a disappearance. Artist called Barke. Director of the Crewe Gallery and so on.'

'Oh that,' rejoined Shaw casually. 'Has he not turned up yet?'

'Look here,' French said firmly, 'how did you know he had gone? What do you know about it all?'

Shaw took his cigarette case from his pocket and held it out. 'Well,' he answered slowly, 'it's this fire, you know. The Thames & Tyne have got stung over it and they're sitting up and taking notice. They've sent me down to see that everything's O.K.'

'I twigged that, strange as it may appear,' declared French as he selected a cigarette. 'What I asked was, how you got on to the Barke affair?'

'You might have twigged that too. I went to see our local heroine, Mrs Stanton, and found her mourning Barke R.A.'s apparent defection. But you haven't told me how you got drawn in.'

'The *Sûreté* rang us up. Barke arrived in Paris from London about four o'clock last Friday afternoon, went to his hotel, booked his room, sent his luggage up, said he had to pay a call and walked out of the hotel. He's not been heard of since.'

'Very pretty vanishing act. What is it? Another woman?'

French shook his head. 'Looks more like murder to me, though of course I don't know yet.'

'That's bad. What's the motive?'

French hesitated. 'I'm not sure,' he answered presently. 'But it's your turn now. You don't suspect this fire's not all O.K., do you?'

'I don't say that. It's what I'm supposed to be looking into, you know.'

'You don't seem very satisfied. Look here, Shaw, I'd like a chat with you about all this. Suppose we have a walk round the top of the lake? It looks attractive under those trees.'

'Suits me. I've been wanting to do it, as a matter of fact, but I've not taken the time.'

'Now,' said French as they set off, 'suppose you begin at the beginning. What is it all about?'

Shaw made a gesture. 'Oh, well, I'd have come in any case, you know. I always examine the site of a fire before we pay.'

French grinned. 'Very good: now get on to it.'

Shaw smiled in his turn. "There's not very much to it,' he answered. 'We hold the insurance of this place, have done for years. Then about a year ago the former owner, Sir Howard Buller, died and for a time they weren't sure who would succeed him. Then they discovered this present man, Sir Geoffrey, in America. He came home, took the title, and settled down here. He is unmarried, and he engaged Mrs Stanton to run the house for him.'

'Where in America was Sir Geoffrey?'

'Chicago, I believe. Then Sir Geoffrey decided he didn't like England—and that he'd sell and go back to the States. I've heard a whisper that he didn't get on with the people here, but I don't know if it's true.'

'Easy to find out.'

'Yes, but I've not had time. Shortly after coming over Sir Geoffrey approached our people to revise the insurance. He said be couldn't find any details about it and didn't believe the place was properly covered. He was quite right. Our people knew the policy wasn't satisfactory, but Sir Howard wouldn't move in the matter. A complete new valuation was therefore made and the premium adjusted accordingly.'

'Well?' French encouraged him.

'Well, he wasn't able to sell, and then,' Shaw paused, adding a trifle grimly, 'there was the fire.'

French thought over this. 'Not absolutely conclusive, you know,' he remarked presently.

'Haven't I said so!' Shaw retorted. 'But a case for investigation and so—here I am.'

'And Barke has disappeared and Barke paid a call here just before it and so—here *I* am. By the way, I've just been asking Relf about his visit, and it seems he saw the pictures and was greatly upset about them. Any theory to cover that?'

'Yes, that may be important. I'll tell you. It seems that

Sir Geoffrey had been getting a lot of pictures cleaned: fifteen to be accurate. Now Barke has a complex about that, normally the very idea sends him off the deep end. There can be no doubt that that was what he didn't like.'

'That would fit in,' French returned. 'Relf saw he was upset about it.'

'That's it.'

French made a gesture of exasperation. 'But was he right?' he asked. 'What's the truth of this cleaning business?'

'Well,' Shaw answered cautiously, 'doctors differ, you know. But there are two things which may be suggestive: first, the pictures he had done were valuable. There was a Van Dyck, a Goya, a Muril—'

'Goya!' French exclaimed with sudden enlightenment.

'What's that?'

'Gorah was what Relf said. I couldn't place it.'

'He meant Goya. Well, that was the first thing: fifteen of the best pictures done. The second was that Wilberforce, our artist who valued the pictures for insurance, tells me that in his opinion none of them wanted cleaning, or not badly at all events.'

French's interest grew keener. This new fact, added to the two he had already known, made a suggestive trio. First, one expert considered that a number of pictures had been cleaned unnecessarily and a second (obviously) that the work had been a disastrous mistake; second, the collection containing these cleaned pictures had been burnt, and third, the expert who had seen what was done had disappeared.

French knew little about pictures. But in the course of his career he had come across more than one case in which cleaned and renovated pictures had been mysteriously burnt. It was an old trick. You own a good picture, and are short of cash. Very well, have it valued and insure it for its full worth: all perfectly correct and above board. Then get it copied. Sell the original secretly to some collector, put the copy in its place and burn down the house. This gives you nearly twice the value of the picture. And if there are many pictures in a like case and your house is also insured for its full value, the profits grow correspondingly. Dangerous if the sales become known? Yes, but only slightly. You have chosen your purchaser carefully and given him something more than a hint of the truth. If you are prosecuted, you will see that he is too. He will keep the transaction dark till you have had time to move elsewhere and adopt a new personality.

But if a qualified judge of pictures has seen your copies before your fire, where do you stand? Your future welfare depends on his discretion, and if you fear this may be inadequate, a certain compulsion is undoubtedly indicated.

'Tell me,' French said earnestly, 'were all those cleanings genuine?'

'No reasons to suppose they weren't, you know. If we could only ask Barke, he could tell us.'

'That's—just it.'

Shaw stared. 'Oh,' he said presently, 'that's what is worrying you, is it? You think he saw too much?'

'The idea passed through my mind,' French admitted. 'But then I have a suspicious nature.'

Shaw stopped and faced round. 'Easy to settle it,' he declared. 'Barke saw the pictures on Monday afternoon and the fire was that night. Then he went to Paris on Friday morning and disappeared on arrival there. That O.K.?'

'Correct.'

'Then if you're right, Sir Geoffrey was in Paris on Friday.'

'Presumably.'

'Easy to find out. But look here, French, suppose your suspicion's right; how would Sir Geoffrey know that Barke wouldn't have told someone what he saw? He'd never have been able to keep it to himself all that time.'

'What matter if he had talked?'

'What matter?'

'It couldn't be used.'

Admiration shone in Shaw's eyes. 'By Jove, I hadn't thought of that! Of course it would be hearsay evidence and inadmissible!'

'So that if Sir Geoffrey had been trying it on, the elimination of Barke would have meant his safety.'

Shaw nodded. 'You're right. Then what about finding out if he was in Paris on Friday?'

'I'll see to it first thing.'

'You, know,' Shaw went on slowly, 'I'm as much interested in all this as you are. If there was any hanky panky, it might save my companies anything up to half a million. And you might get a murderer!'

French lit another cigarette. 'The question of the murder must be settled for both of our inquiries. What about working on it together?'

Shaw, old and hardened as he was, coloured with pleasure. 'Suits me,' he said warmly. 'What do you suggest we should do?'

French considered. 'As a matter of fact, before moving I'd like to be clearer about motive.'

'The motive's simple enough; want of cash.'

'Ah, but how do you know? Can you prove it?'

'No; we'll have to go into it. But apart from the cash he can't have been happy here. Else why did he close down and try to sell?'

'I daresay Mrs Stanton could answer both questions, but I'm not sure if she would.'

'Tell you what I propose,' Shaw declared. 'Gossip in the local pub. A few pints will usually get you what you want.'

'I'm game for that,' French grinned. 'A lot pleasanter than most of my work. Do you suggest waiting till the evening?'

Shaw shook his head. 'No, too many there then. No better time than the present.' As a younger man with less authority than he now possessed, French had on countless occasions used this very plan, though latterly he had favoured the official approach, saying who he was and asking directly for the information he required. But Shaw, he could understand, would have to retain the earlier method, as he was usually working a lone hand, without having behind him, as French had, the backing of the entire British realm.

They retraced their steps to the lodge, and driving to Ockham, went into the bar of the Three Musketeers. It was a cosy room with a big fire blazing on the hearth. Two men were sitting over the latter, while an elderly butler-like man in a pullover and shirtsleeves, leant across the counter. A conversation between the three was evidently in progress, but it closed down as they entered.'

'Afternoon, gentlemen,' Shaw greeted the company, 'Cold today.'

'But not in here,' added French. 'You're very snug, landlord. What'll you have, George?'

'Pint of bitter.' Shaw answered, looking at the fire and rubbing his hands.

'Two pints, please,' said French, also looking at the fire.

The two men seated before it politely took the hint, moving over to make room.

'Thank you, gentlemen,' French answered the movement.

'A very attractive fire on a day like this. Won't you join us? What'll you have?'

The men murmured about pints of bitter, and French went on, 'You too, landlord. I hope you'll join us in your preference?'

The atmosphere grew more cordial. French and Shaw drew chairs to the fire and began a desultory conversation about the last test match which had been played at Melbourne and which England had lost. Presently they wanted more beer. 'This,' said one of the original customers heavily, 'is on me.' They thanked him, drank, and presently ordered a third to go all round.

Up to this they had carefully kept off the subject of the fire, but French now thought the time ripe for a *démarche*.

The two original customers had evidently been drinking for some time, for their tongues were now moving much more freely. Even the landlord had grown unprofessionally mellow.

'That was a nasty fire you had last week,' French therefore essayed. 'We've just been past the place and saw the house all burnt out.'

'Terrible affair,' one of the originals returned, 'but it might have been a lot worse.'

'A lot worse?' Shaw repeated. 'It looked bad enough to me as it was.'

'He doesn't mean that. You don't mean that do you Mr Henson?' put in the other original. 'He means it was a good thing the house was empty.'

'Well, it was, and then again maybe it wasn't,' remarked the landlord. 'It's true when it was empty there could be nobody burnt, but if there'd been someone in it they might have got the fire out.'

'What I mean,' declared the first original ponderously, 'is that if anyone had been burnt it would have been a lot worse. And so it would,' he added as if challenging dissent.

'I fancy we'll agree to that,' French answered. 'It's astonishing,' he went on reminiscently, 'how many of these fine country houses have been burnt in this country within recent years. And many of them empty too. You'd wonder how they'd get alight.'

'Rats at the electric mains,' Shaw suggested.

'I shouldn't be surprised,' the first original pronounced, though looking as if the idea was both new and strange.

'So they say at all events.' Shaw renounced responsibility for the opinion. 'What was supposed to start this one?'

'They don't rightly know,' answered the landlord, appealed to generally as the proper source of local knowledge. 'Some say it was an electric short and some the flue of the central heating, but no one really knows.'

French thought the time had come for another step. 'Hard lines on the owner anyhow,' he said sympathetically. 'Buller, I saw his name was from the paper. Is he a local man?'

This drew the reply he had hoped for, and they were presently discussing Sir Geoffrey with avidity. Shaw's forecast had been correct; they knew all about him, or pretended they did. From the two original customers, backed up with occasional support from the landlord, they learnt that Sir Geoffrey was English, descended from a junior branch of the family, and that he inherited only because of three unexpected deaths having occurred almost simultaneously in the succession. He came home from somewhere in America ('Chicago,' interjected the landlord. 'Told me himself sitting in that chair.') and as he wasn't married, he got Mrs Stanton to run the house for him. ('A nice lady:

140

well spoken of,' from the landlord.) But the whole thing had been a mistake from his own point of view. He hadn't liked living at Forde, for he hadn't hit it off with his neighbours. ("'Damned mountebank!" that's what I overheard Lord Brabazon call him to Mr Cheyney on one occasion. "Damned mountebank," he said, and Mr Cheyney said: "Confounded impertinence! He'll be trying to get into the hunt next!"') No, no one had liked him and he had liked no one. And he was also supposed to be hard up. He had begun by subscribing to the local charities and what not, but later that had dried up and nothing more could be got out of him. These statements were all strongly expressed, and lacked neither in substance nor detail.

However, it was clear to French that if even half of it were true, Sir Geoffrey had a motive for arson. How strong that motive might have been was doubtful, but it was at least certain that the matter could not be left where it was and that further investigation must be carried out. Taking care not to leave the Three Musketeers too abruptly, the two detectives regained their respective cars and drove back to London.

11

The Course of Investigation

On reaching town that afternoon French set to work on a number of small inquiries designed to test the strength of the case he was trying to build up against Sir Geoffrey Buller.

His first call was on Oliphant at the Crewe Gallery. From him he learnt of Charles Barke's interest in the question of cleaning and restoring pictures, of his paper on the subject before the Royal Academy, and of his objection to such work unless absolutely necessary. If Charles had heard, Oliphant was positive, that old masters at Forde Manor had been cleaned, he would have certainly taken the first opportunity of seeing them, if only to satisfy himself that the disastrous results he foresaw in such cases had been duly achieved.

From the Gallery French rang up Betty to ask when she could see him, with the result that an hour later he was shown into the Green House sitting-room.

'I had two reasons for calling,' he explained after inquiring for Agatha. 'First as the bearer of negative news: I regret to say that so far we have heard nothing of Mr Barke.'

'I'm dreadfully sorry. Mrs Barke will be terribly upset, I'm afraid.'

'I'm sorry, too. But Mrs Barke needn't be upset because of this report. Things are no worse than they were.'

Betty smiled wanly. 'It was kind of you to come round at all events.'

'I'm afraid that was only one of the things I wanted. My second object was to ask you a few more questions. Again I'm sorry.'

'I'll answer them as well as I can.'

'I want a sort of background for my report. I want, for instance, to know how often and under what circumstances Mr Barke had previously visited Forde Manor, how you yourself came to go there, and so on. I admit that the exact connection of our questions with our cases is not always obvious, but you'd be surprised how often some vital clue is obtained by asking for apparently irrelevant details.'

Betty smiled again, less wanly. 'It's all right,' she protested. 'I'm not critical.'

'Then let's begin with Mr Barke's previous visits to Forde.'

She told him about this, and he then turned to her own first meeting with Sir Geoffrey. During the discussion he found it easy to slip in questions about the man himself. Thus he learnt about Buller's upbringing and American job and that he had come to Forde Manor with large social ambitions, which he had completely failed to realize. In fact, Betty thought that this disappointment was the reason for his giving up the place.

'What about his financial position?' French asked. 'Death duties often leave an awkward problem for an heir.'

Here Betty couldn't help him. All she knew was that Sir Geoffrey was invariably liberal towards herself. French passed from the point, believing he could get his information from the man's solicitors.

'What about the cleaning of those pictures?' he went on. 'That, I take it, was done to increase their value?'

Betty admitted that this no doubt was the idea.

'But you don't think it succeeded?'

Betty didn't see why he should say that. She was no authority, and though she herself liked the pictures better before they had been done than after, that was merely her personal opinion.

'Mr Barke had seen these restorations. What did he think?' went on French.

'That's what I don't know,' she replied with more interest. 'I don't think anyone does. I didn't see him since the visit and he didn't speak of it to Mrs Barke. He wouldn't have liked them though; he was always against it.'

This, with the name of Sir Geoffrey's London hotel and the fact that she had no idea where Sir Geoffrey was on the Friday of Barke's disappearance, completed Betty's statement.

'Thank you, Mrs Stanton. That's all I want to ask you, but I should like to see Mrs Barke for a moment. Perhaps you would ask her to come down?'

French was impressed by Agatha's personality. Her manner was pleasant and her conversation interesting and she was, he was certain, genuinely good and kind. Obviously she was fond of her husband, and he became more than ever convinced as to the improbability of Barke's having disappeared voluntarily to start another establishment.

French discussed the affair with her in a sympathetic manner, though he learnt little that was new. Then without a change of manner he suddenly changed the subject.

144

'Now,' he asked, 'will you please tell all you can about the circumstances under which Mr Lorrimer left the Crewe Memorial?'

That Agatha was taken aback was obvious. 'Oh,' she exclaimed, 'do you think my husband met Mr Lorrimer in Paris?' Again she paused and her face grew anxious. 'Why do you ask that, Inspector?'

French's manner was reassuring to the verge of fatherliness. 'Just, madam, that we're trying to check up everyone Mr Barke knew in Paris. Mr Lorrimer is believed to be in Paris. I naturally want to know what you can tell me about him. You knew him personally, I suppose?'

'Oh, yes, he's often been to the house.'

Against French's interrogation Agatha had no chance. She did not herself care very much for Lorrimer, who, she thought, was too reserved to invite friendship. But her husband had liked him and they had got on well together. And then with evident regret she revealed the whole story of the man's error and dismissal. 'Then,' asked French, 'Mr Lorrimer was under the impression that if he didn't pay up before the next audit, he would be prosecuted?'

'Yes, my husband thought it would be more of a lesson to him if he didn't know he was safe.'

'Quite.' A few more questions and French politely took his leave.

As he walked to the District Station he wondered if he had solved his problem. Was it conceivable that a man like Lorrimer would have murdered his old chief for a sum of £250? Yet not for £250 only. Prison was at stake, and prison to a man in Lorrimer's position would have meant ruin. If Barke's continued existence meant Lorrimer's ruin, there was certainly a motive for murder.

French tried to picture what might have happened. Barke goes to Paris on some business of which Lorrimer, as his former chief assistant, knows the details. He therefore asks Lorrimer to meet him. Or Lorrimer himself invents the business. At all events the two men meet. Is it possible that at this interview Lorrimer kills the man in whose hands lies his fate?

It might, French thought, depend on the circumstances of the meeting. If Lorrimer saw a way of doing the deed safely, the sudden temptation might have proved too strong for him. Or he might have killed Barke unintentionally. They might have met with the most pacific intention and a quarrel might have broken out, and in the heat of passion Lorrimer might have struck, unwisely but too well.

Lorrimer was a second string to his bow at all events, French thought, or was he the first? Either he or Sir Geoffrey might be guilty, and the cases against both would have to be tested till certainty was reached.

A little later there was a reply from the *Sûreté*. All the persons mentioned in French's communication had been interviewed: without result. All of them except Lorrimer were persons of position and reputation and on *a priori* grounds it was unlikely that any of them should be guilty. In the case of Lorrimer a preliminary investigation had been made—admittedly not exhaustive and he appeared to be innocent. He had an alibi for the critical period which had received a certain amount of corroboration.

French heaved a sigh. That was the exasperating kind of answer he might have foreseen. Probabilities! Why couldn't he for once in a way get something conclusive? He would have to get in touch with the *Sûreté* again.

It was late for speaking to Paris, but on chance he put

through his call and by good luck found someone who knew the details of the case. To this man he repeated his belief that Lorrimer had a motive for murdering Barke, and asked if the alibi could be rechecked from this viewpoint. Then his thoughts returning to Sir Geoffrey, he wired for all available information about him to the Chief of Police at Chicago.

Next morning saw French at Somerset House, where, having tendered his shilling, he inspected the last will and testament of the late Sir Howard Buller. He did not learn as much from it as he had hoped, the figures being extraordinarily complicated, but he did get the impression that the deceased's heir would be left very short of cash to keep up Forde Manor.

He returned to the Yard to attend to some routine details before going on to Messrs Tuffnel, Jinks & Tuffnel, of Arundel Street, Strand, the agents whose name appeared on the 'To be sold' boards at Forde. There he was rung up by Shaw to ask if he had any news.

French in his reply mentioned his next port of call.

'You needn't go to Tuffnel's,' Shaw assured him. 'I've got all they have to tell. I'll come round and give you the dope.'

Half an hour later the man was installed in French's only armchair.

'Well,' he queried, 'so you've got a second line shaping? Tell me more about it.'

For a time they discussed Lorrimer, and then French switched the conversation to Sir Geoffrey. 'You saw those Tuffnel & Jinks birds? What had they to say?'

'Nothing,' Shaw returned, 'except that there was little chance of a sale. During the three months the place was advertised, they hadn't a single offer.'

147

'That might be useful enough,' French answered ruminatively, 'if Buller was hard up.'

'He was hard up all right,' Shaw asserted. 'It seems Sir Howard could only just make ends meet. If so, the death duties would leave Sir Geoffrey practically down and out.'

'That's important,' French declared. 'Can you prove it?'

Shaw shrugged. 'Not exactly, though we might work it out from the probate figures. But I think it's right enough. It was generally accepted in the locality. It's wonderful how these things get out.'

'Not always correctly.'

'They're not usually far wrong. Do you know if Buller brought any money in with him?'

'Shouldn't think so. I'll know for certain when I get a reply from Chicago. It ought to be here any time.'

'It's making quite a case,' Shaw considered.

'Yes, let's sum it up. Here's this man Buller, apparently having come from small beginnings, and he's left this large house and place. He comes over full of eagerness and pleasure and counts on doing the country squire and cutting a dash and entertaining the neighbourhood.'

'And all he gets is disappointment,' interjected Shaw.

'All he gets is disappointment,' French repeated. 'First he finds he's short of cash to run the place, so there's worry to start with. Then he doesn't get on with the local people, he's not received by them, and his dreams of doing the country squire and filling the manor with guests go *phut*.'

'A harder hit than the money.'

'Yes, it touches his pride. Well, he decides on two things; one, to clear out, the other, to overhaul the insurance to cover the whole value of the property.'

Shaw made a gesture of dissent, but French did not stop.

'I know what you're going to say. We don't know which of these conclusions he reached first. That it?'

'That's it,' Shaw agreed. 'It makes quite a difference. If he fixed up the insurance before he decided to leave, it has no particular significance; if *after*, it suggests arson.'

'Very well, let's give Buller the benefit of the doubt,' French continued. 'Assume he has the valuation made in good faith before he realizes he can't carry on. He does at last realize he can't carry on, so he decides to sell.'

'Then he's disappointed again.'

French nodded. 'Exactly. He finds he can't sell. No one has the cash to run a place of that size. Now what's his position? Forde has turned from an asset into a liability. Even when the house is empty there are heavy expenses running on. There's depreciation. There are repairs. The garden must be kept up or a sale will become less likely still. It takes money and he can't find it. Now it's just here that his temptation arises. As you said, if he can't get money through a sale he can get it through a fire.'

'It's certainly plausible.'

'More than plausible, I think. However, arson's your chicken, not mine. But is there a reasonable suspicion of murder? That's not so clear.'

'It involves assuming he's been monkeying with the pictures,' Shaw pointed out. 'You have to assume that those fifteen weren't cleaned but were copied, and that he's sold the originals and is claiming the original price from us.'

'Of course, and also that Barke, during his unexpected visit, tumbled to the trick and so had to be silenced.'

Shaw nodded. 'A good summary,' he approved, 'and it just means further inquiry.'

'My conclusion also,' French agreed. 'Then I'll begin by

finding out where Buller was on the Friday of Barke's disappearance.'

'How will you do it?'

'Ask him. How else?'

'I shouldn't give away that I was interested.'

'What's your method?'

'I'd make up my nephew as a plain clothes man—he's big enough and awkward enough for the job,' Shaw's eyes twinkled, 'and send him to Buller to say that there was an accident on Friday afternoon at such a place, and that his car, which didn't stop, was believed to have caused it. When he gets indignant and says he was nowhere near the place, my nephew would say: "That's all right, sir, but as a matter of pure form, where were you on Friday afternoon?"'

French laughed. 'I'm afraid you've become a moral wreck since you left the force,' he declared. 'You know jolly well I couldn't do that.'

'Perhaps not, but it would be the best way.'

French thought so too as half an hour later he sent up his card to Buller in the Brooklyn Hotel. A moment later he and Sergeant Carter were shown into the man's private sitting-room.

'Good morning, sir. Sorry for this intrusion,' began French, handing over his official card, and explaining that he was inquiring into Barke's disappearance. Sir Geoffrey was polite, but wary and non-committal.

'I'd be grateful,' French went on, 'if you could give me any help. You met Mr Barke once at Forde Manor?'

'Yes,' Sir Geoffrey admitted, 'but I don't see exactly how that's going to help you.'

'May I ask if that was the last time you saw him?'

'Yes, the first and last and only time.'

150

The interrogation went on through its time-honoured stages: French's innocent questions; Sir Geoffrey's demand to know what he was getting at and ascertain that he was not bound to answer; French's agreement and suggestion that such a course would raise undesirable suspicions; Sir Geoffrey's bluster and final capitulation. 'What,' he growled at last, 'do you want to know?'

'Simply, sir, where you were on the afternoon of Friday the fifteenth instant.'

Sir Geoffrey who had been growing more and more upset, looked relieved. He considered for some moments then answered. 'If that's all, and if telling you will save me further annoyance, I'll tell you. But I protest formally against the whole thing.'

'That's all right, sir,' French replied cheerfully. 'I'm sorry for annoying you and I note your protest.'

Sir Geoffrey nodded and took an engagement book from his pocket. 'I may have spoken too quickly,' he said in a pleasanter voice. 'I'll tell you if I can. That was the day I saw my dentist. You want the afternoon?'

'If you please, sir?'

'Well, I don't know that I'll be able to remember everything, but let's see. I lunched here—I suppose that'll be early enough to begin?'

'That'll do nicely.' French felt a shiver of disappointment pass over him. If this were true, he was on the wrong track. However, he might as well hear all the man had to say and make assurance doubly sure.

'After lunch,' Sir Geoffrey went on, 'I read in the lounge and then went out, I should think somewhere about three.'

'Good enough.'

'I did a bit of shopping: two or three things I wanted;

shoes and a waterproof and so on, and then as I had a bit too much time on my hands, I walked to the dentist's. My appointment was for four o'clock and I suppose I was there fifteen minutes altogether. Then let's see, what did I do? I had tea and walked back to the hotel. No, I didn't, not directly. I called for a moment with my solicitors to know if they could yet tell me when I could go back to Capri, a question that I had asked them some days previously. Then I sat in the hotel talking to some Americans till dinner. I dined in the hotel. That enough?'

'Ample, sir. Thank you very much. Now just a name or two and I've done. Who was your dentist?'

Sir Geoffrey frowned. 'Oh, you don't believe me, don't you?'

'I do believe you,' French said with truth, if with regret, 'but you must be aware that we are bound to check every statement we get.'

With a bad grace Sir Geoffrey gave the information. Then French set to work on the corroboration.

First he saw the dentist, Mr Cleveland. Sir Geoffrey had rung him up that morning, asking for an appointment in the afternoon, as he was having pain in a tooth which Cleveland had stopped some months earlier. Cleveland had at considerable inconvenience arranged for four o'clock on the same day. Sir Geoffrey had kept his appointment. The stopping had appeared good, and Cleveland had diagnosed a touch of cold affecting the nerve. The sitting had lasted for about a quarter of an hour.

From the dentist French went to Messrs Quilter, Hepworth & Quilter and there interviewed Mr Rathbone, the partner who had seen Bailer. Once again the alibi was confirmed. Beyond any possible shadow of doubt Sir Geoffrey was in his solicitors' offices between five and five-thirty on the fateful Friday.

Did this entirely eliminate Sir Geoffrey? French thought it did, provided the Barke details as he understood them were correct. Could Barke, for instance, have secretly come back to London? The more he thought over it, the more attractive grew the idea of running over to Paris and getting the local details clear beyond any possibility of doubt. Also he wanted to know more about Lorrimer. He therefore saw Sir Mortimer Ellison, obtained his approval, and after wiring the *Sûreté*, took the night service via Southampton.

Paris was looking very attractive in the bright spring sunshine when about ten o'clock French drove out of the Gare St Lazare. At the *Sûreté* he was greeted with immense courtesy by the Deputy Chief—the Chief being laid up—and introduced to a M. Dieulot, the inspector who had charge of the case. Dieulot, it appeared, had had several years' service at Cannes before being transferred to Paris, and he had learnt English. He was now one of the men to whom were given cases which might have English repercussions.

'He have vanished, thees Meestair Barke, into the thin air, as you say in England,' he explained, evidently proud of the cliché. 'He go out of the Hotel and—' His raised hands and shoulders eloquently covered the remainder of the story.

'And what's your view, M. Dieulot? Do you think it was voluntary or was he murdered?'

Again the shrug, in itself a complete answer.

'We rather incline to the murder view,' French went on, briefly summarizing the reasons. 'But one of our two suspects was in England that afternoon. The other is Lorrimer. We'll come to him in a moment. But first I wanted to be quite sure that Barke really stayed in Paris; I mean, that he wasn't inveigled back to England by some trick.'

As a matter of fact this was not what French wanted. He really wished to know the whole circumstances at first hand and to check what the French police had done, though he didn't care to put this into words. Dieulot, however, volunteered the information, as French had hoped he would.

'As to a return to England,' he answered, 'there ees the passport. But it would be best that you see all.' He opened a cupboard and took out certain articles. 'Behold the passport, the suitcase, the clothes. You see them, then we go to the Vichy. You spik to the manager.'

'That's very kind of you,' French assured him. 'That will cover at once all the questions I wanted to ask you.'

Barke's possessions, which he had left at the hotel, had been brought to the *Sûreté* and French was presently examining them. The passport was undoubtedly Barke's, not only from the details of address and so on, but because the photograph showed the same man as did one which French had already obtained from the Green House. It bore entrance and exit stamps to many countries, and among them was the large purple ring containing the words 'Commissariat Special Débarquement', with 'Boulogne-s/Mer' inside, and below in its rectangular frame across the centre, the date '15 Mars 1939'.

Here was the final proof, had any been needed, that Barke had crossed over on the day in question and by the 9.00 a.m. service from Victoria. The other early services were via Calais. Moreover he had not returned. Without that passport he could neither have left France nor re-entered England.

French passed on to an examination of the suitcase. About this there was nothing of special interest, except the fact that there was nothing of special interest. French had confidently expected some paper or article which would give a hint of the man's business in France, but none was forthcoming. This was more than disappointing. Either Barke had brought nothing of the kind over with him, or he had taken it with him to that urgent appointment to which he had hurried.

In the suitcase was Barke's current chequebook, which French had noted as missing from the Green House. But this threw no light on the affair, as no suggestive cheques had been drawn.

As a routine check French took three or four articles which were stamped with the owner's personality—a dressing-gown, bedroom slippers, a razor case—to make sure they had really been taken from the Green House. In a case where trickery was to be expected, every check, no matter how apparently superfluous, was valuable.'

A visit to the hotel proved equally disappointing. Barke had arrived by taxi just at the time people travelling by that particular cross-channel service do arrive. He had booked his room and signed the register. Then he said, 'I have an engagement just now, so I won't go up to my room till later. Will you please have my luggage sent up.' He had then walked out of the hotel, no one noticing which direction he had taken. The luggage had been duly sent upstairs. That was on the Friday afternoon, and it wasn't till the Sunday that the manager grew sufficiently disturbed about his absence to inform the police. Barke was not known to the clerk, and there was no record of his having stayed at the hotel on previous occasions.

Dieulot then explained what further steps his department had taken. They had quickly traced the taxi which had set

Barke down at the hotel, and found that it had picked up the fare at the Gaze du Nord, one in the crowd obviously pouring out from the English boat train. Barke had been carrying his suitcase: it was not large. Dieulot had been unable to trace him further in the station.

The inquiries usually made in the case of missing persons were then put in hand. Reports of accidents and bodies found were gone into, the hospitals were visited, the men on point duty near the hotel were interrogated, attempts were made to find a taxi which had taken up a likely fare in the neighbourhood, but all without success. Charles Barke had indeed vanished without trace.

'You made a fine job of all that,' French complimented when Dieulot had finished. 'As far as Barke is concerned everything seems clear. Now what about Lorrimer?'

Lorrimer, it seemed, had been easily traced. He had stayed at the hotel he had named to Miss Redpath for a few nights only, and had then moved to a studio in the rue des Couronnes, in the south-east corner of Paris near the Porte d'Ivry. He was engaged on alternate mornings in giving lessons in two ateliers, and in the afternoons he copied pictures at the Louvre and other places. He had been given a good character wherever Dieulot had inquired. Apparently he was working hard and skilfully, was spending little, and must be accumulating money.

On the day in question, he had accounted fully for his time. From 8.30 till noon he had taught in the Atelier Bobillot, he had then lunched and gone out to the Church of St Paul in the rue Blomet, on the west side of the Seine, in the direction of Courbevoie. He had been commissioned by a firm in the rue St Honoré to copy a picture there, and he had already spent a number of afternoons at the work.

On this occasion he started about 1.30. The copy was almost done, and he finished it just before half past three. He found the sacristan, tipped him, and told him he would not be leaving his canvas on that occasion as the picture was done, but that he would be back later to do a second. He left the church about 3.30, walked to the Metro station Pont de Levallois-Bécon, carrying his canvas, and went through to the Porte d'Ivry, changing at the Opera. From the Porte d'Ivry it was about five minutes' walk to his studio. He left the picture there, had a wash and a change, then thinking he had done enough for the day, he took the Metro back to Pont Marie, which was the nearest station to a friend's rooms in the rue de Bagnolet on the north side of the river opposite the rue St Louis. This was a writer named Pierre Charcot, and he reached his rooms about 5.00. He found Charcot with two friends and they all settled down to talk. Later they went to a restaurant for dinner, after which Lorrimer had gone on with some other men to the rooms of one of them. About midnight he had returned to his studio accompanied by a man named Dupuis. Dupuis went in with him for a final drink and saw the picture there.

'That's very interesting,' French commented. 'Do you believe it all?'

Dieulot once again shrugged. 'We have made inquiries, but not complete,' he answered and went on to describe what had been done. He had himself interviewed the sacristan, who fully confirmed Lorrimer's statement. He was sure of the hour of 3.30 at which the painter had left the church. It was a dark building and work could no longer be carried on.

'That suspicious, do you think?' asked French.

Dieulot thought it was natural enough and French agreed

with him. Dieulot continued that he had not himself seen Pierre Charcot, but he had sent a man to interview him, and here again there had been every reasonable corroboration. He was sure of the time Lorrimer had arrived, as Lorrimer had himself asked, had Charcot finished his day's work.

'Once again, was that suspicious?' French repeated.

Once again Dieulot didn't think so. It would be a natural question for Lorrimer to ask. Charcot also confirmed that Lorrimer had been in his presence till he left for his studio shortly before midnight, and that Dupuis had gone with him. Dupuis had also been interviewed, and had fully confirmed the statement. Finally Dieulot said that while Lorrimer's actual journeys had not been made, he estimated that they would take just the time stated.

French thought over this. 'Lorrimer left the church about three-thirty and reached Charcot's about five—so much appears to be established,' he said slowly. 'If he went to his studio during that period he could not have murdered Barke, as the journey would have filled the time. Now suppose he didn't go to his studio. Suppose he got out, say, at the Opera—how long could he have spent there and still reach Charcot's at five?'

'Speaking vaguely, about three-quarters of an hour.'

'In three-quarters of an hour he could easily have murdered Barke, provided he could have found somewhere to do it and to hide the body. Question is, could he have found such a place?'

Dieulot made a gesture of negation. 'A place to commit the murder? Yes, if he could persuade M. Barke to accompany him. A place to hide the body? No! It is this hiding the body, my friend, that is difficult.'

'What about the river?'

'The Seine? But yes, the Seine would hide the body. But this Lorrimer, how does he put the body in? It is still the day, at half past four, is it not?'

'Suppose,' said French, sitting forward and putting his head confidentially on one side, 'they meet near the Opera, and drive to the river—say the Place de la Concorde. They dismount and walk to the bridge. They get down on the quay alongside the water and move beneath the arch. They are pretty well out of sight there. Could Lorrimer not sandbag Barke and slip his body into the water without being seen?'

Dieulot thought it unlikely; while there were few people on the quays, these were not absolutely deserted. The river traffic had also to be considered. Besides the ground under the arches was visible from the roadway on the opposite bank. It would be strange if such a murder were not seen by someone. It would also be strange if a body thrown in at such a place were not found in the river. 'Besides, how does Lorrimer persuade his victim, this Charles Barke, to descend to the quay and promenade beneath the bridge?'

'I don't know,' French admitted. 'He might have made up some story. Oh, I don't know, it doesn't sound very likely.'

'It is not likely, no. And yet it is not impossible. Something of the kind must be kept in view.'

Once again French lapsed into thought. 'Could Lorrimer have taken Barke home with him?' he went on presently. 'Suppose Barke met him at the Opera and they went on together by Metro. He could easily have murdered him in his studio.'

'But not so easily disposed of the body.'

'He wouldn't have disposed of it.' French grew slightly more eager. 'Suppose he hid it and left it there? Then he could have reached Charcot's on time.'

'It is just. But the body, it would remain in the studio.'

'Of course, but in the darkness of the night . . . ?'

Again Dieulot made his gesture of negation. 'In the streets of Paris the nights they are not dark,' he said with a chuckle. 'Besides where could he have taken the body? To the river it is too far. And you cannot hide a body where other persons are—it betrays itself. It is not possible, my friend. No, no; he could find no hiding place.'

'Then your definite opinion is that Lorrimer is innocent?'

'Of murdering Barke in his studio, yes. He could not have done it. Of murdering him near the Opera between four and five—' He shrugged. 'It is possible. But there is something else.'

'Something else?'

'Yes—the picture. The picture was at this Lorrimer's studio at midnight. The sacristan saw it at half past three in the church and Dupuis saw it at midnight. How was it taken from one place to the other?'

'By Lorrimer as he says?'

Dieulot threw up his hands. 'In the end! He was not then murdering Barke! Is it not?'

French was reluctant to accept this view, as Lorrimer was his sole remaining suspect, but the more he thought over the situation the more convinced he grew that Dieulot must be right. If the facts were as stated, Lorrimer could only be guilty if he had not gone home between 3.30 p.m. and 5.00. But the presence of the picture in the studio proved that he had gone home. It seemed conclusive.

'I'm afraid,' he said, 'that I agree with you. At the same

time I think I ought to see Lorrimer. You know what one's superiors are?'

Dieulot made another eloquent gesture. 'But of course!' he cried warmly. 'Lorrimer and the sacristan and Charcot and Dupuis: all of them! Well do I understand your desire. See, I send a man with you. François, a good man. A thousand regrets that I cannot go myself as I should like.'

French was delighted. He had wished for this, but hadn't expected to find Dieulot so compliant.

But the interviews, when they took place, threw no further light on their affair, and French had to admit that Dieulot's investigation had been quite first class. Only in seeing Lorrimer for himself and judging his character from his appearance did he gain fresh information, and that was not helpful to the case he was trying to build up.

When he and François presented themselves at the young man's studio, they found him painting. He was tall and thin and rather stooped and his manner was polite but very reserved. He obviously at once saw what was in French's mind and resented it, but was willing to tell him anything he could. He began by denying that he knew anything about the affair in question. He had been very sorry to hear of the disappearance of Barke, whom he had greatly respected. He was surprised to find that French knew the reason for his leaving the Crewe Gallery, and after showing some further resentment he said he had collected over £100 of the £250 he owed, and only for this unfortunate development, he would before then have forwarded the money to Barke as an instalment. French thought him sullen, but he had to admit to himself that he bore no signs of guilt.

Reluctantly French found himself forced to the conclusion that he might strike Lorrimer off his list of suspects. There was nothing—and never had been anything—against the young man except the possibility of motive, that he might have wished to murder Barke to preserve his secret. Now French saw that this wasn't so convincing as he had supposed. Firstly, Lorrimer could not be sure that Barke had neither mentioned nor made a note of the matter, and if he had, to murder him would be madness. Secondly, if Lorrimer had really collected £100, it was clear that he intended to accept Barke's offer to let the affair drop on the money being repaid. The *a priori* bias against Lorrimer was therefore slight, while of actual evidence there was none. On the other hand several strong reasons suggested his innocence.

French sighed as he settled himself in the train to return to London. So far he had found only two suspects: Sir Geoffrey and Lorrimer, and now both of them must be considered innocent. That unhappily left him where he had started. But he remained convinced that the murder—if murder it was—was a purely Parisian affair. Someone living in Paris had brought Barke over and had tricked him into his power and killed him.

If so, it looked as if the affair was one for the polite Inspector Dieulot and that he, French, might wash his hands of it.

One thing alone was certain: he must either start fresh on some new scent, or he must report a joint failure with the *Sûreté*. Thoroughly disgruntled, he reached Victoria and went home.

12

The Genesis of the Fire

When French reached the Yard next morning he found that a reply had come in from America.

The chief of the Chicago police stated that Geoffrey Buller had been in real estate in the city, but in quite a subordinate position, an employee on a moderate salary. There was no reason to believe that he had been obtaining money from any other source. His character was reputed to be 'ordinary'.

From this it seemed clear that Sir Geoffrey could not have contributed materially to the maintenance of Forde Manor, a fact which undoubtedly strengthened the case for arson.

So much the better for Shaw, thought French, but what of himself? If Buller were not responsible for Charles Barke's disappearance, how and why had that disappearance occurred? What line of investigation into this was now left? For an hour French sat reading and rereading the dossier, pausing over each item to consider if by any means it might point the way to a further advance, and from each passing on disappointed. He could find nothing to grip; nothing to get his teeth into. In so many of his cases the puzzle was to reconcile what appeared to be conflicting facts, but here it was in the absence of facts that his difficulty lay.

He was beginning his second hour of mental struggle when his telephone rang. It was Shaw.

'I'm speaking from Ockham,' the insurance man explained. 'I've come on one or two suggestive points over at Forde Manor. It occurred to me that you might be interested. Care to drop down?' In his present frame of mind the voice came like a message from heaven. 'I'll be with you in an hour,' French replied without hesitation.

'Then bring some overalls and come direct to the Manor.' Once again the day was fine and French enjoyed his run out of town. Relieved to have his exasperating problem postponed, he was in excellent form as he turned the car in at the Manor gates and drove up to what had been the house. Shaw, in a boiler suit and with a smear across his face, appeared through the blackened doorway as the car stopped.

'Glad you were able to come,' he greeted French. 'I think this'll interest you as much as it does me. Bring some old clothes?'

'Overalls; in the back of the car. What have you found?'

'Nothing,' Shaw returned with apparent satisfaction. 'Drawn a complete blank so far.'

A wave of misgiving swept over French. 'Nothing?' he repeated. 'But you didn't bring me down here to tell me you had found nothing?'

Shaw laughed. 'Just what I've done,' he admitted. 'Sounds bad, doesn't it? But perhaps it's not quite so bad as it sounds.'

French conquered his momentary irritation. He threw open the car door. 'Sit down in here,' he invited, 'and tell me about it. Pipe or cigarette?'

'Pipe,' Shaw returned. 'Thanks.' He took French's pouch. 'You were over in Paris?'

'Yesterday,' French answered. 'How did you know?'

'Rang up about this yesterday morning. They said you'd probably be back today. Any news of your little job?'

'None,' French told him, going on to give an account of his expedition.

'Curious thing that,' Shaw ruminated, 'because here it looks—well, you'd better form your own conclusions.'

'Tell me.'

Shaw handed back the pouch and lit his pipe before replying. 'One of my most important jobs,' he went on at last, 'as you know is to find out in a case of fire how the outbreak has originated. Once that's done the question of arson is usually settled.'

'Like finding the body for me. And if there's a knife sticking out of the back we stop wondering whether it's murder.'

'That's right,' Shaw agreed. 'Well, I began by summarizing the available evidence. The first man to see the fire was a farmer's labourer. Smoke was then pouring from the centre block and red flickering was showing through the hall windows. I had some trouble fixing the time of that. I needn't worry you with the details, but I managed it at last. It was a quarter past two.'

'So that it started in the centre block.'

'It started in the centre block. But more than that: at a quarter past two it had got just so far. Very well, various people then came on the scene; the head gardener, some more labourers; Mrs Stanton, a policeman, the fire brigades from Cobham and London and so on. In each case I tried to fix the hour of arrival and the state of the fire at that time, and in that way I've been able to build up a sort of synthetic time study of its progress.'

'Good,' French approved.

'My next move was to find out, mainly from Mrs Stanton, what I may call the building's inflammability. I learned its construction, where there were wooden floors and wall panelling, where the furniture was placed and what it consisted of, how the breaking of the windows might increase the draught—all those sort of things.'

'The deuce of a lot of work.'

'Yes, and of course only estimating at that. But I got it done at last, and then I felt it had been worth the trouble. For I was sure the fire had spread too fast.'

'Too fast?'

'Yes. Of course it was only guesswork, but I have a fair experience of fire and that was my strong opinion.'

'I suppose by that you mean that it was helped?'

'I thought so. I've seen cases where paraffin or petrol has been used with a similar result.'

French was interested. 'Go on,' he urged.

'My next point was: How did the outbreak occur? Well, I went into all the usual possibilities. It wasn't lightning, for there had been no storm. It wasn't accidental focusing of the sun's rays, because it had taken place at night. So far as was known, there had been no explosion. Spontaneous combustion was a more difficult question, but I couldn't find that there had been anything in the place which might have gone up in that way. In the end I eliminated everything but two possibilities which as a matter of fact had been suggested by Mrs Stanton. Those were the central heating and the electric mains.

'I took the mains first. Fortunately the electricity people

had a plan of the house showing the installation, and what with that and seeing their men and discussing the thing with Relf, I was able to trace where the mains had run from their entrance to the master switches. This was in the centre wing admittedly, but it was wholly along brick walls and away from timber or anything inflammable. Further, the electrical people assured me that the wires were properly cased in pipes fixed below ceiling level and that it would have been impossible for rats or mice to have got at them. They were absolutely positive that no fusing or heating could have taken place, and that the current could under no circumstances have Started a fire. The fuse boxes I found; they were beneath an arched flue and were protected. None of them had been blown. I learnt also that all the switches were open, and that the current had not been turned on for some weeks.'

'Pretty conclusive, all that.'

'I thought so and therefore turned to the central heating. The boiler and furnace were in a cellar under that centre wing, so that things looked promising. But here the evidence was just as strong. The cellar was all brick, including the floor, and even if by some miracle hot coals had dropped out of the furnace, there was nothing for them to set alight. Relf, who did the firing, struck me as a competent man, and I have been assured on all hands that he is reliable.

'There remained then the chimney. I made the usual test of putting a smoke up from below, sealing the top, and looking for leaks. I didn't find any, but I wasn't satisfied with that. I examined it all over from ladders, and I can tell you at once it wasn't the chimney. Firstly, nowhere from furnace to cowl was there a bit of timber projecting into it, and secondly, I tore down the brickwork at intervals and it was lined throughout with flue pipes.

French stared. 'What did you do then?' he asked after a pause.

'Rang up and asked you to come down.'

'And now I'm here, what do you propose?'

'That we should search the ruins for the real case.'

For a moment French did not reply. At first he was indignant at what looked like a barefaced attempt to exploit him, to obtain freely the advantage of his knowledge and skill. Then he felt Shaw was not the man to do a thing like that. His irritation passed away and he saw the investigation as indirectly helping his own case. If arson were proved against Buller, he would himself have to revise his conclusions as to his connection with Barke.

'I'd be glad to join with you,' he therefore answered.

'Good,' Shaw replied, getting out of the car. 'Put those blessed overalls on and we'll start. I've got a couple of men to lend a hand.'

As Shaw spoke he moved to the corner of the building and gave a call. Two labourers appeared, and entering through the gaping void which had been the front door, all four got to work.

It proved a tedious task. They began by clearing an area in the centre of the hall block and then piling up on it the surrounding debris as this was examined and passed as innocuous. Gradually the heap grew, but by lunchtime only half the rubbish in the block had been gone over.

Only one item of interest was recorded. At intervals they came across what looked like large splashes of lead or solder. Some soft metal objects had apparently been melted and had poured down in liquid form. There were quite a number of these—at least ten in the area immediately surrounding the hall. No one concerned could throw any light on their origin.

About one o'clock they knocked off and ran down to the Three Musketeers in Ockham, where an agreeable interlude was passed. Then an hour after resuming work Shaw called out. French went over.

'What's that?' Shaw asked, pointing to a piece of what looked like vulcanite or black bakelite. It was rectangular-shaped, about six inches by nine. One edge was straight and even, the others were turned up and irregular.

'It's a part broken off something larger,' French pointed out. 'Better see if we can find the rest.'

Further search produced three more pieces. Shaw fitted them together. They did not build up the entire object, but enough were there to show that it had been a rectangular box with an open top.

'A car battery!' Shaw exclaimed. 'Now what was it used for?' French stood looking down at the remains, considering the suggestion underlying Shaw's remark. A car battery would certainly start a fire, if given a suitable heater. Was there any way in which the matter could be settled?

Suddenly he saw that there was. Wires! No heater could have been operated without wires. Moreover those wires would be copper and wouldn't melt. Therefore their remains should still exist.

'See any wires?' he asked casually.

'If they're here,' Shaw answered grimly, 'we'll find them.'

Presently one of the labourers made an exclamation. 'Looking for wires, sir?' he went on. 'Here you are. Connected to this little knob.'

As he spoke he handed up a tiny object from which hung

a pair of copper wires, bare and discoloured by the fire. The moment he saw it a thrill of excitement ran through French's mind. It was a car cigar lighter. At one end was a miniature coil which grew incandescent when the current was turned on.

He had always thought a lot of Shaw, but now he looked at him with increased respect. 'You've got it, I think,' he said quietly.

'Cigarette lighter?' Shaw returned equally calmly, though his satisfaction was obvious. 'When I saw the battery I thought of it, though I never believed we'd find it. Good work, Sparkes.'

'It's one of those dashboard lighters which are pushed home in a socket to switch on the current,' French pointed out, 'but as you see, the wires from the battery are fixed on permanently. That means something else.'

'A switch!' exclaimed Shaw. 'And there'll be other wires leading to that.'

All four kept on lifting and sifting debris, till at last French announced that he had come on a pair.

Careful work traced them for some feet, and then they came to an end. Shaw rubbed his chin as he stared at them. 'See,' he exclaimed suddenly. 'That beam has broken them. We should pick them up again beyond it.'

Another spell of heaving and barring and tugging and the beam was moved and the surrounding rubbish cleared. Again they came on to the wires. They led to what, Shaw saw from his plan, was a small cellar. In the corner, half buried by rubbish, was some unusual-looking apparatus.

'Let's have that stuff cleared away,' Shaw directed.

It was getting dark as the last of the rubbish was removed and they were able to examine the other subjects. First there was a ten-gallon drum which had evidently been open, as the top was missing. Though discoloured by the fire, it was not otherwise damaged, having been protected by a steel joist which had fallen just above it. In the drum was a copper float, sliding up and down a vertical rod. At the bottom of the drum was a tap.

These in themselves presented an interesting combination, but when blackened and twisted electrical apparatus were attached both to the float and the tap, the searchers' interest grew keener. That on the rod was a Contact, and it was evident that when the float fell to the bottom of the drum, a circuit would be closed. The purpose of the other piece of apparatus was not so clear. It consisted of an electro-magnet, operating the first of a series of levers, the last of which was connected to the tap. Both men stood in silence for a moment, then Shaw slapped his thigh.

'Pretty!' he exclaimed. 'A pretty piece of work. Whoever did it deserved to succeed.'

'What is it?' French asked.

'I have a friend,' Shaw returned with apparent irrelevance, 'in Middleton's, the railway signalling firm, and I've often been over the works with him. He's an enthusiast and he loves explaining his stuff. One of the things he showed me was a signal reverser: that's an apparatus for electrically throwing a mechanically operated signal to danger without putting back the lever in the signal-box. I needn't go into it, but the point is that a very small and weak movement, that of the electro-magnet armature, has to operate a comparatively big and heavy mechanism. It's done by having a hammer-shaped weight swinging on a pivot and held up near the top of its circuit by a trigger. This trigger is attached to the armature, and a movement of an eighth of an inch, when the armature closes, is sufficient to release the weight. The weight crashes down, engaging a heavy lever which is fixed on the same pivot, and its momentum is sufficient to operate the mechanism.'

As he spoke, light was percolating into French's mind.

'Now here,' Shaw went on, 'you have the same mechanism. Here is the magnet and the armature. This is the weight pivoted here, and you can see the trigger would hold it up. You can also see that when it falls it must come into contact with this lever and so open the tap.'

'Very good,' said French. 'It's certainly ingenious.'

'In the signalling affair the putting back of the lever in the box resets the apparatus for the next time, but here,' Shaw's voice grew grimmer, 'no next time was required.'

French nodded. 'Very ingenious,' he repeated. 'Let me get it clear. First the tap would be closed and the weight raised and fixed up with the trigger. Then the drum would be filled with water, carrying the float to the top of the rod. That right?'

'That's right,' Shaw nodded. 'The thing might stay like that for months. Then when the time came someone would send a current through the electro-magnet, the weight would fall, the tap would open, and the water would run out—from the size of the tap, very slowly.'

'Designed to take some hours, I expect,' French suggested.

'Quite; that's the idea. But eventually the float would reach the bottom of the rod and that would close the other contact.'

'Switching the current from the battery on to the lighter,' French added.

'Quite. Someone would switch on the first circuit, then

perhaps six or eight or a dozen hours later, when that person had gone and the place was locked up, the fire would start.'

'And if the bloke hadn't been so clever and put in this delayed action affair, he mightn't have been suspected.'

Shaw shook his head. 'He could scarcely have avoided it,' he pointed out. 'He couldn't have the outbreak discovered too soon after his visit.'

'Well,' French said, 'this is all extraordinarily satisfactory. But we're not finished yet. There's the other electric circuit which operated the magnet. Where did that run?'

'We'll find it,' Shaw declared. 'But it's too dark to do any more tonight. If we store away what we've found and call it a day, I don't think we'll have done so badly.'

French found that his interest in the proceedings had grown too keen to allow him to remain in town and the next morning saw him back again with Shaw at Forde Manor. There they began the search for the second pair of wires which they believed must lead from the drum.

They soon found them. They were not easy to follow, being broken in many places from falls of rubbish. But eventually they traced them to the library, where they came to an end. The flames had here raged with particular fury and no scrap of woodwork was left. Discoloured brass hinges, locks and castors with a coal-box, fire-irons and such like were all that was left of the heavy and expensive library furniture.

As in the region surrounding the great hall, their entire route from service rooms to library had been marked by further splashes of soft metal. These interested both men profoundly, though neither could explain their origin.

For a long time their search was fruitless, then they had

some further luck. They discovered first another car battery, and secondly one spring of a sliding contact.

It was evident then that the impulse which had operated the electro-magnet and opened the tap on the drum had been sent from the library.

'Here's another problem,' exclaimed Shaw as they stood considering this discovery. 'Suppose this contact was made in the library some hours before the fire, who made it? Buller was in Capri.'

'I think,' French returned, 'I can answer that. I'm afraid Mrs Stanton's the villain of the piece.'

Shaw stared.

'As I see it,' French went on, 'that contact was attached to a drawer of an old bureau, so that when the drawer was opened, the circuit was closed and the current flowed. Mrs Stanton opened the drawer on that Monday—for the first time since Sir Geoffrey went to Italy.'

'But why?'

'A letter from Sir Geoffrey asking her to send him a certain paper which was in the drawer.'

Shaw smacked his thigh. 'You've got it! That's it, as sure as we're alive! That's proof that Sir Geoffrey burned down the place for the insurance money.'

'Scarcely that, I'm afraid. You can't prove that he put in that apparatus.'

'Who else could have?'

French shook his head. 'Scarcely enough for court, I'm afraid.'

Shaw remained for some moments lost in thought. 'What was the paper he wrote for?' he asked presently.

'Good,' French approved. 'That's our best chance. Mrs Stanton told me about it. It was a testimonial from his employers in Chicago, and he wanted to show it to the directors of some Italian company, in connection with his getting a seat on the board.'

'Not a very convincing tale. However, it raises some interesting questions to which we'll want the answers.'

'That's right,' French agreed. 'Now, will you get them or shall I?'

Shaw laughed. 'I didn't venture to suppose you would. But if you will, the question is answered. It would be a difficult job for me. I'd have to employ a private agency in Chicago and would probably have to go to Italy myself. Whereas you have only to sit down and write a couple of telegrams.'

'I'll do it,' French decided. 'I should want to in any case because, as you must see, this raises the picture question again and the possible consequent disappearance of Charles Barke.'

'Fine,' Shaw approved, 'and of course I'm interested in the picture question too. If those alleged cleanings were really copies, there's further fraud.'

'That's a second line of inquiry. Who did the alleged cleanings? Have any of the originals been sold? There's a lot of work there.'

'As you're doing the other, I'll take that on,' Shaw offered, 'though it might be convenient later to join forces.'

'You mean,' said French, 'that you'll have a shot at it, and when you fail, you'll shove it on to me.'

'Exactly,' Shaw grinned, 'or in other words, if we need the organization of the Yard, it'll be there.'

Having photographed and removed their finds, both men returned to town, where each began to plan the next stage of the inquiry.

13

The Growth of Certainty

Contrary to his oft-proclaimed principle that he always left business behind him at the Yard, French's thoughts reverted to his case as later that evening he sat over the fire in his parlour. The position was so unsatisfactory that he could not but feel worried. What matter an evening lost from social intercourse or hobbies, if only it advanced him a step towards his goal?

Shaw, he felt, had every reason to be satisfied with his progress. Complete proof that Buller had burnt down his house would no doubt soon be in his hands. But the fate of Charles Barke remained as mysterious as ever. French's own advance had been negligible.

Slowly and systematically he reviewed what he had done up to the present, but he could not keep his thoughts on his own case. They strayed continuously to Shaw's and to the striking discoveries made that day. Then it occurred to him that a promising line of inquiry was awaiting exploitation. If Buller had put in all those electrical fittings, where had he obtained them? It was unlikely that he would have taken a second person into his confidence: therefore had he not made them himself? If so he could scarcely have avoided leaving some trace, and what more helpful than such a trace?

Unhappily this promise was once again connected with arson, not with murder. But now wishful thinking suggested that the cases were probably connected and that what helped one might help the other also. With this in view he rang up Shaw and asked him to call at his house on the following day, which was Sunday. 'It's an idea, certainly,' Shaw said when French had put forward his views. 'I intended to do the workshop in due course, but now I agree there should be no further delay.'

'There's probably a snag,' French pointed out. 'I've got no search warrant and I don't suppose you have either.'

Shaw smiled. 'Not me,' he admitted, 'but then I'm not so faddy as you are. If I want to search a building I just pop in and have a look round.'

'But I can't do that,' French returned. 'You know very well if I broke the rules, the resulting evidence would be rejected in court.'

'The plan for you,' Shaw suggested, 'is to come with me while I make the search. If we find nothing, the matter drops. If there is anything, you get your warrant and find it officially.'

This was what French had hoped for. 'Right,' he agreed. 'You lead on and I'll follow.'

Next morning they drove down in Shaw's car, the better to prove that the business was his and that French was merely a passenger.

The workshop was in one of the haylofts, over the former range of stables and coach-houses. Immediately beneath it was the last of the line of garages, from which it was reached by a staircase. As representative of the Thames & Tyne, Shaw had a key of the former, but when they went up the staircase they found the workshop door locked. Shaw however was second only to French in the cult of the skeleton key, and after some persuasion the lock gave up the struggle.

The workshop would have delighted the heart of any amateur. Lofty and spacious, it was lighted by a continuous window, evidently new, along its north wall. In one corner was a lathe, small in size but elaborate in accessories, in another a universal woodworking machine, while between the two was a boring and slotting machine, a tiny portable hearth and an anvil. A bench ran along in front of the window and racks and shelves on an impressive scale were filled with tools.

Two things were instantly apparent: from the plant, that Buller had here all the appliances necessary to make complicated mechanisms; and from the stores, that he worked not only in wood and metal, but in electrical apparatus. But at first sight there was nothing to indicate that he had made the fittings for the five-gallon drum.

'It's going to take a proper search,' Shaw suggested.

'Right,' French answered, 'if we begin at this corner we can go different ways till we meet.'

'Search warrant no longer a trouble?'

'The less you say about that, the more help you're likely to get,' French retorted as they settled down to work.

For nearly an hour neither spoke and then Shaw called a halt. 'Got anything?' he asked.

'I've got this,' French returned. 'What do you make of it?'

As he spoke he laid on the bench a large glass syringe or

squirt. It had the usual cylinder and piston, the latter being packed, not with a leather or rubber washer, but with a lapping of thread. When full it would probably have held a pint. The only thing remarkable about it was that a bent glass tube had been joined on to the nozzle, making it over a foot long.

Shaw looked at it without speaking, then turned back to French. 'I don't know,' he admitted. 'What do you?'

'I find it suggestive,' French answered, 'but if I'd seen any thin sheet lead, I'd be surer of my ground.'

Shaw stared. 'But I've got that,' he exclaimed. 'Look here.' He pointed to half a dozen tiny cuttings. 'Three pound lead, by the look of it. That's too thin for plumbing or roof work. I wondered what it could be for and that's why I collected it.'

'Where did you find these bits?'

'All in cracks, either between the floorboards or in joints about the bench; I mean hidden from casual view. It looked as if the place had been cleaned and these pieces overlooked.'

French was delighted. 'That's exactly what happened,' he said eagerly. 'In cleaning away his traces Buller missed those, and they're going to cook his goose.'

'One up for you, French, I will say. What exactly's the idea?'

'Put those two things together and you'll see it for yourself,' French answered, 'three things rather: the syringe, those bits of lead, and the melted splashes all over the house. See here. Buller wants to commit arson and he devises an incendiary arrangement which can be operated when he's a couple of thousand miles away. So far, so good. But he spots a danger. If the house is not burnt out, the delayed action mechanism may be discovered. The house therefore must

179

be burnt out. How can this be ensured? No way better than to fill it with little reservoirs of petrol.'

Shaw nodded slowly. 'I see what's in your mind,' he said. 'Go ahead.'

'The rest's surely obvious. Buller buys some sheet lead— lead because it will melt—and makes it into containers. He fills up his car, runs it in below us, and sucks out the petrol with the syringe. Next day he fills up the car at a different station. And so on. He makes and fills his little reservoirs and hides them all over the house, which of course is possible owing to its being unoccupied.'

Shaw was obviously impressed. 'By Jove, French, it's an idea,' he exclaimed, then more doubtfully, 'But do you think he could do that? Where would he hide these containers?'

'I don't know,' French admitted, 'he'd have to think that out. One place occurs to me. The house was full of all sorts of tables, wardrobes, cabinets, chests of drawers and so on. Why couldn't he have made lead containers to fit these drawers, then screwed the drawers up? No one would have any business at any of them while he was away, so the screwing of them up wouldn't be discovered.'

'Ingenious! I will say that.'

'Then,' French went on, his inventive faculty stimulated by praise, 'what would be easier than to take the springs or stuffing out of sofa or chair coverings and replace them by properly shaped containers? I dare say a flat container could have gone under every mattress. There were lots of places.'

'What about the smell?'

'What about it?'

'As you know very well, a petrol container can't be sealed. It gives off vapour continuously.'

French thought. 'He'd have to risk something. The rooms are lofty. I question if there'd be much smell.'

'Probably you're right. It's a great notion anyhow, and I bet it's exactly what he did. If so,' he paused again, 'we should be able to get a conviction out of it.'

'Well, let's see how we'd start. First there's the lead. Anything remarkable about that?'

'It's too light for house work, particularly for a house of this type. Even for poor houses four-pound lead is the lightest commonly used. I should say it was remarkable enough to trace the purchase.'

'Can we estimate how much he must have got?'

'We can be sure of a minimum. All we need do is to weigh some of those splashes and count the splashes.'

French nodded. 'And there are probably any number of splashes we've not seen. Then there's the syringe and all the electrical stuff. We should be able to trace those purchases also.'

'We've got him,' Shaw declared contentedly. 'Worth coming down these last three days, eh?'

'Worth it for you, yes,' French agreed. 'But I've got no further with my case. This is all very interesting no doubt, but it doesn't help to clear up the disappearance of Charles Barke.'

'It makes it more likely that Buller did him in.'

French made a gesture of exasperation. 'I know it does! That's just what's bothering me. But you see, he couldn't have. You can commit arson from a distance of thousands of miles, but you have to be on the spot to commit murder.' He paused as if struck by an idea, then added slowly, 'And then again, you haven't.'

'What do you mean?' Shaw asked sharply.

'I've just remembered one of my own cases. Man poisoned his uncle for an inheritance and'—he leant forward—'now that really is a coincidence.'

'What is?'

'The man was in Italy at the time he did it, near Naples. Just as Buller was when he burnt his house.'

'How did he do it?'

'Left the stuff where it would be taken, of course. But poison's one thing and a disappearance is quite another. No one could inveigle his enemy to his death in the streets of Paris unless he himself was there too.'

'Or his agent?'

'Or his agent of course. No, Shaw, I can't see how Buller could be mixed up with Barke's murder. I'd like to, but I can't.'

They completed the search of the workshop, but without finding anything more of interest. Then returning to town, French set in train inquiries into the purchases of the syringe, the electrical fittings, and the lead respectively.

The last seemed the most hopeful, owing to certain difficulties its purchase would have involved. Normally such a commodity would be delivered by the suppliers. Buller could scarcely have risked this. Probably he would have bought it in small quantities and carried it home in his car. This however would have involved either several calls on one firm, or application to several firms, a repetition which would simply invite discovery.

That French's reasoning was sound was quickly demonstrated. The next day a sergeant rang up to say that he believed he had found the required firm—in Walkover Street, Clapham.

In an hour French was at the place, a large builders' supplies depot.'

'One of our salesmen remembers certain transactions such as your sergeant describes,' the manager told him. 'I'll send for him.'

A smart-looking young fellow presently arriving, French put his questions. It seemed that some three months earlier a man, giving his name as Findlay, called to say that he was building a number of dog kennels and wished to buy some 3-lb sheet lead to roof them. He wanted it cut in strips two feet by ten. These weighed 60 lb, and when rolled a man could just carry one strip comfortably. When asked where it was to be sent, Findlay said that as he was frequently passing the depot, he would call for it himself. He took five rolls that day in his car, repeating the operation on five subsequent occasions. That made 120 superficial feet of lead in all. The salesman said he had been interested in the transaction not only because it was unusual, but also because he thought a two-foot strip too narrow to cover the average kennel roof.

All this was very pleasing to French, but it was not till the salesman picked Buller's photograph out of a dozen others that he was really satisfied.

When he returned to the Yard he found a message from Shaw awaiting him. He had, he reported, weighed several of the splashes of lead and had found that though they varied considerably, they averaged about fourteen pounds. With a further grunt of satisfaction French produced his *Molesworth's Pocket-book of Engineering Formulae* and settled down to calculations.

Buller's rolls of lead were 10 ft by 2 ft, i.e. each contained 20 square feet. On each call he took away five rolls, or 100 sq ft. Altogether he made six calls, so that the total lead he purchased was 600 sq ft. At 3 lb to the square foot, this worked out at 1,800 lb.

But each petrol receptacle weighed about 14 lb or say 15, as there would be some shortage in the amount recovered. 15 into 1,800 went 120 times. So that before the fire some 120 tiny kegs of petrol were distributed through the house!

He wondered could he calculate how much petrol that represented. 15 lb of 3-lb lead equalled 5 sq feet of lead. What size of cube could be made from that?

A little work showed him that one with a side of about 9 inches would meet the case. And how much petrol would that hold? Molesworth told him that there were about 227 cubic inches to a gallon. Then each keg would hold 3 gallons.

Three gallons! 120 kegs! 360 gallons! Or say 300, to allow for varying shapes of kegs. With 300 gallons of petrol distributed throughout the house, it was not much wonder that it burnt, and burnt more quickly than normally!

French realized that there was no direct proof that the lead had been used in this way, but he believed that the indirect evidence would be ample. Buller would be asked what he had done with it. If he had used it innocently, he could say so. If his explanation were unsatisfactory, French's theory would be accepted.

French wondered why the man had used 3-lb lead. The purchase of 4-lb lead, which is in more common use, would have been harder to trace. Then he saw that the heavier stuff would have involved correspondingly more journeys to the shop, and consequently more contacts with outsiders and more chances of discovery. On the whole French thought that the latter would have been the safer course, but Buller had evidently taken the other view.

The question of an arrest now arose and French discussed it thoroughly with Shaw. 'If we don't pull him in,' he summarized his views, 'he may get wind of what we're on to, do a vanishing act, and give us a lot of trouble. On the other hand, I'd rather leave him alone till I've found out about Barke. If there was a confederate in that matter, Buller at liberty might lead me to him.'

'I see that,' Shaw agreed. 'Also if you pulled him in, the confederate might take fright and disappear.'

They agreed accordingly to postpone the arrest, though French decided to put Buller under observation, so as to forestall an attempted dash for freedom.

'I found out something else about Buller,' Shaw went on; 'not much in itself, but with these other things it becomes cumulative evidence. About three months ago, evidently about the time he decided on arson, he sacked his chauffeur. I've seen the chauffeur, and he tells me that there was nothing against him and he showed me an excellent testimonial that Buller gave him, saying that his leaving was through no fault of his own.'

'What reasons did Buller give?'

'That he wanted the job for an old friend who was in low water.'

French smiled. 'He might have thought of something better than that.'

'It went down all right. The chauffeur suspected nothing.'

'It wasn't true, of course?'

'Of course not: Buller didn't replace him. From then he took out the cars himself.'

'The better to carry lead and fill up with petrol. Yes, that's a point.' French considered, then added: 'Anything else?'

'Anything else?' Shaw returned in mock wrath. 'I like that! Anything else yourself!'

'Yes,' French answered unexpectedly; 'the pictures.'

185

Shaw instantly grew serious. 'The cleanings? Yes, I agree. I hadn't forgotten about them. It's a promising line, too.'

'Of course we must be careful,' French pointed out. 'We mustn't forget that our idea's pure guesswork. We haven't a scintilla of proof of fraud.'

'Relf's tale of Barke's displeasure in the gallery?'

'Means nothing. Barke believed that unnecessary cleaning damaged pictures. He might only have been distressed by the damage.'

'I see that,' Shaw admitted. 'Then what do you propose?'

'I think we should ask Buller who cleaned them.'

'Agreed. If we knew that we'd be pretty poor fools if we couldn't find out the rest.'

'And what's more,' went on French, 'I think you're the man to ask him.'

'I've no objection.'

'It would come more naturally from you. You've only to say that your people are considering what difference the cleanings have made in the value of the pictures, and your curiosity is explained.'

'I'll see him,' Shaw nodded and presently took his leave.

Next morning when French reached the Yard, Shaw was waiting for him.

'Bad penny, you are,' French greeted him.

Shaw ignored the remark. 'I've got that information,' he declared. 'Got it without trouble. The cleanings were done in London by a chap called Davenport.'

'Davenport?' French repeated. 'Never heard of him. Where does he hang out?'

'Number 27, Eglington Road. It's not far from Baker Street Station. He has a flat there.'

'Been to see him?'

'No, I called to know if you'd care to join me.'

French considered. If Barke had been murdered by a confederate of Buller's because he had discovered a picture fraud, who more likely to be involved than the confederate artist. Yes, French would very much like to meet Mr Davenport.

'Any time like . . . ?' Shaw queried.

'None,' French returned firmly, 'provided you give me ten minutes to glance over my correspondence.'

The ten minutes had lengthened to nearly thirty before French had finished dictating replies to his letters, and another thirty were occupied in reaching No. 27, Eglington Road. It proved to be a tall Georgian house in a quiet cul-de-sac on the Regent's Park side of Marylebone Road. Davenport's flat was at the top of the house, and the reason for this became evident when they entered his studio and saw that light was supplied from a long skylight with a northerly aspect.

Davenport met them with evident surprise and some apparent embarrassment: or was it a guilty conscience? French's interest was at first keenly aroused, but the man presently grew more normal and French's suspicions became dulled.

'I got your name, sir,' Shaw began, 'from Sir Geoffrey Buller of Forde Manor. I'm acting on behalf of the Thames & Tyne Insurance Company, and I have called about some pictures of Sir Geoffrey's which I understand you cleaned.'

'That's correct,' Davenport answered stepping aside from the door. 'Won't you come in?' he invited, looking inquiringly at French.

'My friend, Chief Inspector French of Scotland Yard,' Shaw answered the look.

'I'm concerned with the disappearance of Mr Charles Barke,' French explained, determined to carry on the interview on Shaw's high level. 'I understand he was specially interested in the cleaning of pictures, and I therefore wondered if you knew him and could tell me anything about him.'

Davenport shook his head. 'I'm afraid I didn't, Chief Inspector,' he answered. 'I know his name of course—who in the world of art doesn't?—but I never had the pleasure of meeting him.'

'In that case I suppose you can tell me nothing that might help to explain his disappearance?'

'I'm afraid I can't,' Davenport said, growing obviously more at ease.

'I scarcely expected you could,' French declared smoothly, 'but I thought I would take the chance.' He turned to Shaw. 'Sorry to have butted in. Shall I wait for you outside?'

Shaw knowing his cue, played up to it. 'No, no; no need,' he replied. 'I've only a question or two to ask and they're not private. It's about the cleaning of those pictures, sir. I wonder if you would tell me just what took place.'

'I thought Sir Geoffrey had already done so?'

'Not exactly,' Shaw returned. 'He gave me your name as the artist who had done the work. I should like something a little more technical, if you don't mind.'

Davenport rubbed his hands. 'I don't mind,' he declared in a tone which irresistibly suggested the Sheep in *Alice through the Looking Glass*. 'Question is what do you want to know?'

'Well, general details—who advised the cleanings, how you and Sir Geoffrey came in touch with one another, how the pictures were transported, what your views are as to their alteration in value, and anything else you can tell me.'

'I can answer those questions I think,' Davenport answered. 'I first met Sir Geoffrey on the *Nicarian*, crossing from New York to Southampton. That was when he was coming to take over his inheritance. We were mere casual acquaintances on board and didn't get really intimate, but I knew of his inheritance and he knew that I was an artist. When we were saying goodbye he gave me the usual vague invitation to look him up. You know. I didn't really intend to do it, but it chanced that one day some weeks later I found myself near Ockham with time on my hands. I thought it would be interesting to see him and Forde Manor, and rang him up. He asked me to lunch and I went. Afterwards he showed me his pictures. He had a lot of very fine stuff and some rubbish.'

'Like most amateur collections,' suggested Shaw as the other paused.

'Quite. It was when we were walking round that Sir Geoffrey raised the question of having the pictures cleaned. He said he had been advised that some of them should be done, and asked me what I thought. I said, was this a professional consultation, as, if so, I should have to take a day or so to examine the pictures. He said no, that it was a question on the general advisability of cleaning. Well, you know, Mr Shaw, I couldn't answer that. It depended solely on the state of the individual picture. Some would be ruined by it, others simply reborn.'

'I can understand that, sir.'

'I was in front of a Goya as I spoke, and I could see that it was in a very bad state. It looked at a casual glance as if it had been revarnished with poor quality varnish which had darkened and cut out a lot of detail. You know. As a rule one would as readily interfere with a Goya as with the Tutankhamen relics, but this was an exceptional case. I said, "Here's a picture that would be the better of a little careful work, and here," I went back to the one I had just looked at, a Hans Holbein, the younger, "is one that would be a crime to touch." He seemed impressed. "That's very interesting," he said. "That's word for word what I've been told by another artist, quite a big man in his profession." Well, we got talking about it; you know; and he finally asked me could I put him on to an artist who would do the work for him.'

'And you did?'

'No. As a matter of fact I had been in America for some years, having gone straight there from Paris, and I wasn't too sure who would be the best English artist to approach. Well, we talked a little more, then he asked me would I do the work myself? I said no, that he knew nothing about me as an artist, and I advised him to go to the Secretary of the National Gallery and get his opinion. However, he said that my views so exactly agreed with those of the man he had originally consulted that he would like me to do the work. I confess it was a temptation. Since starting in London I hadn't had much luck and the fees would be very welcome. Besides, rightly or wrongly, I felt I could do the job. You know. Eventually I agreed to do one of those of less value, and if my work gave satisfaction, to do the rest. Sir Geoffrey had a list of nineteen that his friend thought should be done. As a matter of fact I did fourteen and am at present at work—' he waved his hand vaguely to an easel at the end of the room, 'on the fifteenth.'

'Just what I wanted to know, sir. Thank you very much. How was the transport of the picture arranged?'

Davenport rubbed his hands. 'Sir Geoffrey did it himself. He brought the pictures one by one up here in his car and came for them when they were done.'

'I understand, sir. Now just one last point. What difference in value do you think your cleanings have made to the pictures?'

This proved a fertile subject of discussion. At first Davenport would not be drawn, but eventually admitted that he thought he had increased the value of the collection by several hundred pounds.

'There's one other point,' went on Shaw, when he had noted the other's figures, 'this time really the last. My company would like some artist of standing to inspect the picture you are now working on. Have you any objection?'

'Not the slightest—anyone you like . . . Care to have a look at it?'

Without waiting for a reply Davenport led the way across the studio. 'It's a Flinck,' he went on, 'and rather valuable. But you see the detail that's beginning to come out in that lower left-hand corner.'

The picture was quite a small one and showed an interior with three old men seated round a fire. It was certainly very dark. Where Davenport indicated the colour was lighter. Shadow was still depicted, but through it were faint indications of a chair and table. To French it undoubtedly looked an improvement.

Shaw seemed interested. He first examined the canvas closely, then stepped back and contemplated it with his head on one side. In fact, he stared so long that French's attention wandered, and more from habit than of set purpose he began noting the other objects in the room.

These showed that Davenport was a man of many parts.

In one corner was a stand bearing some object draped with clay-stained cloths, which showed that he did modelling. Pieces of wood and superfine graving tools on a desk indicated woodcuts, and French thought he saw also some of the apparatus of etching. Apparently even these did not exhaust the man's versatility. On another table were blocks of fine rubber, knives like a surgeon's, and a little tray of rubber cuttings, together with coloured pads of various sizes.

French was wondering if this were a new branch of art, when Shaw's voice broke in on his surmisings.

'A very pretty piece of work, if I may say so, sir,' he was remarking. 'I'm sure that's going to be an immense improvement. Thank you for letting me see it.'

Davenport's manner now seemed quite normal. He rubbed his hands together energetically. 'Better when it's finished, I hope,' he smiled. 'But there's a lot more work in it that one would think.'

'You seem to do all kinds of work, sir,' French put in. 'I don't know anything about art, but I seem to see clay modelling, woodcut work and etching, as well as something to do with rubber stamping, which I've never seen before.'

For a moment Davenport looked annoyed and French wondered if he had given offence. But his brow quickly cleared.

'You're quite correct, Chief Inspector,' he admitted. 'I do all those things. Jack of All Trades, with, I'm afraid, its contingent limitation. You know.' He hesitated as if in' doubt, then apparently deciding to be friendly, went on, 'That rubber cutting that you remarked on is my own idea, so I'm not surprised you haven't seen it before. I make rough try-outs of my woodcuts in rubber. The reason is that they can be done quickly and I can go on making a succession of the same subject till I get one that pleases me. From that I do the wood block. It perhaps seems a long way round, but I think it saves time in the end.'

Both men thought it an admirable idea, and having arranged a day on which the artist might be brought to inspect the cleaning, they took their leave.

14

The Relinquishment of a Theory

Disappointment was the feeling uppermost in French's mind after his call on Davenport. He had hoped to obtain proof that the painter was Barke's murderer, but of this he had discovered no particle of evidence. Indeed, as he thought over the interview, he felt that he might eliminate Davenport from further consideration. Except for that first slight embarrassment—or was it fear?—the artist's manner had been normal throughout. He had described his association with Buller and his cleaning of the pictures in a straightforward way, and there was no reason whatever to doubt his good faith.

But if he believed Davenport, the whole case he had been trying to build up as to the disappearance of Barke crashed to the ground. If Davenport were an honest man the pictures had been cleaned and not copied, and there was therefore no reason why either he or Buller should be interested in Barke's silence.

And yet French had felt an instinctive distrust of the man. He could not tell why, nor could he recall any specific look or gesture which had given the suspicion birth. He reminded himself that such a feeling was not evidence and that his reason rather than his emotions must be his guide. Yet he could not but remember that on previous occasions similar impressions had not always proved at fault.

In the end this fact, together with the more pressing consideration that Davenport was his last hope, decided him to put through two more inquiries before coming to a final conclusion. He wired the American police to know if they could trace the artist, and he called on Betty Stanton in the hope that she had met him and to learn her views.

Betty seemed glad to see him and began by asking about his progress. 'It's now twelve days since Mr Barke disappeared,' she said earnestly. 'Do you think there's any hope that he may still be alive?'

French did his best to reassure her on those familiar lines which, however well meant, never convince. She smiled in a sickly way and drew her own conclusions.

'Did you ever hear, Mrs Stanton,' French went on in due course, 'of an artist named Davenport?'

'Yes, of course. He crossed on the *Nicarian* with Sir Geoffrey, at least so I heard, and he came to lunch one day at Forde.'

'Were you aware that it was he who had cleaned the pictures?' Betty's face registered unqualified surprise. 'You don't say so!' she exclaimed. 'I had no idea of it.'

'I can see that,' French returned with a chuckle. 'I have therefore wondered whether, since Mr Barke was interested in the cleaning of pictures, the two men had ever come into contact?'

'Why not ask Mr Davenport?'

'Naturally,' French prevaricated. 'But I should also like your views. You saw Mr Davenport at Forde, you say?'

Betty promptly told of his visit to the Manor. She did not feel called on to mention his sister Joan's story about his conversation with Buller during the gale, but French's systematic questioning soon brought it out.

This tale, together with the reply from America, which he received on the following day, made a deep impression on French. Davenport had been traced to Chicago. The Chief of Police in that city reported that he had lived there for six years prior to leaving for Europe some eleven months previously. He was, it was believed, an Englishman who had studied in Italy and Paris, and he had been employed by the Mayor of Chicago to paint a series of panels in the new city library. He had obtained this work in open competition, and had carried it out to the satisfaction of all concerned. Since then he had apparently lived by painting, having rented a studio in the suburbs. He was reputed to be a talented artist, but not to have been too successful financially.

Here it was that the Chief of Police inserted a sentence which interested French more than all that had gone before. 'Davenport,' he wrote, 'was believed to be a close associate of that other man Scotland Yard recently inquired about, Geoffrey Buller.'

Then Mrs Stanton's sister had been right and there was something between these two, something underhand which needed to be hidden! All French's suspicions poured back in a flood. He could not now leave the affair as it was. He would have to know more, much more, about Davenport and his relations with the baronet.

The crucial question indeed was reopened: had Davenport murdered Barke in Paris? That must now be answered, and without possibility of error.

On reaching the Yard French dispatched a constable to Eglington Road, telling him to watch No. 27 and ring him up if Davenport went out. An hour later the summons came and French, with Sergeant Carter, hurried to the house.

When, as he had expected, he found there was no one in the studio, he went to the basement and asked to see the landlady, for the constable had found out that the house was not really divided into service flats, but into lodgers' apartments attended by the owner. Mrs Maine was of the faded gentlewomen type and looked as if the cares of her calling had robbed her of all vitality. French felt that an exaggerated politeness would be his trump card.

He apologized for troubling her, explained who he was, and said he was looking for Mr Davenport in the hope of getting some information as to his whereabouts on 15 February last. 'These motor accident cases are sometimes very troublesome,' he added truthfully, if not with complete candour. As Mr Davenport appeared to be out and he didn't want to have to come back, he wondered if she could possibly help him? Could she tell him if Mr Davenport was at home on the date in question?

Rather to his surprise, she said she could. Going to a fine old bureau, another relic of faded gentility, she opened an exercise book and slowly turned the pages.

'That was a Friday, wasn't it?' she said tonelessly, and when French agreed, she went on. 'I have to note comings and goings for making out my bills,' She found a page. 'Mr Davenport was away from home, so he can't give you the information you want.'

French wondered what the information was which he was missing. However, she seemed quite satisfied about it, and went on automatically: 'He went away on Thursday:

to Paris, I think he said, and he wasn't back till after eleven on Friday night.'

A thrill shot through French's mind. Was this what he had been seeking since the case began? However, he was careful not to betray his jubilation. Thanking Mrs Maine gravely, he took his leave.

Now he and Carter took on themselves the role the constable had borne before their arrival. Strolling up and down Marylebone Road, they watched the end of Eglington Road. It was a considerable time since French had personally done such a job, and though he had lost none of his old cunning, he found his patience was not what it had been. Hanging about indeed grew so irksome, that he could scarcely force himself to remain.

Then, just two hours and ten minutes after he had left the house, he had his reward. He saw Davenport approaching Eglington Road from the opposite direction.

Quickly collecting Carter, who had been strolling about by himself, he walked to No. 27 and put up his hand as if to knock. Glancing round he recognized Davenport with evident surprise and lowered his hand.

'Good evening, Mr Davenport. Sorry to trouble you, but I was just coming to ask you a question I overlooked yesterday. May we come up for a moment?'

'Of course, Chief Inspector; though,' he smiled slightly, 'if you can think of any question you didn't ask me yesterday, I'll admit you're a clever man.'

French smiled in his turn. 'I hope I wasn't as bad as that, sir,' he protested. 'But I defy anyone at a first interview to think of all the points that should be covered.'

'No doubt,' Davenport returned dryly, throwing open the door. 'Won't you come in?'

French kept up a rather inconsequent monologue until they had reached the studio and been accommodated with chairs. Then his manner became grave and official, while Carter ostentatiously produced his notebook.

'I'm sorry, sir,' he said, 'if my question is offensive to you, but I have to ask it, and I have to make it clear that you are not bound to answer it unless you like. In brief, it has been suggested to us that when in Paris on Friday, 15 inst., you met Mr Barke. I should like to ask if you would care to make any comment on this suggestion?'

Once again there flashed into the painter's eyes that fleeting look which might have been fear. However he quickly registered indignation, though whether it was genuine or assumed French could not decide. 'None!' he answered angrily, 'except that your informant is deliberately lying.'

'You mean that you didn't meet Mr Barke?'

'Of course I mean it. Isn't that what I say? Who told you such a tale?'

'"Information received" is the phrase we use,' French returned smoothly. 'But you needn't be upset, Mr Davenport. I've not suggested it was true. I've simply asked a question. And here's another. Were you in Paris then, or is that equally false?'

'No, that part of it's true enough,' Davenport answered more mildly. 'I went over on the Thursday afternoon, and returned by the afternoon service on Friday.'

Then the man was definitely in Paris when Barke arrived. This would require careful handling. French settled down to it.

'Thank you, sir,' that's very satisfactory. Now you must know that in possible murder cases we are forced to test all statements. It's no reflection on you that we shall have to test this of yours. If you will kindly give us details of what you did on that Friday, particularly during the hour before you left Paris, I shall be grateful.'

Davenport for a moment looked daggers, but presently the expression changed. 'I was going to say, "Why should I?" but after all I suppose you've the authority to ask these questions?'

'No power to make you answer, sir. But of course a refusal would mean suspicions and a lot of unnecessary work. I hope you'll save us that.'

Davenport shrugged. 'I can't complain of your attitude,' he said judicially. 'All the same, you leave me in a difficulty. My business was private, and if it were to become known it might injure me professionally to quite a considerable extent. You know. Before mentioning it I'll want a guarantee that you'll respect my confidence.'

'I can only give you my word,' French said with sinking heart. This looked as if Davenport's business was unconnected with his own. 'I promise that what you tell me will be kept secret, unless it is required as evidence in a criminal case.'

Davenport rubbed his hands. 'I'll accept that. The truth is that I wanted advice as to the treatment of that picture.' He indicated with a gesture the Flinck on the easel. 'Though it was one of lesser value than others of Sir Geoffrey's, I still wanted to be sure that what I proposed was the best thing. You know. I took it to my old atelier and consulted my two former masters. It may interest you to know that my diagnosis and proposed treatment met with their approval.'

'That's certainly interesting, sir,' French commented. 'But I don't understand your secrecy clause. Why do you think the knowledge that you asked for advice should damage you professionally?'

'People would say I should have known what to do myself.'

'I should have thought that a reputation for cautiousness would be even more valuable.'

'I dare say, but experience has taught me otherwise.'

'Was it your habit, sir, to consult these people about your cleanings?'

Davenport hesitated. 'Yes and no,' he presently returned. 'I had done so on two previous occasions, but I did twelve other pictures on my own responsibility. You know. I only went over when I was in doubt, either as to the advisability of doing anything, or as to just what should be done.'

'That's very clear. Would you mind giving me your friends' names?'

'M. Gassot is the principal and M. Guérineau his partner. I consulted them both.'

'And the atelier?'

'The Atelier Voges in the rue des Écoles off the Boul' Mich'.'

'Thanks,' said French as Carter made his notes. 'And when did you see them?'

'On Friday morning. As I told you I went over on Thursday afternoon. I stayed at the Hôtel du Maréchal Ney in the Boulevard Magenta. It's rather a huge place, but it's close to the station.'

'The Gare du Nord?'

'Yes. I went over to the atelier at—I don't know exactly— between nine and ten.'

'Quite, sir. And then?'

'We spent a couple of hours discussing the thing and

trying one or two experiments; you know. Then I brought the picture back and returned it to the management. I should explain that I had had it put in the hotel strong room the night before.'

'And you lunched?'

'I lunched at Les Quatre Plumes in the rue Royale. I had nothing to do, you know, and rather than stay in' the hotel I strolled down to the restaurant. It's a fashionable place, as you no doubt know, and the people are always worth looking at.'

French nodded. 'I've been there,' he declared. 'Then after lunch?'

'I don't know that I can tell you—certainly not exactly. I wasn't expecting to have to account for my every moment like this. You know. I had a leisurely lunch, strolled about for a bit—it was a day of bright sun and Paris was looking charming. But I was bothered with a rather nasty headache and I presently wandered back to the hotel, went up to my room and lay down on the bed till it was time to start for the station.'

'Could you tell me when you reached and left the hotel?'

'I'm afraid not. Perhaps though I could estimate it backwards. I had reserved a seat in the 4.25, so I didn't go very early to the station. But I had plenty of time to stroll over to a bookstall and choose something to read and to take my place without hurrying. You know. I probably arrived with ten minutes in hand.'

'Arrived at the station at 4.15. That would mean leaving the hotel—?'

'It's only a two or three minutes' run, but what with waiting for the taxi and getting my picture and so on into it, I think you might say five or six minutes.'

'Right. Left the hotel about 4.10. And you left your room?'

'Oh, five or ten minutes before that. I rang down to have my picture ready, but I thought there might be a delay, so I came down a few minutes before it was time to start.'

'Five, ten, fifteen? I'm sorry, sir, but all this is important.'

'I appreciate the point,' Davenport said dryly, rubbing his hands. 'You mean that I might have been murdering Barke at this time? Well, so I might, I suppose, but I wasn't.'

'I am hoping that your statements may close the matter. Can you tell me approximately the hour at which you left your room?'

'I can't Chief Inspector. I estimate that I was in the hall about ten minutes, which would make it exactly four o'clock, but this is only an estimate and I can't say exactly.'

French saw that if the man was guilty, this was all he would get, and if he were innocent it was all he could expect. 'Thank you,' he said. 'Now there's the one other point. Can you estimate when you returned to the hotel? That is, how long you were in your room?'

Davenport remained silent for some moments. 'About an hour,' he said at last. 'I think I returned shortly before three. But if it's important I can tell you,' he brightened up a little, 'how you may be able to find out—though again I suppose it's unlikely after so long. When I went into my room the chambermaid was there. She had made up the bed. I told her I was afraid I was going to disarrange it, as I wasn't feeling well and I was going to lie down till my train. I gave her a few francs. You know. She may remember.'

'Thank you,' said French again. 'That's all, at last. If you'll let me have a look at your passport, it'll complete my business.'

The story, as he later considered it, struck French as

satisfactory from Davenport's point of view, but just the opposite from his own. It was eminently reasonable; in all probability it was what the man had done. Yet equally possibly it might be a partial invention. The question of Davenport's guilt remained unsettled.

Certainty depended upon confirmation of the statement during that vital period between the arrival of Barke's train at 3.48 and the departure of Davenport's at 4.25. All the same, the more French thought over it, the less likely it seemed that Davenport would have had time to commit the murder. And not only the murder: the disposal of the body also. With unlimited time this latter would be difficult; surely in that available to Davenport it would have been utterly impossible?

Yet Davenport was his only suspect. French felt that he could not leave the matter in its present state. He must run over to Paris and check up on that last half-hour of Davenport's stay.

Having reported to Sir Mortimer Ellison, French that night crossed the Channel and next morning was once again discussing the case over coffee with Inspector Dieulot of the *Sûreté*.

'The affair,' Dieulot summarized his own contribution with an expressive shrug, 'It does not march.'

'I'm not getting on too well myself,' French admitted. 'I have gone carefully into Barke's life and I have rejected every solution but murder. Of possible murderers I could find only three: Lorrimer, the artist, Sir Geoffrey Buller, and this man Davenport. Lorrimer we jointly eliminated, Sir Geoffrey was definitely in England on the day in question, which leaves only Davenport. It's to settle about Davenport that I've come over.'

Dieulot made sounds indicative of interest and desire to help. 'I'm obviously concerned only with the thirty-seven minutes between Barke's arrival at 3.48 and Davenport's departure at 4.25,' French concluded when he had repeated to the Frenchman Davenport's statement.

Dieulot again expressed his interest. 'Is it certain,' he asked, 'that these men they come and go at the times you say?'

'Well,' French answered, taking out his notebook, 'let's go into that. First Barke. On the Thursday Barke told his wife and the people in his house that he was crossing next morning to Paris on business. He packed his bag and started off next morning in time to catch the 9.00 from Victoria. He arrived at the Hôtel Vichy near the Place de Lafayette at a minute or two before four: just at the time arrivals by the English boat train were expected. In his suitcase you found his passport, stamped as having entered France at Boulogne on that day, Boulogne being the port of entry for that service. In the suitcase were various objects, such as bedroom slippers and a dressing gown which the maid at his house in London had seen there on the previous evening. He had given his name at the hotel and registered. Admittedly the name was hurriedly written, but then he had been in a hurry. What do you make of that?'

Dieulot shrugged. 'It is just,' he admitted with something of sadness in his tone.

'As to Davenport,' French continued, 'we have yet to check his statement, but it is so easy to check that I'm assuming it must be true. He was in Paris on genuine business, and spent the morning of that Friday with two artists on the South Bank. He'd never dare to say that if it wasn't true. Now when did he return to London? His hotel almost certainly will be able to check the train. He arrived at his flat in London shortly after eleven, just when that 4.25 train gets in.'

'He wait here for two-three hours, cross then by air, and arrive at the flat as you say? *Hein?*' Dieulot suggested.

'No, he didn't,' French answered. 'I've seen his passport. He went out of France on that date through Boulogne.'

'In the end,' Dieulot exclaimed with an impressive shrug, 'that settles it. Only by taking the 16.25 could he pass that day through Boulogne.'

'That's what I thought.'

Dieulot shook his head with gravity. 'Then, my friend, you think no longer of this Davenport. He is innocent of this crime.'

'I'd like to be sure.'

'Perfectly. See, monsieur, the affair arranges itself. Barke he comes to the Gare du Nord at 15.48, or as you say, 3.48 pee emm; the train it arrives that day, as you say, on the teek. He walks out, gets a taxi, drives to the Vichy, registers, has his little conversation about his appointment. Is it not? How long does that take him, think you?'

'Ten to twelve minutes at the least.'

'At the least,' Dieulot emphasized. 'Let us say twelve. That makes it just four o'clock when he leaves the hotel. Is it not?'

'Correct,' French nodded.

'Then this other man, this Davenport, when would he leave his hotel, the Maréchal Ney?'

'He said about ten minutes past four.'

'Good. It could not be much later. But, say a quarter past. Now . . .'

'Steady a moment,' French intervened. 'We've overlooked

something. Davenport said that he came down from his room about four, or at least that he was in the reception hall for about ten minutes, waiting while his picture was being got out of the strong room.'

Dieulot threw up his hands in despair. 'But that, it ends the affair!' he cried. 'When then could he have met this Barke? Why it take him five minutes to go from one hotel to the other. Is it not?'

'I feel that too,' French said despondently.

'And if they meet, what about the murder? *Hein?* Does this Davenport shoot him there on the pavement? And the body? Does it vanish itself away into the air? No, my friend, you have not this time hit the oil. If this Davenport voyage at these hours, he is not, as you say, our man.'

French sighed. 'I'm afraid you're right. All the same, we must check the statement.'

'Perfectly. When you like. I am at your disposal.'

After three strenuous hours, every checkable point of Davenport's story had been checked. He had visited the Atelier Voges and consulted Messrs Gassot and Guérineau on the cleaning of the Flinck. He had returned to the Maréchal Ney between twelve and one, and asked that his picture should again be placed in the strong room. He had gone out for lunch, but had returned later. The precise hour of his return could not be established, but the chambermaid remembered his conversation and tip, and thought it had taken place between half past two and three. Finally the following facts were established. That about four Davenport had telephoned from his room that he was ready to leave for the train' and asking that the picture be brought from the strong room, that he had claimed it in the hall, and that he had left in reasonable time to catch the train. The exact times of these various operations could not be established, nor could this be expected. But enough was established to prove beyond the slightest doubt that Davenport had acted as he said.

It was a despondent French who that night returned to London. After nearly a fortnight's intensive work he was precisely as far on as when he had started the case. And in no direction could he see a ray of light. When he reached home he was grumpy even to his Em, though Mrs French recognized the cause and smiled forgivingly.

15

The Continuance of Mystification

The interview next morning at which French reported progress to Sir Mortimer Ellison did little to relieve his gloom. He had indeed a bad fit of the blues. So far as his case was concerned, his past work had resulted in Failure with a large F; he was at present at a Dead Lock, while a glance into the future revealed No Single Gleam of Light.

Still another promising line of inquiry had proved a washout. The Chicago police wired that Buller's employers had given him a testimonial, and those in Rome that the man had been in treaty with some Americans about starting a company for running American oil to Italy. The Americans reported that Buller had wished to join the board, if the company were formed, but added that no question of a testimonial had arisen.

This evidence, French realized, neither supported nor rebutted Buller's statement. He might well have himself started the discussions for the simple purpose of supporting his prospective alibi. If challenged about the testimonial, he need only say he wanted to have it in reserve. True or false, this was certainly plausible. Disgustedly French watched the evidence crumble under his analysis.

During the morning Shaw looked in at the Yard, listening despondently to French's report.

'What will you do now?' he asked with a surprising lapse from his usual standard of tact.

'Do?' French retorted bitterly. 'Why, start again. What else? It's clear that this fire and picture stuff of yours has nothing to do with it.'

'It looked like it at first.'

'It's some other trouble connected with neither Buller nor Davenport. It means another search of Barke's papers.'

'Sort of job I loathe,' Shaw commiserated.

'I don't mind that if I get anything out of it,' French returned. 'What upsets me is all the time I've wasted with that Forde Manor nonsense.'

'You couldn't help yourself there. There was a suspicion, and till that was cleared up, you couldn't leave it.'

French, who was growing ashamed of his grousing, agreed with a better grace.

'By the way,' went on Shaw, 'I went yesterday with Dalton—you know, the artist the Academy Director recommended—to see that picture Davenport is cleaning. He says the work is O.K.'

French nodded wearily. 'I was expecting that. It works in with what I learnt in France. Davenport's not our man.'

'Dalton said the work was desirable and was being skilfully done, and that the picture will be much improved thereby. He's positive also that it's the genuine picture that's being done.'

'No question of its being copied, and no question of our

finding out the truth. Sorry, Shaw, but I'm fed up at the moment and it looks as if I was going to remain so.'

French's prognostication proved accurate. There now followed for him a period of anxiety and worry, during which he put in a lot of work, but made practically no progress.

He called again at the Green House and the Crewe Gallery and went through Barke's papers in much greater detail. Again he questioned Agatha Barke, Betty Stanton, Oliphant, and Miss Redpath. He even returned to Paris and with Inspector Dieulot visited every person and firm whose name appeared among the missing man's papers. But all was to no purpose. Nowhere could he find anything A helpful.

Dieulot also seemed dissatisfied with his own results. He hemmed and hawed in a way quite unlike him, till French stopped in the middle of a sentence and asked him what was the matter.

'There is nothing,' the Frenchman answered in a slight surprised tone. 'It is that I have been thinking much of Lorrimer.'

'Of Lorrimer? What about him?'

Dieulot grew more confidential. 'You remember we find he leave the church of the picture at half past three and reach the house of Charcot at five. Is it not?'

'It was definitely proved.'

'Perfectly. And we find that if he went to his *appartement* inside that time, he could not have committed the murder.'

'That seemed equally certain.'

'And that he must have gone there inside that time because of the picture.'

'That's right. The picture was at the church at half past three and it was in his studio at twelve midnight. It could only have been brought by him, and before five.'

Dieulot moved impressively. 'But that, Meestair French, it is not so. I think afterwards. It does not follow.'

French stared. It had been Dieulot who had been so sure of the alibi.

Dieulot leant forward and tapped him on the knee. 'See, my friend, might not this have been—what do you say?—a prearranged alibi?'

French felt puzzled. 'Yes, I think so,' he answered. 'Lorrimer might have written some yarn to Barke to bring him over. If so, he would know all about Barke's movements.'

Dieulot nodded several times in a self-satisfied way. 'I think so too. Now,' he wagged a heavy forefinger, 'suppose the good Lorrimer he paint two pictures. He is a quick worker and easily could he prevent the sacristan from guessing what he does. Good. He finish one copy and almost finish the second on the day before Barke comes over. The finished copy he takes home and leaves it on an easel. On the Friday he finish the second copy, and the sacristan see him leaving with it at half past three. It is not a large picture and once out of the church he cuts it out of the frame and tears it into strips. He has to cross the Seine to the Metro and what easier than to throw frame and strips into the river? He gets out at the Opera, somehow murders Barke and goes direct to Charcot. But when he gets home at twelve that night the picture is in his room.'

French sat motionless while he considered this new idea. Granted that Lorrimer had known sufficiently early that Barke was coming to Paris, he certainly could have carried out such a trick. And if he himself had invented the story which brought Barke over, he would obviously have known. Could this at last be the truth?

He still kept silence, thinking deeply. Was Lorrimer the

sort of man who could invent and carry through a trick of this kind, subtle and ingenious? On the whole French thought he was. He was certainly both clever and efficient, reticent to the extent of secretiveness, and with a stolid manner which might well cloak excitement or fear. And if he could think out such a scheme, he could certainly make up a story which would bring Barke to the necessary rendezvous.

'I congratulate you, monsieur,' he said at last. 'That's very ingenious. You've shown how the alibi might have been faked, but doesn't the second difficulty still remain: how Lorrimer could have got rid of the body?'

'That? It is difficult, yes. But it was you who thought he might have dropped it into the Seine, is it not? You remember the walk on the quays beneath the bridge?'

French shook his head regretfully. 'I did suggest that,' he agreed, 'but I admit it's not very likely.' He paused, as an idea struck him. 'Suppose Lorrimer paid his hundred pounds to the Crewe?' he went on. 'Wouldn't that be proof—of innocence?'

Dieulot nodded. 'If he paid, it would be proof of innocence, for to avoid paying would be the motive for murder, yes. But not so otherwise. If he did not pay, it would not be proof of guilt.'

'You're right,' French admitted.

They discussed the matter for another hour, but without reaching any further conclusion. Eventually French had to return to London, the question still unsettled.

Next morning he found out by veiled inquiries that no communication of any kind had been received from Lorrimer, either at the Crewe or by Agatha. All that day he brooded over the problem, trying desperately to find some test which might establish the truth. But without success.

Then at last there came some fresh evidence, and from an unexpected source. The London Central Hospital rang up the Yard to ask for the officer who was dealing with the Barke case, and when French answered, he was told that a patient, a Mr Wellesley, wished to make a statement.

Half an hour later French was talking to the house surgeon. 'Under normal circumstances I never should have permitted your visit,' the latter declared, but with a disarming smile, 'as Mr Wellesley is still very weak and is really not fit for the interview. But he is so anxious to get his statement off his chest that I am afraid to thwart him. I must warn you to be careful. Hear what he has to say and pretend to be satisfied with it, even if you're not. Under no circumstances attempt any questioning.'

'I understand,' French agreed.

'I hope you do,' the house surgeon returned, again with his disarming smile. 'I tell you quite straight that if you excite or worry him, you may have his death on your conscience.'

'Straight enough, doctor. I'll be careful.'

A passing nurse was commandeered to take French to Mr Wellesley's private ward, where he was handed over to the sister-in-charge. A pleasantly mannered woman with a kindly smile, her very appearance inspired confidence.

'Mr Wellesley met with a serious accident,' she explained, pausing outside the door. 'He was knocked down by a car and sustained a fractured leg and head injuries. However, his condition is satisfactory so far. But he mustn't be excited. The doctor warned you, I suppose?'

'He certainly did,' French smiled.

'This morning Mr Wellesley was allowed for the first time to see his letters.1 gave them to him myself and then I had occasion to leave the ward. When I came back he was very much upset, "Sister," he said when I went over, "I've just had some bad news. Will you do something for me? Will you ring up Scotland Yard and ask the officer who is in charge of the Charles Barke case to come and see me?" He grew very excited and at last to pacify him I told him I would speak to the doctor.'

'Quite right, sister,' French smiled, reading her face.

She smiled also. 'I appreciate your sympathy,' she said dryly. 'The doctor was doubtful, but at last he said it would be better to do as he wished. Hence the message.'

'And hence me,' French added.

They entered the ward. Wellesley was lying with his eyes closed. He was a man of about sixty, with an aquiline nose and tightly compressed thin lips. The upper part of his head was swathed in bandages and his thin drawn face was the colour of old parchment.

'I think he's awake,' said the sister. She moved over to the bed. 'Are you awake, Mr Wellesley?' she asked in her soft pleasant voice. The man's eyes opened and passed from her to French.

'This is the gentleman from Scotland Yard that you asked for,' she went on. 'Sit down here, Mr French.' She turned again to Wellesley. 'Talk as little as you can,' she urged him, 'and if you let Mr French tire you, I shall be very much displeased with you both.' She smiled, nodded and moved silently away.

'Nice woman,' Wellesley said in a weak voice, following her with his eyes. 'They're very good to you here.'

'Sorry to hear of your accident, Mr Wellesley. I hope you're feeling better?'

'Yes, oh yes, thanks. Well,' he went on feebly, 'I'm not

allowed to talk much so I'd better get on with what I have to say. I understand Charles Barke has disappeared?'

'Yes, sir, I'm afraid so. On Friday, the fifteenth of last month.'

'A terrible thing! I just learnt of it today. It was mentioned incidentally in a letter, also that Scotland Yard had been called in. I'm his solicitor: the senior partner.'

French could have kicked himself. When he called on Messrs Quilter, Hepworth & Quilter to inquire about Barke, he had seen Mr Rathbone, the second partner, who had mentioned that his colleague, who usually did Barke's business, was ill. Now French came to think of it, he had mentioned the name Wellesley, but French had not specially noted the fact, since Mr Rathbone was giving him all the information he required. He apologized.

'Probably it was because my name is not in the firm's,' Wellesley replied. 'The firm goes back for over two hundred years, and no one now likes to alter it.'

It was quiet in the private ward, otherwise French might not have heard all that the solicitor said, so weak was his voice. He looked terribly fragile and French felt the doctor's warning was by no means unnecessary.

'It was stupid of me all the same, sir,' he said quietly. 'However, I'll be glad to hear anything you may be able to tell me.'

'It's about Barke's reason for going to Paris. He consulted me about it.'

French's interest had been mildly aroused from the first; now it suddenly reached boiling point. 'That would be most helpful. It's just what we've been wanting to know.'

'That surprises me. I should have thought you would have known all about it.'

'We didn't, sir. We couldn't find out anything.'

'Didn't the Thames & Tyne people tell you? They knew all about it.'

French in his bewilderment was about to deny the suggestion and bombard the man with questions, but he remembered the doctor's warning in time.

'I'm afraid there has been some misunderstanding,' he said smoothly. 'Perhaps if you would tell me about your interview with Mr Barke, we might see how it has come about.'

Wellesley remained silent for a moment as if marshalling his facts, then began to speak, still in that scarcely audible voice and pausing for rest at intervals.

'It was on the Thursday, the day before he was leaving for Paris that we met after lunch at the club. He came in just as I was about to leave, called me aside, and said that he had been coming round to my office that afternoon to consult me professionally, and that it would save him a journey if we could have our talk there. I agreed of course, and we went to a deserted corner of the smoking-room.

'He asked me had I seen about the fire at Forde Manor. I had read of it of course like everyone else, but I had no particular knowledge of it. He said he had become involved, and he wanted to consult me as to his proper action.'

French's interest was now at a white heat. Did this mean that he had been on the right track after all and that Buller or Davenport or both were guilty of murder?

'I can see, sir, that you've a good deal to tell me,' he said gently. 'But please don't be in a hurry. Stop and rest when you feel like it. The day's long and there's plenty of time.'

'I appreciate your thoughtfulness,' Wellesley returned, 'as I'm sure you're a busy man. But I'll be as quick as I can.

Mr Barke said that there was a fine collection of pictures at Forde Manor, and that owing to his being acquainted with the lady housekeeper, he had recently seen them twice. On the first occasion he and Mrs Barke had lunched with Sir Geoffrey Buller and the housekeeper, Mrs Stanton, and Sir Geoffrey had himself shown him the pictures. The second visit was paid on the day before the fire, and it was paid alone. His wife was laid up with 'flu, and when he arrived he found that Mrs Stanton had also just gone down with it.'

'I heard that part of it from Mrs Stanton,' French put in.

'That's all right. You'll understand better what's coming. Did Mrs Stanton tell you about the cleaning of the pictures?'

'She told me that some fifteen had been cleaned, also that it was a subject in which Mr Barke was specially interested.'

'That is so; he has read papers about it. She had told him that they had been done and he was interested to see the result; in fact he had really gone to Forde Manor for that purpose. When therefore he found that Mrs Stanton could not show him over the galleries, he asked the caretaker, a man called Relf, to do so. This Relf readily agreed to. Have you heard all this?'

'To that point, sir, but no further. Anything you can tell me now will be new to me.'

'Well, Mr Barke saw the pictures and he didn't like them. At first he thought simply that the work had been extraordinarily badly done, and then he grew suspicious. He got rid of Relf for a few moments, and examined one of the canvases in detail. He found evidence that the painting was quite recent; he did tell me what it was, but I needn't go into that even if I remembered it correctly. It followed, of course, that it wasn't a cleaning at all, but a copy.'

A feeling not far removed from triumph was now rising in French's mind. Then they were both in it! Davenport had joined Buller in his attempt to cheat the insurance company. A plausible ruffian, that Davenport! To himself French admitted that he had been deceived by his talk in the studio.

But if this were so, must they not be guilty of the murder also? It looked like it, and yet it didn't seem possible. If either were, they were a lot cleverer than he had given them credit for. No, he simply didn't see how the thing could have been done.

He had quite a time to consider the problem, for at intervals, and this was one, Wellesley remained silent, evidently to fight off his exhaustion. But he presently resumed.

'Mr Barke was worried by his discovery. It looked suspicious, though there was no actual evidence of fraud. The pictures were Sir Geoffrey's own property, and if he wanted ready money, it was legitimate for him to sell them and have them replaced by copies. The loss was his alone; the originals were not damaged and were still available to the world. In any case it was not Mr Barke's business, but Sir Geoffrey's only.

'Then another possibility occurred to Mr Barke. Sir Geoffrey might know nothing about the affair, but might himself have been defrauded. The artist he had employed to clean the pictures might have secretly made copies and stolen and sold the originals.

'Mr Barke wondered whether he ought to tell Sir Geoffrey what he had noticed. Then next day he read the account of the fire and that all the pictures were burnt, and he wondered still further. The idea of a fraud on the insurance company suggested itself, though he rejected it immediately.

He had no reason to suspect that Sir Geoffrey was not a perfectly honourable man and that if he knew of the copies he would not advise the insurance company accordingly.'

'All very natural.'

'Yes, but delicate. He felt, you understand, that he was probably the only outsider who knew of the substitution, and that he should inform Sir Geoffrey. But he felt also that the interview might be unpleasant.'

'I follow you, sir,' French assured him. 'He would feel that he must prevent a fraud, and yet he would wish to avoid anything that would look like suspicion of Sir Geoffrey.'

'Exactly. Well, at that time, that was Tuesday, he took no step, having come to no decision.'

Like a shadow the sister was there, smiling and competent, but just a little critical. Mr Wellesley mustn't talk too much. She thought the interview had gone on long enough. If he hadn't finished with French, French could come back tomorrow.

'No, please,' Wellesley begged, a look of alarm appearing on his face. 'I must finish. It won't take much longer.'

She hesitated. 'Very well,' she said at last, 'but Mr French must go away for an hour while you have some rest. An hour,' she repeated to French, smiling, but inexorable, 'then if Mr Wellesley's awake you can see him again.'

'That will be quite satisfactory to me,' French said untruthfully. 'All right, Mr Wellesley, your story's just what I wanted. I'll come back later.'

When he returned Wellesley was looking better. 'I've been asleep,' he explained. 'Had a hot drink and went to sleep. You do nothing else in this place. Sit down, Chief Inspector. I want to give you all the details I can, as nearly as possible in Mr Barke's own words, even if it takes a little time.'

'Very good of you, sir. That's just what I should like, if you can do it without tiring yourself too much.'

'I'll do my best. Let me see now: where was I? Yes, I remember.' He went on hesitatingly in his weak voice. 'That afternoon Mr Barke was rung up by a Mr Vincent, who said he was speaking on behalf of the Thames & Tyne Insurance Company and Sir Geoffrey Buller of Forde Manor, in connection with some pictures which were destroyed in the fire. He said that he understood from the caretaker that Mr Barke had seen the galleries on the previous day, and was that so? Mr Barke said it was. "I don't want to go into details over the phone," Vincent went on, "but if you happened to notice anything unusual about the pictures, you will guess what our business is." "I noticed something," Mr Barke answered. "Then you could be of the greatest help to both of us," Vincent assured him, going on to invite him to join Sir Geoffrey and himself at lunch on the following day at the Holly Restaurant to discuss the matter. He then asked had Mr Barke mentioned what he had seen, and when Mr Barke rather indignantly denied it, begged him to say nothing till after their meeting.'

Again Wellesley paused while French sat waiting till he should recover energy to proceed.

'Mr Barke duly kept the appointment. Vincent was waiting for him in a private room, and he explained that he was a partner in the Thames & Tyne, that an awkward point had arisen in connection with the insurance of the Forde Manor pictures, and that if Mr Barke could help them, both his company and Sir Geoffrey would be very grateful. He was surprised that Sir Geoffrey had not turned up, but if Mr

Barke would not mind waiting a minute or two for lunch, he should not be long.

'They waited for about ten minutes, then Vincent was called to the phone. He came back with a long face, explaining that Sir Geoffrey had just rung up to say that he had had an accident with his car and would be unable to come to lunch, and would Vincent get on with the business.

'They had lunch accordingly, and after it Vincent explained that it had come to the knowledge of the Thames & Tyne that a number of the pictures at Forde Manor had been ostensibly cleaned, but their information was that instead they had been removed and copies had been substituted. The Thames & Tyne immediately initiated steps to find out the truth, but before they could complete their inquiries the fire took place. They then appealed to Sir Geoffrey for information and he had been completely open with them. He explained that he had had the pictures cleaned in Paris by a M. Picoux, in whom he had every confidence, but that under the circumstances he of course wished every step to be taken to set the matter at rest. That was what they wanted from Mr Barke: could he tell them if these were the originals or copies?'

Once again Wellesley closed his eyes and lay for some moments without speaking. The story, though not going quite as French had expected, was still easy enough to account for. Evidently Buller had learnt of Barke's visit from Relf and when the Thames & Tyne had approached him he had seen his danger. Any attempt to hush the matter up would obviously be fatal, so he had simulated the open and candid employer, anxious to reveal all the facts, though puzzled, as he didn't believe his employee could have let him down.

The only unexpected part was about having the work done by M. Picoux in Paris. Who, he wondered, was lying? Or was it possible in some way to harmonize this statement with Davenport's? This at all events suggested an interesting line of inquiry. He should ask—But there, Wellesley was speaking again.

'Mr Barke didn't at all like the position. Buller had been his host and he would have given a good deal not to be mixed up in the affair. However there was nothing for it but to tell the truth. He said that he had been suspicious of a number of the pictures, but that only in one case was he sure; in that case the picture was a copy.

'Vincent seemed pleased. He thanked Mr Barke and said his statement would be most valuable both to Sir Geoffrey and the Thames & Tyne, and that he was sorry that Sir Geoffrey had not been there to hear it for himself. Then he hemmed and hawed and at last asked Mr Barke if he would be so good as to undertake some professional work for the Thames & Tyne? Would he come over with himself and Sir Geoffrey to Paris and call on M. Picoux, partly to discuss the affair with him, but principally to see two of the Forde Manor pictures which he was then cleaning? His fee and of course all expenses would be met.

'Mr Barke told me that he was so much interested in the affair that there was nothing he would have liked better. However he kept all eagerness out of his tone as he agreed to go.

'"Then would the nine o'clock from Victoria on tomorrow, Friday, morning suit you?" asked Vincent. Mr Barke said it would, and Vincent added that he and Sir Geoffrey would travel by the same service and would take the tickets. "Just one thing, Mr Barke," went on Vincent, "if all this got out there might be unpleasant rumours which might affect Sir Geoffrey adversely. Might I beg you to say nothing about it till we've seen Picoux? If possible, all concerned would like the affair settled privately." Mr Barke gave his word.

'And that's the story,' Wellesley concluded. '"I'm not too happy about the whole thing," Barke went on to me. "I thought I'd just tell you about it, and if you have any advice to give me I should be glad of it."'

'And did you advise him?' asked French, forgetting the doctor's instructions.

'No, I only told him what he already knew: to volunteer nothing, to offer no opinions, and to tell the whole truth in reply to any questions he was asked. I warned him that he might have to repeat what he said in court.'

'Sound advice for the journey through life, sir,' French smiled. 'Now I just want to ask you one question, if it wouldn't tire you too much: Did Mr Barke mention M. Picoux's address?'

'No, I'm afraid he didn't.'

'Never mind, I'll get it from Sir Geoffrey. I'm extremely grateful for your clear statement and I hope you'll soon be about again.'

Before settling down to consider Wellesley's statement in detail, French felt that he must make two obvious inquiries. First, he rang up the manager of the Thames & Tyne, only to be told, as he had expected, that there was no one in their employment of the name of Vincent, that none of their staff had lunched with Mr Barke on that Wednesday or any other day, and that they had never heard of any artist named Picoux in Paris or anywhere else.

Next he went round to the Brooklyn and saw Sir Geoffrey. The baronet was obviously amazed at the story. He also had never heard either of Vincent or Picoux and he had never made any arrangements to lunch or go to Paris with Barke.

'What does it mean, Chief Inspector?' he asked. 'I feel as if I were in a nightmare. Am I to assume from this that some trick was played and that these pictures really were substitutes?'

'Certainly not, Sir Geoffrey,' French returned heartily. 'If you take my advice you won't assume anything. The part of the story about you and Vincent was false: why not that part also? No, the whole thing was an obvious trick to get Mr Barke over to Paris, where his murder had evidently been arranged.'

As a result of the information gained by these two inquiries, French made a third call: to the *Sûreté*: Could Inspector Dieulot tell him if there was an artist named Picoux in Paris, and if so, any details that he could learn about him? Again French was not surprised when there was a reply to say that the name was unknown.

Barke, then, had been hoaxed at that lunch. But who had hoaxed him? French's first thought had been that Vincent was really Davenport and that Picoux was the creation of his fertile brain. But in he thought over the matter more carefully, this theory seemed to grow less likely.

If Davenport had masqueraded as Vincent in order to get Barke over to Paris to meet his death, who had murdered him? Not Davenport and of course not Buller either. The theory then involved some accomplice of these two who would commit the actual deed. But was this likely? If someone else were going to commit the murder, why should Davenport have taken part? Why shouldn't Vincent be the Paris murderer?

This point of view was further strengthened by the fact that neither Davenport nor Sir Geoffrey had travelled to Paris by the nine a.m. service on the day in question. Davenport had crossed on the previous day—his passport proved that—and Sir Geoffrey had not gone at all. Vincent, whoever he was, must surely then have travelled with Barke. If no one had turned up at Victoria, Barke would scarcely have gone alone.

Once again French's thoughts turned to Lorrimer and then to a possible hired thug. But once again he re-abandoned these ideas. The difficulties of detail would have been too great.

Who then was this mysterious individual whose shadow lurked at the back of this most puzzling case? Was nothing known about him?

Quickly French saw that there was one thing, and that a point which might prove of the utmost importance. The unknown, whoever he was, knew a good deal about Forde Manor, Sir Geoffrey, the collection of pictures, and the fact that doubtful cleanings had been done, as well as that Barke had been down on Monday and seen the treated canvases. The people who fulfilled these conditions must be few in number, and what was more, did not he, French, know them all?

Incidentally they ruled out both Lorrimer and the thug. Who else was a possible? With something approaching horror French's thoughts swung towards Betty Stanton: not as the murderer of course; she had not been in Paris. But was she not the only other person who could have passed on the necessary information to Vincent? Who was Vincent? This was now a vital question, and to learn the answer must be French's next business.

Could Vincent be Lorrimer? If so, there was Dieulot's theory as to how he might have faked his alibi. Unlikely, French thought, but he supposed it possible.

Once again he rang up Dieulot. And then his question was answered. In the ordinary course of investigation the Frenchman had already ascertained Lorrimer's whereabouts during every day between the fire and murder. He had been in Paris on all of them.

French's thoughts swung back in exasperation. Against all this theorizing there was one outstanding fact which he felt he was in danger of forgetting. It was Buller who had committed arson. It was Buller who faced ruin if Barke talked about the substitutions. It was Buller who was interested in the artist's death . . . But Buller had not gone to Paris . . .

'Damn!' French muttered, as he twisted unhappily at his desk. All the same he regretfully decided that he must make some further inquiries about Mrs Stanton.

16

The Elimination of a Suspect

When French settled down to consider his programme in relation to Betty Stanton, he recalled immediately a significant and disquieting fact.

At this first interview with her when Agatha Barke was ill, before ever he had told her anything about Barke's disappearance, she had seemed apprehensive. With many persons the mere visit of the police produces a certain nervousness, but Mrs Stanton was certainly not of this type. Yet her nervousness had undoubtedly been considerable. What had caused it? Then when he had mentioned Barke's disappearance she had been powerfully affected. For a moment she had looked as if she were going to faint. At the time he had supposed that this was due to her friendship for the Barkes, but now he thought her emotion had come too quickly, before she could have realized the implications of his statement. If so, once again, what had caused it?

At the time he had been impressed with her personality. She had seemed an extremely estimable type of woman and he had not for a moment supposed she could be involved in anything shady. Now he wondered had he not leaped too quickly to conclusions. After all, her uprightness had been his impression, her emotion was a fact. He now realized that there was here an undoubted case for inquiry, and the sooner he set about it, the sooner he would reach a result.

What should be his first step? Well, the obvious thing was to find out if she had passed any information about Forde Manor on to Vincent. At the time she had been staying at the lodge. Would that help him?

He went down once again to Forde and saw Mrs Relf. 'I'm still,' he explained after a little judicious conversation had got her into a friendly mood, 'working on this affair of Mr Barke's disappearance and I'm trying to account for all the letters, telegrams and messages of all kinds that he got during the last few days before he went to France. You follow?'

'Yes, sir,' she answered with just the bemused reaction he wished for.

'Quite. Now you didn't yourself write to him or send him any message?'

She looked shocked. 'No, sir. I had no message to send.'

'No, I suppose not. What about your husband? Do you think he did?'

'I'm quite certain he didn't.'

'I didn't suppose so either, but I had to ask. Now who else is there down here that I ought to see? I have to see Mrs Stanton of course, but perhaps you can tell me about her?'

'I know nothing of her private affairs, sir.' There was reproof in her tones.

'No, of course not,' French answered easily. 'I don't expect

it and wouldn't ask it. But that's no reason,' he smiled, 'why
you shouldn't tell me if she had a caller or sent any telephone message or telegram or urgent letter or anything of
that kind.'

'I understand, sir. She had no callers here, but she had a
telegram the night before she left.'

'Thank you,' said French, manfully concealing his satisfaction. 'But I'm afraid that doesn't interest me. It's not
what she received I want to know of, but what she sent.
You don't know of any message?'

Mrs Relf knew of none, and after a suitable rounding up
of the interview, French took his leave.

He was delighted with his success. If Mrs Stanton received
a telegram, it might well be in answer to one she had sent.
He drove to the local post office and asked to see the postmaster.

The question of seeing telegraph and telephone records
was always a matter of delicate negotiation. Postmasters,
like other specimens of the human race, varied. Some held
strictly to the letter of the law, saying their job was to
maintain in inviolable secrecy what had been entrusted to
them by the public. Others were willing for the general
good to help the officers of justice by disclosing information,
knowing that a refusal could be met with a Home Office
order which they would have to obey.

Fortunately for French, the present officer belonged to
the second category, and after a short search he was reading
with thrilled attention: 'Unexpectedly crossing Paris
tomorrow. Have wired Roland to meet me. If you desire
will advance him money if satisfied with scheme. You refund
me later. Charles.'

'Thank you,' French went on, 'I shall want this message

and shall therefore get you the necessary order. Was there by any chance a reply to this?'

The postmaster held out another form: 'Please do as you suggest. Immensely grateful. Betty.'

Having taken copies, French drove back to London. In spite of his previous cogitations, he was surprised—and strangely, a little disappointed—by what he had found. Mrs Stanton knew more about Barke's journey than she had admitted; in fact, she had quite deliberately kept her information back. Why? That was a question in which he was going to be much interested.

Wishing he could have avoided an unpleasant job, he called at the Green House and asked to see Betty. She met him with some eagerness.

'Any news?' she asked hopefully as she invited him to sit down.

French shook his head. 'About Mr Barke? None, I am sorry to say. But Mrs Stanton, I have to tell you that some facts have come to my knowledge which will, if I am to be satisfied, require a pretty complete explanation from you. I have also to tell you that you are not legally bound to answer my questions, though of course if you don't, it may raise unpleasant suspicions in my mind.'

Betty stared at him, her face slowly whitening. He noted it with an added distaste for his job.

'What do you want to know?' she asked in a low, troubled voice.

'Two things,' he answered. 'First, I want to know the details of the financial business Mr Barke was doing for you in Paris, and second, I want to know why you kept this back when I asked what Mr Barke had gone for?'

For a moment Betty did not reply. Her face was ghastly

231

and she instinctively moistened her dry lips. 'I don't know how you know about this,' she said at last in a curiously small voice, 'but it is true that Mr Barke was going to make a payment for me in Paris.'

'Yes?' French prompted as she stopped.

She seemed to make an effort to continue. 'The matter was purely personal and could not possibly have had anything to do with Mr Barke's disappearance.'

'You can't be sure of that.'

'I think I can. At all events that was one reason why I didn't feel called on to mention it, and the second was that it was not the business which had taken him over. If you must know, he telegraphed to me to say that he was going over and would I like him to do this small commission which we had talked of earlier. So you see, he was going in any case on business of which I knew nothing—his principal business. So I think I answered you perfectly truly.'

'Yes,' French declared, 'I'm not questioning your good faith. But you cannot ask me to believe, Mrs Stanton, that you did not know that you should have mentioned this commission. A court would take a very serious view of that.'

'But I assure you it wasn't what took Mr Barke to France.'

'I accept that also. But you must be well aware that that didn't excuse your action. Now what was the commission you gave to Mr Barke?'

He could see that she was extremely upset and also undecided as to her course of action. Though he had told her the absolute truth in saying she was to blame for keeping back her information, he could not even now believe that she had been a party to murder, and he hated causing her this anxiety. However, he could not act otherwise. Presently he went on in a pleasanter tone.

'Let me try to clear up the situation. You're not bound to answer my question, but if you don't do so, I'll be forced to assume that your commission was connected in some way with Mr Barke's disappearance, perhaps his murder. If the latter proved true, you would then be arrested as an accessory. So you see, I'm not exaggerating its importance. On the other hand, if you tell me the whole thing, I undertake, unless it proves to be material evidence, to keep it entirely secret.'

Her face remained ghastly and she gave a little moan when he mentioned the word 'murder'. For Betty indeed it was a horrible situation. She had no idea how much French knew. She longed above everything to keep Roland's name out of the affair, but she was well aware that if she did so, and French then learnt of his existence, her efforts would have the very opposite effect to that she wished. She would have dearly liked time to think it over, but delay was equally dangerous. Feeling hunted and driven, she came quickly to a decision—right or wrong.

'I admit, Chief Inspector, that I wanted to keep the matter secret,' she said, 'because it is one that is very painful to me, involving, as it does, the failure and disgrace of my twin brother. But I can see now it would be worse for both of us if I kept back the information. I can see that it would cause the very suspicions which I'm most anxious to avoid. I've therefore decided to tell you everything.'

French received this with mixed feelings. As he had really all the time believed, there was going to be nothing against Mrs Stanton, for which his personal and human self was glad. At the same time, another promising line of investigation seemed to be going west, which officially was a disaster. He told her gravely that he was sure that she was doing the right thing.

'It's my brother, Roland Brand,' went on Betty. 'He's been a failure. He has the artistic temperament and he couldn't stick regular business.' She felt her plan was to make the case as black as possible. 'He had a good banking job, but he lost it through carelessness and inattention. He always loved acting, and he drifted to Paris and got a part in a troupe there. It was a miserable affair, they only did turns in the lowest music halls. For a long time he was practically down and out, then I'm glad to say he began to pull himself together. He worked harder and began to save. Then he discovered that there was an opening in the better class music halls for a superior kind of troupe, and he decided to try to form one. He got the people and the promises of employment, but he couldn't raise the capital for costumes and properties and so on. His share came to £120, and I thought that, as he had steadied down so much, he should have his chance. I had talked it over with Mr Barke, who took a very kindly interest in my affairs. Before paying the money I wanted him to be satisfied that Roland's scheme was promising, and I suggested that the next time he went to Paris he should see Roland, have a chat with him, and if he thought it was all right, pass on to him the money I should have already given him. On that Thursday afternoon he telegraphed to me that he was unexpectedly going next morning to Paris, and asked me would I like him to see Roland, saying that as there wasn't time for me to send him the money, he would advance it himself, and I could refund him later. I agreed thankfully, and that, Chief Inspector, is the entire story without any reservation whatever.'

French believed it absolutely; he had too much experience of witnesses not to know when he was being told the truth. But unhappily for this nice woman, the truth in this case by no means ended the affair. A situation might well have arisen in which this Roland Brand might have murdered Barke for the £120. Suppose Barke had unwisely begun by saying he had the money with him, and then on getting details of the scheme had refused to hand it over, might not the disappointment have led to a fatal assault? And French, in spite of his liking for Betty, was not at all sure that her silence had not been due to fear of this very contingency.

'Thank you,' he said. 'I'm glad you've told me that. You should have done it before, but as you've done it now I may tell you that I accept every word of it. All the same, as you probably know, it will be my duty to check it. What is your brother's address please?'

'27 rue de Tanger. It's a little street near the P.L.M. station at Charenton.'

'And the bank he was in?'

'Lloyds' Clayton Street Branch.'

On his way back to the Yard, French called at the bank and found that the manager remembered Brand. He was, he said, a likeable chap, but not cut out for business. He was interested in amateur theatricals and would take endless trouble in making up a character or building a stage set, but he couldn't bear the monotony and regularity of banking life. His work was below the required standard, and his hot temper created endless difficulties. Eventually they had had to ask him to resign.

French saw that the matter was so important that he dared not leave the inquiry to Dieulot. He therefore rang

235

up the Frenchman and that afternoon once again crossed the Channel.

'I hope it's not another Lorrimer,' he declared when next morning he was once more seated in Dieulot's room, 'but this new line strikes me as the most promising we've yet struck. You see, the £120 might have made all the difference to Brand. And if he first thought he was going to get it and then found he wasn't, with his hot temper he might have seen red and lost his self control.'

'It is just,' Dieulot returned amicably. 'But, my friend, we shall soon learn the truth. The rue de Tanger—let us see.'

He crossed the room to where a large map of Paris hung on the wall, then pointed. 'Behold, it is here.' His finger moved to the southeast corner and stopped. 'The Charenton Station; and here,' the finger moved slightly, 'is the street. We go there, is it not?'

'I'm ready,' French answered, getting up.

Dieulot, having telephoned for a car, led the way. They drove across Paris, and passing outside the fortifications at the Porte de Charenton, ran down the rue de Paris to the crossroads at the rue Gabrielle. A few hundred yards further brought them to the rue de Tanger.

No. 27 was a tall old house, let in apartments. Dieulot inquired from the woman concierge.

'No. 12, monsieur. On the third floor to the back.'

They knocked at No. 12. A man's voice called '*Entrez*' and they pushed open the door.

The room was of fair size, though poor and dilapidated both as to decoration and furnishing. A threadbare rug covered the area of the floor in' front of an old-fashioned tiled stove and on it were two deck chairs and a small deal table. In one corner was a small folding bedstead, and close by was a rather good wardrobe which, however, had seen better days. On a desk in another corner were a gramophone, a stack of records, and a pile of books and papers.

Lounging in one of the deck chairs was a man whose startling resemblance to Betty Stanton instantly showed his relationship. He was poorly but neatly dressed, was properly shaven, and looked fit and fairly prosperous. In the other chair lay a girl, a pretty dark-complexioned creature, simply dressed and with something of the same air of mild prosperity. Both held what seemed to be the scripts of a play. Brand levered himself out of his chair when he saw his visitors and stood waiting expectantly.

'Mr Brand?' said French. 'I've come over from England to see you. I am Chief Inspector French from Scotland Yard, and this is M. Dieulot of the *Sûreté*.'

French watched keenly the reaction to this. Brand's expression showed the most acute surprise, but French couldn't say that it was mingled with fear.

'Oh,' he said. 'Well, won't you sit down,' continuing in French: 'Give them that chair, will you, Loo? They probably won't be long. Your business is not private, I presume, gentlemen?'

'I think it should go no further than yourself, Mr Brand. Perhaps the lady would excuse us for a few moments?'

'Certainly. You clear out, Loo. Go and fix up those alterations with François: you have to do that in any case.'

The girl got up slowly but without speaking, and with a resentful look at French, passed from the room. Obeying Brand's gesture the men sat down in the deck chairs, while Brand pulled round the table and perched himself on it.

'We want your help in an inquiry,' French went on, still

watching his host. 'It's about Mr Barke. You knew that he had disappeared?'

'What?' Brand exclaimed. 'Disappeared? No, I didn't know that.'

If his surprise was not genuine, it was uncommonly well done. But then, thought French, the man was an actor. Then his expression slowly changed. Undoubtedly he was now feeling apprehension.

French said nothing. A silence under such circumstances was often more impressive than speech.

It seemed in this case to produce its effect, for Brand moved uneasily. 'Tell me about it. I know nothing. What has happened?'

'Don't you read the papers, Mr Brand? The case was fully reported.'

'I'm afraid only by fits and starts. I certainly missed this.'

'Well, I'll tell you. But first I should like to ask you a question or two. You knew Mr Barke?'

'Oh, yes. He was my sister's friend really: he and his wife. But I've met him several times.'

'Have you seen him recently?'

'Not very. I suppose not for four or five months.'

'You used to meet him when he came over to Paris?'

'Sometimes. He often asked me to dine with him. It was my sister of course. She wanted him to tell her how I was.'

'I understand. Now Mr Barke was over in Paris three weeks ago: on Friday, the 15th of last month. Do I understand you to say you didn't see him then?'

'No, I didn't see him. I wondered if he had come over.'

'You wondered? Why was that, Mr Brand?'

238

'Because I got a wire from him to hold myself in readiness to meet him.'

'Oh: have you got it still?'

Brand swung off the table and went over to his desk. 'I don't think so, but I haven't tidied my desk for some time and it may be here.'

He searched rapidly through the accumulation of papers that covered its top. Except for the rustling of the sheets, the silence remained unbroken. Finally just as French was deciding to lend a hand, Brand gave a grunt. 'Got it, though I didn't expect to.'

The message had been handed in at a post office near the Green House late on the Thursday evening, and had been delivered early on the Friday. It read: 'Crossing Paris Friday by nine from Victoria. Anxious to see you. Don't know movements so stand by telephone in afternoon.'

'He had your number?'

'Yes, he had the number of this house. The phone is in Madame Thevenet's in the basement, and she calls anyone who is wanted.'

'I follow. And did you stand by that afternoon?'

'Yes, I waited here for the entire afternoon and evening up till bedtime. But no one rang up.'

'Do you mean that you got no further message?'

'None.'

'And did you not think that rather strange?'

'Not very. I presumed that Mr Barke had been prevented crossing and that I would hear from him again later.'

'You're sure that the message didn't come to Madame Thevenet?'

Brand shrugged. 'One has to take the chance of that,' he answered. 'I can't afford a special installation up here.'

'Did you write to Mr Barke asking what was wrong?'

'No. Why should I? It was he that was managing the affair and I felt sure I should hear again in due course.'

All this was quite reasonable, but it did not get French much further. It might well be the exact truth. On the other hand, if Brand had murdered Barke, it was exactly the kind of story he would tell. The telegram proved nothing. If it were genuine, as French thought likely, it only meant that there was a confederate in London who had sent it for the precise purpose for which it had been used: perhaps Vincent.

A further possibility occurred to French. Could Brand have murdered Barke, but not for the £120? Could he have done it as the tool of Buller, for some vastly greater sum? Not very probable, perhaps, yet the possibility must be kept in view.

'You say you were here in this building all the afternoon and evening of that Thursday, Mr Brand. Now I'm not questioning your statement, but can anyone corroborate it?'

There was now no doubt of the man's apprehension. Indeed, naked fear showed in his eyes. For some moments he did not reply. Then he said in a lower tone, 'I don't know that anyone can.'

'Well,' French said more cheerily, 'let's see what you can do about it. Madame Thevenet will remember about the telephone perhaps?'

Roland looked appraisingly at French. 'Yes, she may, though I doubt if she'll remember what day it was. But would that be any use to you?' Again he paused unhappily. 'I with you'd tell me what happened, as you said.'

'Certainly,' French agreed. 'Mr Barke came to Paris that day, leaving London at 9.00 a.m. and reaching Paris at 3.48.

He went direct to the Hôtel Vichy, booked a room, walked out of the hotel, and was never heard of again.'

Brand stared, his face still further paling. 'My God!' he said brokenly. 'And you think that I—'

'We think nothing,' French interrupted decisively. 'We're only trying to get information. Tell me, Mr Brand, about the new troupe you propose to get together.'

The fear in his eyes died down. 'That was Louise Gerard,' he said, 'who was here. She would be one of us if the thing came off. She's absolutely top hole. And there are four others who would join, all first class. But you've got your question wrong; "Propose" is not the word.'

'Then what should I have said?'

'That I'd like to get it together. I can't afford the preliminary outlay.'

'How much would it take?'

'About a hundred and twenty each.'

'Have you tried to get it?'

For the first time in the interview Brand smiled. 'Have I tried to get it?' he asked scornfully. 'Well, what do you think, Chief Inspector?'

'I suppose you have. Did you try to get it from Mr Barke?'

Brand shook his head, again resentful. 'Not likely. I don't know him well enough for that. I've tried a lot of people over here. Couldn't get them interested.'

'Mrs Stanton?'

'Betty would have helped me if she could have afforded it. But she hadn't the money to spare. She's been hard hit herself lately.'

It was evident, French thought after some more questions in the same strain, either that Brand really had no idea that Barke was bringing him the money, or that he was a magnificent actor and a very clever man. Gradually French was coming to the belief that he was innocent, but here again it was his opinion only and there was no proof. That this was the exasperating position in which French so often found himself did nothing to make it more satisfactory.

As a little later they were leaving the house, they met the young woman Louise Gerard returning. French stopped.

'We've been hearing about your proposed troupe, mademoiselle,' he said politely in English, 'but we forgot to ask Mr Brand when you are actually starting. Can you tell us?'

She understood and replied in the same language. 'But it is not finished,' she said in accents of surprise. 'Mr Brand, he has not got the money. He cannot get it.'

She patently believed what she was saying and French thought he might take it as the truth. It was unlikely then that the money had passed between Barke and Brand. Though officially it would still be necessary to keep an open mind about the actor, he had little doubt privately. The man was innocent. Dieulot, when later they discussed the affair in detail, held the same view. Disgruntled, though glad for Mrs Stanton's sake, French once again bade his temporary colleague farewell, returning to London by the afternoon train.

17

The Beginning of the End

With Brand eliminated from the case, French's thoughts turned back to his former suspects. There still remained this strange personality, Vincent, and of course suspicion still hung unsatisfactorily over Buller and Davenport. Granted that neither of the latter was the actual murderer, could they not have used Vincent as their agent? Could Barke's elimination not have been effected by a conspiracy between the three?

From Wellesley's statement French had already concluded that Barke—unless he had received some later communication—would not have crossed to France alone, and that as neither Buller nor Davenport went with him, his companion must have been Vincent. Now he began to wonder whether Barke would have gone with Vincent without having first seen Buller. Barke had been asked to lunch at the Holly to meet Buller, but Buller had not appeared. Barke had been told Buller was going to France with them. If only Vincent had turned up at Victoria, would Barke not become suspicious and insist on postponing the journey until he had made sure of Vincent's bona fides?

With the possibility of such an obvious hitch to their schemes, would Buller not have taken steps to reassure Barke? If so, how better could this be done than by a personal interview?

Had Buller and Barke then met between 3.30 pm. on the Thursday when, according to Wellesley, Barke left his club, and 9.00 a.m. on the following morning at Victoria? It surely should not be hard to find out. Half an hour later French was once again seated with Miss Redpath in her room at the Crewe Gallery. Could she possibly help him on two points: first, had Mr Barke received any private message on the Thursday afternoon? And second, at what hour had he left the building?

Miss Redpath, rather to his surprise, was able to answer both questions. Barke had had no caller nor letter nor message after lunch that day, and he had left, ostensibly for home, at 5.30. She remembered this because it was Barke's last day, and also because his slightly early departure had enabled her to catch the 6.02 train instead of her usual one at 6.17.

'How did Mr Barke usually go home?' French asked, hoping his luck would hold.

It did. Barke went home by bus from Piccadilly Circus to King's Road, walking the few hundred yards from the nearest stop to his house. Miss Redpath had no reason to suppose he had departed from his custom on the evening in question.

French left the Gallery, noting the time. He paced at a moderate speed up Regent Street to Piccadilly Circus, took the first bus that came along, got down at a suitable stop in King's Road, walked to Green House, and again looked at his watch. It had taken twenty-three minutes.

At Green House he had more difficulty. No one at first was able to help him. But he was persistent in suggesting clues, and at last Agatha Barke recalled that her husband had reached home on the evening in question a quarter of an hour earlier than usual. Generally he arrived at five minutes past six; this time it was about ten minutes before the hour. She remembered because she was ill and bored and was watching the clock till he should come; also, like Miss Redpath, because it was his last evening.

Both she and the maid were positive that he had had no callers or messages either that night or before he left next day. The maid had herself got a taxi at twenty minutes to nine in the morning and had seen him drive off—alone.

If all this testimony were correct, and there was no reason to doubt it, Buller had not communicated with Barke until he reached Victoria. Had he done so then?

French's luck now seemed to have run out. He spent a long time at the station, armed with both Barke's and Buller's photographs, questioning everyone whom he thought might help him, but without success.

Deciding to try another line, he went to the Brooklyn Hotel and saw the head waiter.

'I want to meet Sir Geoffrey Buller at breakfast one of these mornings,' he explained. 'Can you tell me what time he comes down?'

The head waiter referred him to an underling. This man said it was usually about nine o'clock.

'Thank you,' said French, slipping over a form. 'Just one other question. Do you remember if Sir Geoffrey was specially early or late some days ago?'

But this was too much: the waiter couldn't tell. Then he made a prodigious effort of memory. 'He wasn't in at all one morning about the time you mention,' he declared, but when pressed further he could not remember the date.

The suggestion interested French. He went back to the entrance lounge and buttonholed one of the accounts clerks. 'A little bit of confidential information,' he begged, handing over his official card. 'You have a note here of what meals your visitors take?'

'Certainly,' the young woman answered with a slight suggestion of humouring a halfwit. 'We require the information to make up the accounts.'

It seemed an occasion for bluff. 'I thought so,' French went on. 'It's about Sir Geoffrey Buller. He told me that he paid a certain call one morning about three weeks ago, which necessitated his going out before breakfast. But he couldn't remember which day it was. Can you tell me from his records?'

The clerk nodded. 'Easily,' she answered. 'Though Sir Geoffrey is on a weekly rate we note meals and extras just the same.' As she spoke she ran her finger down a sheet. 'Here it is. It was on Friday 15 March.'

So far, so good! French now turned to the head porter, jingling money in his pocket the while. He had been discussing some matters with Sir Geoffrey Buller and he was trying to fix the hours at which Sir Geoffrey left for and returned from an engagement on Friday morning, 15 March. Could the porter by any chance help him?

At first French was met by a blank negative, but his persistent suggestions met once again with perhaps more than their reward. His success was due to a page. 'Wasn't that the day the phone message came for Sir Geoffrey?' he asked his superior. 'You remember I couldn't find him and you booked the message to give him when he came in.'

The porter remembered the incident, but neither the day nor the time at which it had occurred. All he could tell was that the message had been handed to Sir Geoffrey the moment he came in, and that he had gone immediately to the telephone.

'What was the message?' asked French.

'Simply for him to ring up a certain number directly he came in.'

'No record of the number?'

It appeared that the porter had noted it in his book, from which he had filled the memorandum form for Buller. Some few seconds search produced it: Paddington 0743.

'Fine,' said French. 'Thank you very much.' The money passed. One more inquiry and he felt he would have his information. He went into a street call box and dialled Paddington 0743. In a few minutes a voice said: 'Jones & Henderson speaking.'

'Sorry,' returned French promptly. 'Wrong number,' and rang off.

Looking up the directory he found that Jones & Henderson were garage proprietors in George Street, north of Marble Arch. This was close by and in a few minutes French reached the place and asked for the manager.

'A little bit of confidential information, please,' he asked again as he handed over his official card: it was a useful gambit. 'It's not connected with you or anyone in the garage,' and he explained what he wanted.

At first the manager couldn't remember the circumstances, but by dint of consulting his clerks and looking up records he was able to give French the information. Sir Geoffrey had left his Rolls Royce with the firm to be sold and it happened that on that Friday morning an offer for it had been made. It was to discuss this that they had rung him up.

The settling of the time at which Sir Geoffrey's reply had been received proved less easy, though eventually French's suggestive questions brought it out. The boy who took the message had done so just as he was preparing to go for an early lunch, and it had delayed him. That had been at 12.20.

'Thank you, that's very satisfactory,' said French. 'Tell me, does Sir Geoffrey garage all his cars here?'

'There are two here: the Rolls and an Austin 10. I think he has only those two.'

'Either of them out on that Friday?" This meant another search of records, but it was presently established that neither had been.

Sir Geoffrey then had been out on some business from before 9.00 till 12.20 on the fateful day. Where, French wondered, had he gone and what had he done?

For dealing with cases of insufficient evidence there was a well established procedure: to imagine all the things which might have happened and to investigate these one after another till the right one was found.

Adopting this plan, the first thing that French thought of was that Buller might have travelled with the artist as far as Folkestone.

This at all events could be tested easily. French turned into a hotel and looked up Bradshaw. It did not give the time at which the 9.00 am. boat train reached Boulogne, but the steamer left at 10.55, so that the train must have been in several minutes earlier. Then as to up trains. One left Folkestone Central at 11.10, which the baronet could easily have caught. It arrived at Charing Cross at 12.30. From Charing Cross to the Fifth Avenue by taxi would have taken, say, fifteen minutes. The message could scarcely have been sent before 12.50. Could the garage office boy have received Buller's telephone message at 12.50 instead of 12.20?

Not if his statement as to his movements were correct. At first French was afraid he would have to check it item by item. Then he thought of a quicker way.

Going again to Victoria he saw the head booking clerk. No tickets for Folkestone had been issued by the train in question; all were for places beyond Boulogne.

So that was that. French's first guess had been wrong. What else might Buller have done? Gone to his club or his lawyers or the Crewe Gallery or to see Mrs Stanton? No. A series of telephone inquiries proved that he had done none of these things.

What then? At first French could make no more suggestions.

Then he wondered could the man have taken some excursion by road, some secret journey for which his own car could not be used? It seemed a long shot and yet what other possibilities were there? French decided to see if it led anywhere.

Next morning he began by sending some men to all the large garages—large because in them transactions cause less comment—in the Marble Arch and Victoria areas, to inquire about all cars on hire during the critical hours. If this inquiry failed, he would try further afield.

It succeeded beyond his hopes. Within an hour a man rang up, calling French to the Plutarch Garage in Vauxhall Bridge Road. There he learned that a black Colorado saloon No. ARK0040 had been hired on the Thursday afternoon for a couple of days, and had actually been out on the road between the hours named. The assistant who dealt with the matter moreover had picked out Sir Geoffrey's photograph as that of his client, though the latter had given his name as Morton.

Delighted with his good luck, French obtained details. It appeared that Sir Geoffrey had asked for a car with a large boot, as he was bringing a party of actor friends to town to do a charity sketch, and they had a lot of luggage. They had supplied him with the Colorado, which had the largest luggage space of any car in the place. He had refused to take a chauffeur, saying there would only be room for his friends if he drove himself. He had therefore made a substantial deposit, which was returned to him when he gave up the car. He had not taken the car with him on the Thursday, but had called for it at 8.30 on Friday morning and returned it about 12 noon on the same day.

'I thought you said he had it for a couple of days?' French pointed out.

'So he had. When he left it in he said he would require it again that night, as he wanted to take his friends down to the country after their show. He called for it about 11.30.'

'And when did he bring it back the second time?'

'About 8.30 next morning, Saturday.'

'That the last run he had?'

'Yes, he only took it out twice.'

'I follow. Did you note the mileage down on each trip?'

The assistant nodded. 'As a matter of fact we did, though only by mistake, and if it's important, it was a lucky mistake for you. As a rule we only note the mileage at the beginning and end of a hiring, but this time our foreman thought the car was finished with when it came in about midday on Friday and he read the mileage.'

'Lucky for me, as you say,' French agreed. 'What were the figures?'

Again books were looked up. 'The first time the car was out, between 8.30 and 12.00 noon on the Friday, it had done fifty-eight miles. The second time, between 11.30 on Friday night and 8.30 on Saturday morning it had done fifty-three. Total 111 miles.'

Full of renewed rigour and satisfaction, French took his next step. He issued a general call to all police stations within a radius of twenty-nine miles from Victoria, asking had a black Colorado, No. ARK0040, been seen between the hours of 9.00 a.m. and 12.00 noon on the Friday morning, or at any time on the Friday night, and giving a description of Sir Geoffrey as the probable driver.

A few hours later there were two replies. The first was from Croydon. The book of a car-park attendant showed that the car had been there on the date in question, and the position of the block among those used that day suggested that the ticket had been issued during the middle of the morning. The park was close to the airport, though not that commonly used by cars attending the planes.

The second reply was from a constable who had been on patrol duty during Friday night. At about 4.00 a.m. he was passing down a narrow road on Ockley Common when he saw the car. It was drawn into the trees near a small lake, a well-known beauty spot. Its lights were off, which however was correct, as it was clear of the road. He looked into it—the night was not very dark—and saw a man asleep in the back seat. This man answered to the given description. There had been nothing to interest him in the matter, and as soon as he had noted the number and satisfied himself that everything was in order, he passed on. When he returned just before eight, the car had gone.

All this was puzzling though obviously significant, and French retired to his room to consider it.

Of the Ockley Common report he could make nothing whatever. Why Sir Geoffrey should hire a car and drive at night into the country, park in a wood and go to sleep there, when he was paying for a good bed in an hotel, he could not imagine. It was true of course that Ockley Common was close to Forde Manor, but French could see no significance in the fact.

The Croydon story seemed more promising. The obvious suggestion was that someone had gone somewhere by plane. On that morning Buller had returned to London and Barke had gone by rail and steamer to Paris, while Davenport was with his painting friends in the atelier. Apparently, therefore, the air-minded traveller could only have been Vincent.

French dimly began to visualize Buller meeting Barke and Vincent at Victoria, making some excuse to Barke why he and Vincent could not accompany him to Paris, and perhaps fixing up the appointment for Barke immediately after his arrival at the Hôtel Vichy. Then hurrying Vincent to Croydon so that he could reach Paris quickly. Vincent would doubtless make his preparations and be waiting at the Paris rendezvous, where he would see to the elimination of Barke on the latter's arrival in the trap.

French was delighted with his theory for two reasons. First, because he thought it was the truth, and second, because it should lead him to Vincent. The names of all travellers were on record, and if he couldn't pick the man out at once from the lists, he should be able to trace him from Le Bourget.

He went to the offices first of Imperial Airways and then of Air France, but though he was supplied with the names of everyone who crossed to Paris on that day, none awakened any responsive chord. Disappointed, he set off for Croydon to continue his inquiries on the ground.

For some time he drew a blank. He checked the lists of passengers, lest someone joining at Croydon should have been omitted from the London copies. He made every inquiry he could think of, but it was only when he produced photographs of Sir Geoffrey, Barke, and Davenport, that he began to make progress.

A baggage clerk picked up Sir Geoffrey's. 'I've seen that man somewhere,' he said thoughtfully, 'but where or when I've no idea.'

This was encouraging. French did not press him, but let him think quietly. But it was no good. In spite of all his efforts, he could not remember.

It looked like another deadlock after all. French fumed and fretted internally, while speaking soft words of encouragement and cheer. But in the end it was French's own perspicacity which brought the desired light.

This clerk, he thought, was a baggage clerk. What did that mean? Why, that he attended not to passengers but to baggage? Was that his solution? Had Buller brought, not a passenger for Paris, but a package?

Two minutes later he was going into the records with the clerk. In another two his eyes had caught a name, and he was staring, motionless, with feelings both of bewilderment and delight.

The name was Roland Brand.

It appeared that A. F. Vincent of 'Cheddar', Appletree Road, St John's Wood, had sent two suitcases, one small and one medium-sized, to Roland Brand, Le Bourget Aerodrome, by the Air France plane leaving Croydon at 12 noon on the day in question. They were marked 'To be called for', and as no inquiries had been received about them, it was to be presumed that they had been duly received by Brand.

'I've got it now!' added the clerk, slapping his thigh and picking up Sir Geoffrey's photograph. 'That's Vincent. The whole thing comes back to me. He stood there, just where you are, making a big point that the stuff should go by the noon plane. That's your man. Is it anything important?'

'Important?' French repeated vaguely. He felt utterly befogged. 'Oh yes, in a way. It may be a help to me later.'

So Vincent was Buller! Was it possible?

But of course it wasn't! Barke had met Vincent at lunch at the Holly and Barke knew Buller. Vincent must be someone unknown to Barke.

One thing, however, was clear. Buller knew Vincent, and they were both concerned in this business of getting Barke to Paris, presumably that he might be killed. Well, French could put his hands on Buller at any moment, and through Buller he would soon get Vincent also.

The Croydon business was puzzling enough, but when French thought of the Paris end of the affair he felt at a complete loss. Roland Brand was mixed up in it too! Was it possible after all that he was the actual murderer? When French had finished that part of the investigation he had felt reasonably satisfied as to the actor's innocence, but now he wondered if he had been wrong. He could scarcely believe that he and Dieulot had been duped, yet he supposed it was not impossible.

But though the details of the affair were obscure, there

was little doubt as to its main features. Barke had been murdered, and in some way Buller was responsible. Brand, Vincent, and probably Davenport were his accomplices. Though French could not say how, he was satisfied that between them Barke had met his end.

Yet was not this an absurdity on the face of it? Surely no one, wishing to commit murder, would have entrusted his secret to three other persons? Besides, what inducement could he possibly have offered them to join him in such a risk? Most things can be bought with money, but murder is seldom one of them. And what else had Buller to give?

The one thing that was uncomfortably evident in the whole affair was that he himself had so far failed to get to the bottom of it. None of his theories was satisfactory. To each there seemed some overwhelming objection. What he required was more information. He must learn more details of what had occurred and in their light revise his conclusions.

And as to the learning of those details? Well, two inquiries were staring him in the face, shouting out to be made.

Almost automatically he rang up the St John's Wood local police station and asked for all the information they could give him about A. F. Vincent, of 'Cheddar', Appletree Road, and he was not greatly surprised to hear in reply that there was no such road in the area.

The second inquiry appeared more promising. Who had met the plane at Le Bourget and collected the suitcases? What was in them, and what had been done with the contents?

French felt that if he knew the answers to these questions, he would be nearer his solution.

For some time he wondered whether he should simply

ask Dieulot to get the information. Finally he decided that the matter was so important that he ought to go over himself. He therefore rang up Dieulot and fixed up an appointment for the following day.

That night he once again crossed the Channel.

18

The Emergence of the Truth

Dieulot was waiting for French when next morning he reached the *Sûreté*. 'It is the ill wind that blows you here, is it not?' he beamed with the most polite intention.

'More than an ill wind, monsieur,' French smiled back. 'There's a spot of work that I'd like to get done over this side.'

'A spot? A small area? A place? Work in a small place? *Hein?*' French continued smiling. 'I'm afraid it's only a way of speaking,' he explained, 'like your ill wind.'

The puzzled Dieulot stared, then nodded his head several times. 'Ah, yes,' he declared, 'it is clevair, is that one. What?'

'Quite,' French made the only reply he could think of, then decided that a business discussion would be less of a strain. 'I've got some information for you, M. Dieulot, and I want some from you in return. I've discovered,' and he went on to tell about the suitcases sent by Sir Geoffrey to Roland Brand. 'I'd like to find out if Brand received those suitcases, and if so, what he did with them.'

Dieulot nodded with evident anxiety to oblige. 'Perfectly,'

he declared. 'The affair arranges itself. We go first to Le Bourget and then to the house of Brand. Is it not?'

It was just what French wanted. Though Dieulot's English was at times a little difficult, he was a fine collaborator.

They were received with courtesy at the aerodrome, which became obsequiousness when Dieulot explained his position. 'The matter,' he went on, 'is a small one. My English colleague wishes to trace two suitcases sent here from Croydon by the twelve o'clock Air France plane on Friday, fifteenth March. Can you tell us what became of them?'

The answer was. quickly forthcoming. The suitcases in question had been addressed to a M. Roland Brand, to be called for at La Bourget. The incident was not remembered: that could scarcely be expected, but it was evident that M. Brand had received them, for behold, here was his signature on the waybill.

French beheld the signature, first with his naked eye and secondly with the aid of a lens. It undoubtedly read Roland Brand, but his suspicious mind was ever seeking for flaws and frauds and forgeries. This time he thought he had found all three. Practice had made him an acute judge of hand-writing and this looked as if it had been written slowly and painfully, instead of with careless ease. It was backhand to start with. There was of course nothing intrinsically suspicious in backhand—many perfectly honourable people habitually use it—but French could not but remember that it is the inexperienced forger's first choice. Backhand however was not the only peculiarity of this writing. It was irregular. Some down strokes had been leant on more heavily than others, while the degree of curvature of the letters varied. These appearances were not conclusive evidence, but they were extraordinarily suggestive.

'How does that writing strike you, M. Dieulot?' he asked.

Dieulot, not to be outdone, produced another lens and subjected the signature to an even more profound scrutiny. Then he shook his head and shrugged, throwing up his hands. The action expressed exactly French's own view. The signature was questionable, but no more.

'Can we take it along?' French asked, and as soon as a copy was made and attested by Dieulot, they left the aerodrome.

'Now for Friend Brand,' said French as he climbed into the waiting car. They drove practically across Paris, turning off the main road at the Charenton Station. Brand was in his room, alone this time, but once more immersed in the script of a play.

'Sorry to trouble you again, Mr Brand,' French began, 'but one or two questions have arisen since we met. I hope you'll answer them for us, but it's my duty to warn you that you needn't do so unless you like.'

This had curiously divergent effects on French's hearers. While Brand paled and grew obviously anxious, Dieulot's eyes goggled in amazement. Then he shrugged as if to indicate that for so great a madness as French's nothing could be done. Neither spoke and French presently went on, 'Perhaps one question will be enough. Can you tell me where you were at a quarter past one on Friday, 15 March, the day of Mr Barke's visit which we have already discussed?'

As he spoke, French carefully watched the actor. Once again he could see no special signs of guilt, but only of nervousness and mystification.

'But—but,' Brand hesitated, 'I understood you to say that Mr Barke did not reach Paris till nearly 4.00?'

'I didn't say my question was connected with Mr Barke,' French returned gravely.

Brand showed some confusion as well as relief. 'No, no, of course not. But I supposed that you had come on the same business as before.'

'Can you answer the question, Mr Brand?'

Brand hesitated still longer. 'I don't know that I can, Chief Inspector. It's a good while ago: nearly a month, I suppose.'

'It was the day you got the telegram from Mr Barke,' French prompted. 'Perhaps that will help you. What time did it come?'

'Oh early: about 9.00 or 9.30. It must have been sent the night before.'

'Then you waited in for Mr Barke's telephone?'

'Yes, but not until nearly 4.00.'

French was very patient and very persistent, and Roland was obviously anxious to help. But he declared he could not remember how he had filled the morning. He had almost certainly rehearsed and lunched at his usual restaurant, Perosi's, in the main street. But he couldn't prove this, and neither could any of his friends nor the staff of the restaurant, which Dieulot presently interrogated.

French felt exasperated. He had come all the way from London to settle this point, and now it was not settled. Yet his impression was that the man was innocent. Brand denied absolutely having ever seen or communicated with Buller, Vincent or Davenport, adding that he had never even heard of the latter pair. He had shown no reaction other than surprise when French had asked if he had recently been to La Bourget, and the idea of calling there for suitcases seemed to touch no answering chord of memory. Of course, once again, the man was an actor.

French thought that on the whole he must assume him innocent. Certainly he could prove nothing against him.

And the fact that he had no alibi actually counted in his favour. If Brand had met the suitcases, he would certainly have worked out some answer to the questions he would naturally expect.

Dieulot, though less convinced than French, agreed that the probabilities were in Brand's favour and that French would have to look elsewhere for his man.

'I wanted that business of Brand cleared out of the way,' French declared as they reached the *Sûreté*, 'before we took up the next point. Has it occurred to you that from Davenport's statement he could very well have met the suitcases?'

'But yes! That had occurred to me also, my friend. It is that we next address ourselves to the matter, is it not?'

'Let us see just what he said.' French turned the leaves of his notebook. 'And first let's get the times in connection with the plane. It leaves Croydon at 12.00 noon and reaches La Bourget at 1.15. A bus—for another plane—leaves the Place Lafayette at 12.30, reaching Le Bourget, I suppose, in a quarter of an hour. The bus connecting with our plane arrives back at the Place Lafayette at 1.45.'

Dieulot nodded. 'Correct, monsieur. To leave the Place Lafayette, collect the suitcases and return to the Place would take an hour and a quarter: from 12.30 to 1.45. Is it not?'

'That's right. Now let's check up the statement. Davenport went to the Atelier Voges between 9.00 and 10.00 and stayed a couple of hours. Then he brought his picture back to the Hôtel du Maréchal Ney. From his own statement therefore he should have reached the hotel about 12.00 or a little later, and you remember this was confirmed by the hotel people, who said he arrived between 12.00 and 1.00. The hotel is quite close to the Place Lafayette, so he could have returned his picture and caught that bus at 12.30.'

'He could have left even later by taxi.'

'Of course he could, or if he wanted to cover his traces, he could have hired a car. Well, Davenport stated he lunched at Les Quatre Plumes in the rue Royale, strolled about, and returned to the hotel about 3.00. We neither proved nor could expect to prove that, and we have to consider whether this failure isn't suggestive. At all events he would have ample time to go to La Bourget and collect the suitcases.'

'And to dispose of them,' added Dieulot, 'for it is evident that he didn't take them to the hotel.'

'I suppose not,' French admitted. 'I hadn't thought of that.'

They continued discussing the affair till French, feeling they had exhausted it, changed the subject. 'What about a spot of lunch?' he suggested.

'A spot! A little place for lunch. Ah! that is good.' Dieulot laughed, then suddenly grew serious again. 'But, my friend, I am desolated! Already I have a lunch engagement. I did not know that you were coming, otherwise it should not be so.'

'That's all right. Don't apologize. But I should like to see you again before I go back.'

'I shall be busy till four o'clock, then at your service.'

French strolled down the boulevards till he came to Les Quatre Plumes. He knew it as a first class restaurant and turned in with pleasant anticipations about lunch. He chose a table in an alcove with an excellent view of all that went on. There he sat, alone for the most part, entertained by the unfamiliar scene, and there while the place gradually emptied he remained on, slowly sipping his coffee and smoking French cigarettes with proper British contempt.

For a time he had banished his case from his mind, but

now it once again filled his thoughts. Had Davenport met the suitcases? If so, what had he done with them? These were the questions. If he could solve them they might throw light on the entire affair.

He sat pondering till the place was nearly empty and to justify himself he called for more coffee. Those suitcases! What could have been in them? Their weight gave him no hint: the clerk had assured him it was normal. He racked his brains, but without result. He could make nothing of the suitcases and presently he turned to another point.

It was one he had thought of before leaving London, but he had not time to consider it in detail. It was the question of Buller's car mileages, and he had dropped a road map into his bag, intending to study the matter if circumstances permitted.

Buller had taken out his hired car twice. On the first occasion, when on the Friday morning he had called at Croydon, he had done fifty-eight miles, and on the second, when that night he had visited Ockley Common, he had done fifty-three. Could anything be deduced from that?

There was little to be learnt in the case of the Friday night, except that Buller must have gone fairly directly to and from the Common. French worked out the distance. He made it about twenty-five miles. There and back would therefore be about fifty miles, and as the car had only been out for fifty-three, slight deviations from the direct route would alone have been possible. Buller could, of course, have gone on to Forde Manor within the mileage, but French couldn't see why he should have done so.

On the Friday morning, however, some movements, still undisclosed, must have taken place. The car travelled fifty-eight miles that morning, but from the garage to and from

Croydon was only, according to his map, twenty-one or twenty-two. How were the other thirty-six to be accounted for?

For a solid hour French sat puzzling his brains over this smaller problem and then over the equally baffling main conundrum. His second lot of coffee grew as cold as that it had replaced. The waiter looked more and more pointedly at him and then with a flourish produced his bill, but still French sat on. Then just as he began to feel that he really could not occupy his corner any longer, an idea shot into his mind.

He sat motionless considering it, weighing its implications, following out its ramifications. As he did so he found that facts which had hitherto been contradictory, began slipping one by one into place. A delightful excitement slowly grew in his mind. At long last he was on to something satisfactory. He could now see why Buller drove secretly to Croydon and sent those suitcases to Paris. He could even tell what was in them. But he still couldn't explain the Ockley Common incident—or, yes, he could! He saw it now! He realized why Buller must spend those hours of darkness in his car, but not asleep: no, he would wager the man was not asleep. But he would simulate sleep to avoid embarrassing questions should a police patrol pass.

French could scarcely sit still. It seemed too good to be true, but at last he realized that he had solved his problem! Admittedly certain details still remained obscure, but of the main facts there could no longer be any doubt. Now for the first time he saw the sequence of events from Buller's arrival in England right up to the disappearance of Barke.

Proof? No, not yet. But one thing at a time. When you

know just what to look for and where it is likely to be, inquiries become short and effective. He would return to Lon—

His train of thought ceased abruptly, while the bottom seemed slowly to drop out of his world. No: he was wrong after all! One point he had overlooked, but it was vital. One small point, but it upset his entire case.

Calling for still more coffee, he concentrated on that single obstacle. Everything else fitted so perfectly that it must be possible to harmonize it also.

The third lot of coffee grew cold in its turn while French continued racking his brains on the devastating problem. But he could obtain no light on it, and unless it were somehow cleared up, he would remain as far from a solution as ever.

Then he wondered if still another inquiry would help him. As there was nothing to keep him in Paris, the sooner he got back to the Yard the better. He could ask his question on the way home. It concerned the stamping of Barke's passport at Boulogne, and if he went by the 4.25 train, there might be time to see the officials and catch the connecting boat.

He was waiting at the *Sûreté* when Dieulot came in at about a quarter to four.

'I'd like to go by this 4.25 train,' he announced, 'and I want a word with the passport officers at Boulogne on the way. Will you do two things for me? Will you ring up the officers to introduce me, and will you lend me Barke's passport?'

Dieulot was delighted to render any assistance, and French was presently in the train with the passport and assured of prompt and courteous attention when he reached the port.

He received it, but he found that the officers were too busy to attend to him till the boat had left.

'I want you,' he explained when at last he was seated with the senior officer in his office, 'to have a look at this passport. You will see that the holder entered France at Boulogne on Friday 15 March last.'

The officer turned the pages and came on the Boulogne stamp. He glanced at it, nodded, then examined it more carefully, as if struck by some doubt. Finally he nodded again. 'That is correct, monsieur,' he agreed in admirable English, but still with apparent reserve.

'Now,' French bluffed smoothly, 'there is reason to suppose that stamp is a forgery. Have you any way of testing it?'

The official stared, first at French, then again at the passport. He grew obviously uneasy. 'I thought it looked a little strange,' he said with hesitation. 'You see? It is—what you call "rough". Not quite so—perfect? Well finished?—as it might be. But then these roughnesses: they were so little. I thought again that it was all right.'

'I agree with you, monsieur,' declared French. 'But is there any absolute test?'

'There is a test, yes,' the official admitted with a shrug, 'but it is only partial. If this impression is a fraud, it might prove it, but then again it might not.'

'Perhaps, monsieur, you would apply the test and let me know the result?'

'But certainly. This stamp, you see, is a ring with "Commissariat Spécial" above and "Débarquement" below in a curve following the shape of the ring. Beneath the upper curved letters is the name "Boulogne-s/Mer", printed horizontally. Beneath that, across the centre of the circle, is the date "15 Mars 1939", also printed horizontally and between two horizontal lines. All these printings are correct. See for yourself.'

He seized a stamp and made an impression. Save for the almost microscopic irregularities, it seemed identical with the other.

'But,' he went on, demonstrating with his finger, 'there is another marking, a number, below the date. This may or may not give what we want. You see, my stamp is No.14, that in the passport is No. 6. What that number stands for is confidential. I will tell you in confidence if you wish, but it may not be necessary. Excuse me while I look up our records.'

A brief search produced an astonishing change in the officer's expression and manner. From doubtful it had grown horror stricken. 'I can't understand it,' he exclaimed. 'It is beyond comprehension, but you are right. This stamp was not affixed on the date in question. No. 6 was not in use on that day.'

A wave of overwhelming delight swept over French. He had hoped that this indeed might be the fact, but he had never expected to be able to prove it.

'Nothing like coming to the fountain head, monsieur,' he said diplomatically. 'In Paris we all looked at it and assumed it was all right. Then we take it to you and you find the flaw. I can't say how grateful I am.'

The official looked as if he resented the diplomacy. 'This, monsieur,' he explained anxiously, 'is an extremely serious matter. Our stamp appears to have been copied. And our officer passed the copy. A very serious matter for us.'

French felt he should be sympathetic. 'That side of it needn't come out,' he declared. 'It will be enough if you will testify that the stamp is a forgery. The copy will not be used again and we're not interested as to how it was obtained.'

'My superiors will be,' the man pointed out grimly. French, anxious to be alone, made encouraging murmurs and took his leave. It was with the most profound satisfaction that he strolled up to the Town Station to inquire if he could get to Dunkerque that night. He had succeeded better than he could have hoped. The snag in an otherwise almost perfect case had been overcome! Once again he was going to triumph over an ugly problem! Once again he would maintain his own high reputation at the Yard!

There was a train at 9.12, and French filled up his time by dining at the Station restaurant. He caught the ferry at Dunkerque and next morning was in London.

19

The Peak of Achievement

After dealing with his correspondence and making a formal report to Sir Mortimer Ellison, French settled down in his room to consider his next step in the light of the theory he had evolved in Les Quatre Plumes. First out of politeness he wrote to Dieulot, telling him what he had learnt at Boulogne, though he did not think the information would be of much use to him. Then pulling towards him a large-scale map of Forde Manor, he began to study it.

He had not been working long when there was a knock at his door. French glared up with an expression that boded ill for his caller's welcome. The door opened and in walked Shaw.

'Constable told me you were here,' he announced calmly, then after a glance at French he added, 'How're things?'

'Things,' said French, suddenly feeling that he could do with a spot of sympathy, 'are all right. What about yourself?'

'Bad,' Shaw declared, putting down his hat and pulling out a chair. 'I've not got any further with that confounded puzzle.'

'I have,' French returned, trying to keep the triumph out of his voice.

'You have? What's the latest?'

'The latest,' French could not avoid a slight pomposity, 'is the solution of the whole darned box of tricks.'

Shaw stared. 'Do you mean you've got your man?'

'I mean I know who he is and that I can get the proof.'

Shaw swore—a satisfying oath which relieved his feelings. 'Who?' he breathed gently.

'Look here,' French swung round. 'I'll tell you what I've learnt the last couple of days and you'll see it for yourself.'

'I'd rather you'd tell me the answer right away.'

'No, it's an interesting problem. I told you about Wellesley and Vincent, but I didn't tell you of the Colorado Buller hired, nor of all that I learnt in Paris. Quite a lot I've learnt since we met. I'll tell it to you now.'

Shaw sat drinking in the tale while French recounted his recent activities. 'Now,' he ended up, 'you know everything I know. You can get the entire solution from this.'*

Shaw moved uneasily. 'Hang it all, French,' he protested, 'don't ask riddles. Who's the man?'

French grinned. He couldn't help it, but he felt like a mischievous child. 'Tell you what,' he said, 'I'm going down to Forde Manor presently to have a look round. Come with me. With luck you'll be interested. Excuse me while I fix up about the car. Here's a map of the estate you may find interesting in the light of what I've just told you.'

He went out of the room, delighted to observe in Shaw's expression bewilderment and irritation struggling for the mastery.

---

* So can the reader. F.W.C.

'Carter,' he said when he had run the sergeant to earth, 'what are you doing?'

'Clyde's evidence in the Battersea case, sir.'

'Then drop it and come along with me. Get another man,' and French gave instructions about personnel, car, and equipment. 'When can you be ready?'

'Ten minutes, sir.'

'Good.'

Some quarter of an hour later a large car left the Yard with French at the wheel. Beside him was Shaw and in the back were Carter and Constable Grayson, with some tools of strange design not unlike the outfit of a Brobdingnagian chimney sweep. The morning was bright if a trifle cold, and French found the run refreshing after his night in the train. He was still feeling rather like a child, intensely, supremely interested in his quest and eager to get to work. Shaw admitted he was completely mystified, but he asked no questions. He knew French well enough to be sure not only that the secret would in due course be revealed, but also that when it was, it would be worth hearing.

French glanced at his watch as they turned into the back drive, which led to the house through the trees near the head of the lake. 'I telegraphed to Relf to meet us at twelve,' he observed, stopping the car at the shell of the great building. 'Let's get out and stretch our legs while Carter puts the things together. Now, Shaw,' he went on as they strolled away from the car, 'I want you to answer a question. Suppose you were the owner of this place and you had something you wanted to hide, where would you put it?'

'What sort of thing?' Shaw parried.

'Any sort of thing,' French returned comprehensively.

271

'Well, it would depend. I shouldn't hide a brooch or a diamond ring in the same place as a ton of coal.'

French grinned. 'Why not? If you didn't want either of them to be found again.'

'You didn't say that,' Shaw protested, getting deeper into the mire.

'I say it now. Where would you hide them?'

Shaw hesitated. 'Plenty of places. I might dig a hole and bury them. If they were heavier than water I might throw them into the lake. I might pack them up and post them to some imaginary address in Lapland. I don't know what I might do.'

'I know one thing you wouldn't do,' French chuckled, 'and that's post a ton of coal to Lapland. No, Shaw, I'm serious. If you wanted to hide an object here on the estate, how would you do it?'

'Would it burn?'

'No.'

'Then the lake, I suppose, if it didn't float.'

'Light objects can be weighted,' French pointed out. 'Very well, let us say the lake. That's what I lent you the map for. I went over every inch of it this morning before you came in and I also plumped for the lake. That's why Carter has brought the drags.'

Shaw whistled. 'Then we're going to make a day of it?'

'Well, I expect it'll take as much of the day as is left. 'Morning, Relf. Got the keys?'

The caretaker touched his cap. 'The boathouse is open, sir. Everything's ready for you.'

'Good. Then let's go down.'

The boathouse was on the narrow upper end of the lake, deeply secluded among the trees. It was a modern building of purplish red brick, with an L-shaped floor, surrounding on two sides the water basin. There were no windows, illumination by day being obtained from a large central roof light, and by night from two electric light bulbs swinging beneath large reflectors.

'Money no object,' remarked French. 'Fancy running down a special cable just for those two lights! Tell me, Relf, if those were turned on at night, would they show through the skylight?'

Relf shook his head. 'No, sir. You couldn't tell from outside whether the light was on or off. The reflectors keep direct light off the glass.'

French nodded as he passed through the door. On the floor lay three boats, a punt, a long narrow skiff and a yacht's tiny dinghy, the latter nearest the basin. Two sets of conveyors with light chain blocks and gunwale grips showed how these could be lifted in and out of the water. The door to the lake was solid and worked on the portcullis principle, being raised and lowered by a Windlass.

'Job to get these boats in and out,' said French, examining the apparatus.

'Not so bad, sir,' Relf returned. 'If one of you gentlemen would lend a hand I'll guarantee to have all three floating in ten minutes.'

'It would take two people?'

'Not necessarily, but with the punt and skiff it would be quicker. The little dinghy one man could handle easily.'

'Let's see you do it,' French invited, glancing at his watch. 'I'd like to time you. Start—now!'

The dinghy, which had only one central thwart besides the bow and stem seats, was right below one of the conveyors. Relf took down from the wall a set of four light chain slings connected at one end to a ring and ending at the other in grips. These he hooked to the gunwale, two at each side, threw the ring over the hook of the chain blocks, and began to wind up the chain. In less than a minute, the boat was swinging clear of the ground. By pulling another chain, Relf then moved the blocks along the conveyor beam, till the dinghy was hanging over the water. To lower it till it floated was a matter of another minute. Relf stepped into it, unhooked the grips, and coming ashore again, drew the chains back out of the way.

'Four and a half minutes,' said French. 'Not bad. And I suppose the same time to get it out again?'

'Say five, sir,' Relf returned. 'There'd be more lifting to do.'

'Ten altogether. Well, that's good. When did you tidy up this place last, Relf?'

'I do it every week, sir; every Saturday morning.'

'Now tell me, when you did it on the Saturday after the fire, did you notice anything unusual?'

'Unusual, sir?'

'Yes: anything you might not have expected? Any sign of anyone having been in the house, or any of the boats or oars wet?'

Relf stared. 'Come to think of it, sir, I did see some marks of damp on the floor. I noticed them particularly and wondered how they had got there. I thought maybe rain was blowing in through the louver and I intended to look, but I forgot.'

'Whereabouts were the marks?'

Relf pointed to the space between where the dinghy had been lying and the edge of the basin.

There was triumph in the look French exchanged with Shaw. 'Want to ask Relf anything?' he inquired.

Shaw shook his head.

French turned back to Relf. 'Thank you. Then I think that's all we want in the meantime. Come down again at dusk to lock up.' He waited till the man had gone. 'Well, Shaw, what do you think of that? Water on the floor! That shows we're right.'

'It looks as if a boat had been used right enough,' Shaw admitted. 'But I don't know what you're expecting to find.'

'You wait and see,' French returned in high good humour. He turned towards the others. 'Now, men, we think someone's hidden a package in the lake and we want to find it. Take out the punt and have a try with the grabs.'

Then began a long and tedious search. French walked along the bank sticking posts into the ground to act as guides, while the others swept across the water in parallel lines. All that afternoon they worked till the early twilight closed down and they had to desist.

'Disappointing,' murmured Shaw.

'We're not beaten yet,' French returned. 'Tomorrow morning at nine. We'll have another shot at it when we're fresh.'

He put a watchman on that night and next morning saw the scene re-enacted. They had by this time covered all the deeper portions of the lake and were working up nearer the boathouse.

'More chance up here,' Shaw said encouragingly. 'If I were going to get rid of something I'd do it here surrounded by all these trees and not down there in the open.'

'Probably you're right,' French answered. 'Well, we'll soon know.'

All that day the search dragged on interminably. Next morning they went at it again, French growing steadily more depressed and his comments shorter and less polite. Then at last, just before the first signs of dusk appeared, he had his reward. The constable gave a shout, 'Something here, sir!'

It took a deal of work to get it up. They manoeuvred the end of the punt over the place, and while Shaw and Relf held it steady, the others got their drags beneath the object and began to lift. But it was heavy and they could not get it up into the punt. They therefore propelled it to the shore and beached it. Then Carter and the constable, slipping off their shoes, waded into the water and pulled it ashore.

As they looked at it there were exclamations of surprise from the officers and of horror from Relf. But French was neither surprised nor horror-stricken. Abundant satisfaction was his sole feeling. He had been right in his theory and he had won his case!

For the object was the body of a man, a man whom Relf identified in awestruck tones. 'Bless my soul,' he shouted, 'it's Mr Barke!'

It was small and insignificant-looking as it lay there on the lake bank. The bulk due to clothes was lacking, for it was dressed in undergarments only: shirt, pants and shoes. Round it was coiled several turns of heavy chain, fully accounting for the difficulty they had had in lifting it.

For a time all stood motionless, looking down at the ghastly object; then French roused himself. 'Slip away, one of you men, for an ambulance and get it moved to the mortuary. Then get your doctor on to it. Maybe, Shaw, you'll stay and see it though? And you,' he turned to Relf, 'not one word about this before tomorrow. Understand?'

French hurried back to the car and drove furiously for town, stopping at the first telephone box to speak to the

Yard. As a result, men and warrants were waiting for him, and that night Sir Geoffrey Buller and Basil Davenport were arrested, the former on a charge of murdering, the latter of conspiring to murder, Charles Gresham Barke.

It was with deeper misgivings than was usual under such circumstances that French in the small hours of the next morning reached his home. For once his customary sense of achievement on making an arrest was absent, and instead anxiety gnawed in his mind. With regard to Buller he felt safe, but he had no proof of any kind against Davenport. Yet he had burnt his boats. If he could not obtain evidence demonstrating the artist's complicity, he would have laid himself open to serious criticism.

Anxiety and eagerness were therefore balanced in his mind as early next morning he again went down to Ockham. With Shaw acting as a sort of indeterminate liaison officer, the local police had taken charge. Their doctor had examined the remains and their coroner had fixed the hour of the inquest, which was to be held that afternoon.

The doctor reported that Barke had died as the result of a blow on the back of the head, rather towards the right side, from a soft heavy weapon such as a sandbag. The skull was fractured, but the skin was not broken, so that there had been no blood at the scene of the crime. He could not say precisely how long the body had been in the water, but he estimated about the period since Barke had disappeared.

The chain was found to consist of four pieces each weighing some thirty pounds. The sections were wired together to form a single length, which was wrapped round the body from the ankles to the neck. The remains would therefore never have floated, no matter what chemical changes had afterwards taken place.

French seized eagerly on the chain, which he thought might produce valuable evidence. It was obviously new, as the links showed no sign of wear and but little rust. Relf was positive that there had been no such chain about the estate: therefore presumably Buller had bought it. One of French's earliest steps was to have inquiries made in all likely shops in the London area, in the hope of tracing its purchase.

At the inquest evidence of identification was given by Oliphant from the Crewe Gallery, in order to spare Agatha Barke. He also told of Barke's disappearance. French described the finding of the body: 'Acting on information received I proceeded to the lake at Forde Manor.' The doctor was first technical about the injuries, afterwards by request translating into the vulgar tongue, and finally declaring that neither accident nor suicide was a possibility. The coroner, refusing to consider suggestions of possible guilt, confined the inquiry to the questions of who had died and how, and the jury obediently brought in the obvious verdict of wilful murder by some person or persons unknown.

Shaw hung about with a faintly disapproving air. 'You know, French,' he said, 'I can't give up my case just because you've found a murderer. It's absolutely necessary that the arson should be proved. It means hundreds of thousands to my Company. I'd like to talk it over with you before making my report. And, of course,' he added as an after-thought, 'I want to hear the story of what you did.'

French grinned. 'Don't worry, Shaw. You'll get your verdict all right. The arson is part of the murder case. And as to my story, let's kill two birds with one telling. You want the facts and I want a check on my deductions from them. We might have a go at it this evening. What about coming home with me and having a bit of supper first?'

Shaw seemed pleased. 'Very good of you, French. I'd like to.'

'Right then. Say seven o'clock. Or will you call at the Yard at six-fifteen and we can go home together?'

'At the Yard,' Shaw decided, as the two men parted.

20

The Conclusion of the Affair

Till after supper that night not another word about the case was spoken. It was not till they were settled in armchairs before the fire and Mrs French as a tribute to her guest had brought in coffee, that French deemed the hour had come.

'Pipe drawing properly?' he asked. 'Well, the sooner we get at this thing, the sooner we'll be finished. I've got the dossier in case some question arises.'

'Good,' Shaw approved. 'And I'm to be counsel for the defence?'

'Not quite so drastic as that,' French returned. 'But if you see any flaws, shout out.'

'A watching brief? Right. Then go ahead.'

French laid his open notebook on his knee, paused for a moment as if to arrange his thoughts, and then began: 'The first thing is that I'm really worried about pulling in those two men. Or rather about Davenport. Buller's all right. He's guilty and I can prove it. But I can't prove Davenport's guilt.'

'You're morally certain of it?'

'Moral certainty isn't evidence. I have enough to justify an arrest, but not to go into court.'

'You'll get your verdict all right,' Shaw declared easily. 'Go ahead and let's hear the tale.'

'Very well, this is how it looks to me. Here's this Geoffrey Buller, a very ordinary young man, working in a house agent's office in Plymouth. For some reason he goes out to Chicago and starts in the same line. He does neither very well nor very badly: holds his job, but misses promotion, proving his mediocre qualities. Then this old boy over here dies and he suddenly becomes a British baronet with a large estate in Surrey. He throws up his job and comes home, full of large ideas about playing the country squire and filling his house with people in his new social sphere.

'Unhappily he has neither the manner nor the training for the job, and he fails to make the contacts he expected. He is disappointed, and as he is lonely, his disappointment festers. He finds that his predecessor was not a businessman and that the estate has been run in a haphazard way, and he begins to put this right and see where he stands. He has, for instance, an inventory made for insurance purposes, and the premium is adjusted to give adequate cover. You'll see I'm giving him the benefit of the doubt and assuming that this was not a deliberate prelude to fraud.'

'That's wise. It's the sort of thing that counts with a jury.'

'It might even be true. Well, his researches lead to a further discovery, much more serious and fundamental. He's short of cash. He expected a fortune with the estate, but death duties have seen to that and he finds he hasn't enough to keep the place going.

'But he has an immense potential source of wealth—his

pictures. He hasn't realized how valuable they are till the inventory opens his eyes.'

French poured out second cups of coffee.

'Now,' he resumed, 'we come to a hiatus. Somehow, whether out of his own inner consciousness or, as I should imagine, as the result of a suggestion from Davenport, he decides on the substitutions. Probably his first intention is merely to sell, and knowing nothing of art, he commissions Davenport to conduct the sale. Probably it was in the subsequent conversation that the suggestion was made. That's guesswork, but in some way it is arranged that Davenport will make the copies, presumably selling the originals and dividing the spoils. So far the intention need not necessarily have been fraudulent.'

'Plausible at all events.'

'That has to be cleared up. Then we go back to certainty. All this shortage of money and worry about the pictures, for it must have been a worry, still further increases Buller's disappointment. It grows so bitter in fact that he determines to give up the Manor and go back to America. His hopes and his dreams are dead and he hates the place and everyone connected with it. He decides to sell. Then he has a third disappointment—the greatest of the three. He can't sell; no one wants so large a house. He is left with a white elephant on his hands.

'But one thing runs on—his expenditure. To keep up the place, even untenanted, will take more money than he has. He grows desperate. Then comes another hiatus, though I think we can bridge it in our minds. Buller might have reasoned—if all legal action leads to bankruptcy, why not try illegal? Somehow the arson idea is born, either through him or through Davenport. At all events Buller burns his house down after making elaborate plans to avoid suspicion.'

'Also destroying the evidence of the substitutions.'

'Quite. Whether the substitutions had been fraudulent from the start or not, they become so now. When the camel of the greater crime is being swallowed, why strain at the gnat of the lesser? What were those copied pictures worth?'

'About forty thousand. But Davenport couldn't have sold them secretly for that. Say twenty or twenty-five.'

'There you are. Why lose twenty-five thousand when you can get it as safely as the rest?'

'I agree. You mean then that Buller's shortage of cash drove him to arson?'

'I mean it was his only hope. Arson would change a huge liability into a still vaster asset. And if he had scruples, he would know that the loss would fall heavily on no one, owing to its wide distribution. Your people reinsured, I suppose?'

'Oh Lord, yes. we only covered about a tenth of the liability ourselves. No firm would take on so big a risk.'

'I thought so. Well, the plan works perfectly. While Buller is in Italy the house is burnt down. He comes home, sees you and your manager on the ground, and says that in due course he will put in a claim for the damage. The pictures are actually discussed, their great value being mentioned, but Buller says nothing about the substitutions. And in that omission lay, in my opinion, the seeds of the murder.'

'That's right. His silence could only mean that he intended to defraud us.'

'Quite. Then a new factor arises. Buller learns that Barke has seen the substituted pictures. There's no chance that a man of Barke's qualifications will be taken in, nor any doubt but that he'll tell what he has seen. What's to be done?'

'Nothing for him but to put Barke out of the way.'

'That's as I see it. In a way it doesn't matter if Barke has told what he has seen. No statement that he might have made would be evidence, so if he was out of the way, Buller and Davenport would be safe.'

Shaw nodded, but without conviction. French glanced at him doubtfully, then with some hesitation went on.

'Are you sure that's sound, Shaw, or is there a flaw? Could Buller not still have gone to your company and admitted the substitutions?'

Shaw considered this. 'I don't think he could,' he said at last. 'If Buller told about the substitutions after having kept it back in the first instance, our manager would ask himself why in both cases. He would hear of Barke's visit and spot the answer. It would suggest fraud. He would reason. If there was fraud about the pictures, why not about the fire? And I can tell you that if our manager once grew suspicious of the fire, he'd stick at it till he found out the truth. Buller daren't risk it.'

French was listening with satisfaction. 'That's what I thought but I'm glad to hear you confirm it. You mean that if Buller confessed about the substitutions he'd fear it would lead to the discovery of the arson?'

'Exactly.'

'And if the arson was discovered, instead of going to the States with about half a million sterling, he'd lose his fortune and have a long stretch in a British prison. Quite, there's a motive there, all right.'

'To my way of thinking it would depend on whether he believed he could get Barke out of the way without risk.'

French nodded approvingly. 'That's it. You've got it now. Which was the greater risk: to raise a suspicion of arson, or to do Barke in? I'm satisfied he thought the murder absolutely safe.'

'I agree. And Davenport?'

'Party to both substitution and murder.'

Shaw leant forward, knocked out his pipe, and began to refill it. 'This is a good story, French,' he declared. 'I wouldn't have missed it for worlds. Carry on.'

'Directly Buller learns that Barke has seen the substitutions, we may presume he gets in touch with Davenport, and together they work out their scheme. And a very ingenious scheme it is, and only for you discovering the arson, they might easily have got off with it.'

Shaw made a gesture of dissent. 'Handsome, French,' he acknowledged, 'very. But not true. We both know how they've been caught.'

'Well, we needn't quarrel over it. Their first difficulty is to find out whether Barke has already passed on his information, because even though his statement can't be used in court, there's the vital point you make about raising your manager's suspicion.'

'The probabilities would be against Barke speaking.'

'That's right. Firstly, because he hasn't seen Mrs Stanton, who is the only really interested person, and second, because making copies of masterpieces and selling the originals is a common and perfectly legitimate way of realizing money. Fraud will only arise if the insurance is claimed. Barke will therefore wait to see what is done before speaking.

'But Buller and Davenport will wish to prevent him speaking—if he hasn't already done so. And how can this be better accomplished than by taking away the motive for speech; in other words, by making him believe that Buller has himself reported the substitutions to the Thames & Tyne? Buller cannot move in the matter, as he is known to Barke. But Davenport can. So we have the lunch with the representative of the Thames & Tyne, which Buller is prevented from attending by a motor accident. Buller can thus deny any knowledge of the affair.'

'And thus Davenport demonstrates that he is an accessory before the fact.'

'Yes, if we can prove it. If someone in the Holly can identify him as Barke's host, we're all right. But after a month will anyone do so?'

'There's a chance at all events.'

'I hope so. Well, Davenport finds out that Barke has kept his observations to himself, going on to satisfy him that there are no fraudulent intentions in connection with the pictures. Then he offers him a job at his own fee. He says the pictures were done by a M. Picoux in Paris, and will Barke go over with himself and Buller to inspect two pictures on which Picoux is then actually at work? Finally he pledges him to silence until they have seen Picoux, on the ground that a distorted view of the story might give rise to unpleasant rumours. This is a good enough tale to satisfy Barke, who agrees to meet the others at Victoria in time for the nine o'clock train on the following morning.'

'Very plausible,' Shaw, commented again. 'You can't blame Barke for getting hooked.'

'No, particularly as he appears to have been a kindly trustful sort of chap who wouldn't expect well-mannered people to be crooks. Very well, that lunch takes place on the Thursday, and Davenport crosses to Paris by the four-thirty service that afternoon. He takes with him the picture he was then about to copy, ostensibly to consult his former art masters about its restoration, actually to provide a motive for the journey as well as an alibi for the next day. That Friday morning he spends at the Atelier Voges, really discussing the picture, and in the afternoon he returns to London by the four twenty-five train. But between these two activities there's a blank period which enables him to carry out his part of the plot.

'Meanwhile Buller is making his contribution. So far he has been able to deny his connection with the affair. There is nothing to connect him with the lunch, and he can always say, if challenged, that "Vincent" has used his name improperly. He wishes to remain uncompromised, therefore for his Friday motoring he can't use his own car. On the Thursday he hires a Colorado in a garage not far from Victoria. As you know, this American car has an unusually large boot, and Buller, on the excuse that he wants to carry the equipment of a theatrical party, satisfies himself that this sample is no exception to the rule. On this Thursday he also buys a small second-hand suitcase.

'On Friday morning he calls for the car, drives to Victoria, parks, and meets Barke on the platform. What he says to him we don't know, but we may imagine that it is something to the effect that a cleaned picture has been discovered unburnt at Forde Manor, and he would like him to see it before crossing: at all events he makes some excuse to get Barke to Forde. This meeting with Buller will reassure Barke as to "Vincent's" bona fides, had he doubted it, and Buller will probably say that "Vincent" will meet them either at Forde or in Paris.'

'Very plausible. Nothing suspicious so far.'

'No, it will all look quite natural. Now here we come to

another hiatus. Somewhere on that journey down to Forde, Buller murders Barke. Whether he actually reaches Forde or makes some excuse for turning elsewhere, we don't know. What we are sure of is that he drives to some deserted place where he gets Barke out of the car and sandbags him.'

'Risky, that part of it.'

'It's a risk he has to take. But when the rest of the scheme is so good, it's unlikely that he'll fail here. In fact, as we know, he *doesn't* fail.'

'You're right. Carry on.'

'Now he strips the body of the outer clothing, which with Barke's passport, keys and the other articles in the pockets, he puts in the small suitcase he has bought. Then we see the need for the large boot. He puts the body in and locks the boot. He has reckoned that Barke is a small-sized man. He drives to Croydon and books the two suitcases, the one he has bought, and Barke's own, to Davenport at Le Bourget. They have arranged to use the name "Roland Brand", about whom Mrs Stanton must obviously have talked to Buller, partly that the name should be in a directory, and partly to shift any suspicion which may be aroused on to someone connected with the case.'

'Dirty, that.'

'I don't think so. They will know that nothing can be proved against Brand. Buller then drives back to the garage, leaving the car till the evening. The body of course is inside, but the boot is locked.'

French paused to rake the fire together. 'Throw on a log or two, will you?' he directed, as he got up and crossed the room. 'I think the time has come for a drink,' he went on, busying himself with bottles and glasses. 'What do you say, Shaw?'

Very politely Shaw indicated that it was overdue. 'Nice situation,' he went on, reverting to French's exposition. 'A car in a busy garage, worked at by the staff—we know at least that someone read the trip mileage; and probably it was dusted down—and all the time there's the body of a murdered man within a foot or two of them. Sort of dramatic when you come to think of it.'

French grunted. 'It's what must have happened,' he asserted; 'nothing else will account for the facts. Now,' he went on with a change of tone, 'let's switch over to Davenport. He does his picture stunt at the atelier, setting up as much of his alibi as he can. Then instead of lunching at Les Quatre Plumes, he goes out to Le Bourget, claims the suitcases as Roland Brand, and comes back to Paris. Another slight hiatus here. We don't know what he does with Barke's: probably pushes it into the consigne at the Gare du Nord. But he returns to the Maréchal Ney with the small suitcase containing Barke's outer clothes and passport, going to his room openly, ostensibly to lie down because of his headache. For all of this we have no proof, but it just must have taken place.

'In his room he changes into Barke's clothes—they are much of a size—and no doubt makes up to look as like Barke as possible. Then he used something which he has no doubt made before leaving London: a passport stamp. You remember he has developed picture stamping in rubber as an aid to his woodblock work, and it will probably be easy for him to make a stamp for registering entry into France at Boulogne. Doubtless he has a sample to work from in Butler's passport, if not in his own. Whether he has some photographic process to cut the rubber with chemicals, or whether he builds it up from rings and type, I don't know, though an investigation of his studio may tell us. All I'm sure of—and can't prove—is that he has made it, and there in the Hôtel du Maréchal Ney he stamps Barke's passport and misleads us all.'

'You'll get proof of that later.'

'I hope so, for I'm afraid what's coming now is also guesswork. Made up as Barke and with Barke's passport in his pocket, Davenport walks out of the Maréchal Ney. As you know, it's a big place with two sets of lifts and a continual stream of people passing in and out. Having taken care to use one set as Davenport, he is unlikely to be recognized if he uses the other as Barke. It's a risk, of course, but he must take it.

'He now gets Barke's suitcase, goes to the Gare du Nord and meets the train at 3.48, mingles with the stream of people coming from it, and takes a taxi to the Vichy. In the taxi he puts Barke's passport into Barke's suitcase. At the Vichy he does the play acting we know about: arriving as Barke, registering, sending his luggage up to his room, saying he has an appointment and walking out. It's only five minutes back to the Maréchal Ney, and he slips up to his room as he came down, immediately telephoning the office to get his picture ready. He quickly changes back to his normal exterior, goes down to the lounge, gets his picture, and leaves for London.'

Shaw removed his pipe from his mouth and moved round in his chair as if to make a pronouncement. 'I do congratulate you, French,' he said with deliberation, 'I really do. That's about the best reconstruction I've ever heard. And I'd bet a hundred to one in flyers it's the truth.'

'It's going to be the mischief to prove all that about Davenport.'

'I congratulate those two also,' went on Shaw judicially. 'Their scheme was good and it deserved to succeed.'

'I expect they thought it invincible. Just consider it as they would see it. Buller is safe because Barke disappears in Paris and Buller never leaves London. Davenport is safe because he can't be charged with murder unless the body is produced, and the body is not in France. Oh yes, it was a good scheme all right.'

For some days French's anxiety remained acute, then gradually subsided as one item of information after another came in.

In the case of Buller the final proof of guilt was given by the discovery of his purchase of the chains in which the body of Barke was wrapped. Buller had made the mistake of having the chain cut into four pieces: probably because he could not otherwise have carried it. This fixed his personality on the salesman's mind, with the result that in the time-honoured manner he picked out first his customer's portrait from French's gallery and later the man himself from an identification parade.

A somewhat longer shot on similar lines brought the evidence French wanted, in the case of Davenport. A search of his studio showed no photographic method for making rubber impressions, but did bring to light mechanical apparatus for engraving the rubber in straight lines and circles. It seemed to French, therefore, that Davenport could have made all of the Boulogne stamp except the lettering. Accordingly he had inquiries made as to the purchase of rubber letters. From three shops in the City he had answers. At these a man, identified in two of them as Davenport, had called on the morning of Thursday, 14 March, bringing no less than five samples of lettering and asking if similar letters could be supplied. Between the three they made up the required fonts. What specially pleased French was that Davenport had also obtained two E's with acute accents. These of course he would have wanted for the words 'Spécial' and 'Débarquement'. He had also obtained certain numerals. In most cases the salesman remembered the type chosen, and when French saw that these were similar to those used on the Boulogne stamp, he felt he need go no further.

But though he believed this purchase of letters would give him all the proof he needed, it turned out that he was able—or Dieulot was able for him—to obtain something even more satisfying. Dieulot, feeling that so far French detection had not scintillated with the brilliancy of English, had gone out to Le Bourget and interviewed the clerk who had handed over the suitcases to 'Roland Brand'. By dint of judicious suggestion he had so stimulated the man's memory that he suddenly declared that he recalled 'Brand'. A telephone conversation with French followed, and that afternoon the clerk flew over to London, and at a parade in Brixton prison unhesitatingly picked out Davenport as the man.

At the ensuing trial defending counsel made a brilliant fight for his clients' lives, but the weight of evidence amassed by French was overwhelming, and both men' received the supreme sentence of the law. During the trial the arson was proved up to the hilt, so that Shaw and his company were well satisfied with the result. Buller accepted his fate, but Davenport appealed on the ground that he was overborne by his stronger partner. This plea failed, and at the end both men met their death bravely.

When he saw that nothing could save him, Davenport made a confession which cleared up the one or two points of which French was still in doubt.

It appeared that the conspiracy was deeper and more deliberate than even French had imagined. Buller and Davenport had been in the same set in Chicago, and as both desired expensive pleasures and neither could afford them, both were chronically hard up. One night they were playing in a friend's rooms, when Buller, having taken more than was good for him, plumped wildly and lost to his friend more than he could pay. Davenport had not pressed for the money, though he had used the debt as a lever to force Buller into helping him in one or two small swindles, which, however, they had managed to keep secret. Davenport had always paid Butler his agreed share in these adventures and the partnership had grown strong and intimate.

Then came Buller's legacy. He received the news with mixed feelings. He had grown fond of America and had no desire to return to England, while English society and the life of an English county magnate were anathema to him. What he wanted was money. The bars of luxury cruising liners and of palace hotels at Miami or Palm Beach were what really drew him, and from the very beginning his only idea was to change his inheritance into cash.

In all this Davenport, the stronger spirit of the two, saw a heaven-sent opportunity. He declared that if Buller would let him in on the thing to a strictly limited extent, he would forget the debt and do all in his power to help in the turning of the estate into money. Buller, who wanted a companion and really liked Davenport, agreed readily enough. They set off together from America, booking their passages on the *Nicarian*.

Buller, however, had foreseen the difficulties which might arise through death duties and lack of purchasers, and it was then, before ever they left their rooms in Chicago, that Davenport suggested arson. It was, he advised, only to be treated as a last resource. If the place could be turned into money legally, so much the better. But if honest methods failed, they would burn down the house, collect the insurance, cut their losses on the land, and clear out with the swag.

At first Buller demurred, but the stronger Davenport talked him over, and having done so, took charge of the proceedings. It was he who decreed that from the very beginning precautions against suspicion should be taken. Thus, their association was to remain unknown in England, so that Davenport could the better help on the good work. Buller was to arrive enthusiastic to see and take over the property, and to let it be known that he intended to settle down at Forde Manor and take his share in the life of the community. It was for this reason that he was so anxious to engage Betty, whose presence at the Manor would, he felt, help on the deception. Davenport was to account for himself by taking a studio in London and continuing his painting, and they were to meet secretly as occasion offered to discuss subsequent steps.

The first of these steps was naturally to increase the insurance on the property, and both believed that Buller had done this without giving rise to suspicion. Then occurred the first of the difficulties which Buller had foreseen. The death duties really had robbed him of sufficient cash to carry on.

At this point they made their fundamental mistake. Davenport suggested the picture substitution, to which, against his better judgement. Buller agreed. Davenport's motive was sheer greed. He knew that he could sell the originals at reasonably good prices to collectors who would ask no questions, but who would understand enough of what they were doing to keep the transactions secret for a year or two—at least until he and Buller had vanished, and taken on new personalities. It was a risk of course, but every picture done meant thousands of pounds more for the conspirators. As confirmatory evidence of the cleanings, should such be required, Davenport took three pictures over to his old masters in Paris, ostensibly for consultation as to the best way of carrying out the work. Incidentally this fact was afterwards used to supply a motive for Davenport's visit to Paris to help with the carrying out of the murder.

When Buller reached the Manor after the fire he met the manager of the Thames & Tyne and discussed the loss of the pictures without mentioning the substitutions. Naturally he later asked questions as to visitors to the galleries, and when he heard that Barke had seen the pictures on the day before the fire, he realized that danger threatened. That Wednesday evening he had a long discussion with Davenport. Their problem was whether to confess the substitutions to the Thames & Tyne, thus losing some £25,000 and inevitably arousing suspicion of arson, or in some way to silence Barke. Buller was for the former, Davenport for the latter, and as always, the stronger personality won.

The details of the murder were practically as French had surmised. Davenport worked most of the Wednesday night at his passport stamp, obtaining the necessary type to complete it on Thursday morning. He had foreseen the possibility of rubber stamps being needed to forge official documents in connection with their fraud, and had adopted the scheme for testing woodblock work as a screen for such activities. This suggested the faking of the passport. The lunch with Barke was that day, and Davenport left for Paris in the afternoon.

Next morning Buller met Barke at Victoria and told him that one of the cleaned pictures had escaped the fire. It had just arrived from M. Picoux in Paris and was in his workshop. He wanted Barke to inspect it before interviewing Picoux, explaining that the delay would be trifling, as they could go on by the next service. Barke was quite willing, but asked where was Vincent? Buller said he had crossed on the previous night.

They drove towards Forde Manor, Barke sitting in front with Buller. When crossing Ockham Common near the lake, a place practically deserted at that time of the year, Buller looked both ways, saw that no one was in sight, glanced out of Barke's side window, cried, 'Why, there's Relf! Can you attract his attention?' and stopped the car. Barke turned his back towards his companion to look for the elusive caretaker. Buller, seizing a lead pipe which he had covered with a soft cloth, struck, killing his victim instantaneously. Buller then backed the car in among the trees, took the outer clothes off the body, and put it in the boot, as French had suggested. This was the only real risk he ran, but he could not see how to avoid it.

That night Buller drove down to Forde Manor, entering by the back drive gate, and parking among the pines near the lake. On the Thursday he had bought the chain. Hiring another car, he had that night taken it down to the lake at Forde and hidden it in the water near the boathouse. He now wrapped it round the body, and taking out the dinghy dropped the body into the water. Then during the remainder of the night he feigned sleep on Ockham Common.

Two matters alone remain to be mentioned. The first was the congratulations received by French from Sir Mortimer Ellison himself, ending up, 'You'll be glad to be done with trips to Paris and such nonsense and to get back to your beloved East End slums,' for which French dutifully grinned his appreciation.

The second matter was that Betty Stanton's book proved, if not a best, at least a very good seller, and with delight she signed an agreement to give her publisher the first refusal of her next three efforts. Agatha Barke wishing to leave London, the two women settled down together near San Remo, at which place the subsequent masterpieces were to achieve birth.

By the same author

Inspector French: Found Floating

The Carrington family, victims of a strange poisoning, take an Olympic cruise from Glasgow to help them recover. At Creuta one member goes ashore and does not return. Their body is next day found floating in the Straits of Gibraltar. Joining the ship at Marseilles, can Inspector French solve the mystery before they reach Athens?

Introduced by Tony Medawar, this classic Inspector French novel includes unique interludes by Superintendent Walter Hambrook of Scotland Yard, who provides a real-life detective commentary on the case as the mystery unfolds.

'*I doubt whether Inspector French has had a more difficult problem to solve than that of the body 'Found Floating' in the Mediterranean.'* SUNDAY TIMES